Snow Angels, Secrets & Christmas Cake

Sue Watson

Bookouture

Published by Bookouture

An imprint of Storyfire Ltd.
Carmelite House
50 Victoria Embankment
London EC4Y 0DZ

www.bookouture.com

ISBN: 978-1-909490-76-5
eBook ISBN: 978-1-909490-75-8

Acknowledgements

To all my family and friends for their love, support and laughter throughout the year - and for all the Christmases they've made special just by being there. Thank you!

Thank you to the wonderful team at Bookouture, Oliver Rhodes, Kim Nash, Emily Ruston, Jade Craddock and everyone who has been involved in turning this into a glittery bauble of a book.

But the story doesn't end there – I have been writing now for several years and have met so many people through books, but I want to say a special thank you to my book blogging friends.

In their own time, for no payment these people have read and reviewed my books, taking the trouble to write reviews on their blogs and websites. My book blogging friends Tweet and Facebook, write and shout about my books and are always there supporting me, cheering me on and embracing the world of books and authors. There are many, many book bloggers out there and I wanted to thank them all and give each one a mention.

Like Santa I made a list and checked it twice – but there may be one or two bloggers who have reviewed my books and haven't got a mention. If that's the case, I'm so sorry - please shout at me on Twitter and sulk on Facebook to let me know, and I will make sure to give a mention in the acknowledgements of my next book.

So to my wonderful book blogger friends Thank you!

Here they are – in no particular order – they are equally wonderful.

Dr Ananda @ This Chick Reads

Kat @ Best Books To Read

Dawn @ Crooks on Books

Sara @ Chick Lit Central

Melissa @ Chick Lit Central

Paris @ Paris Baker's Book Nook

Jo @ Comet Babes Books

Lauri @ Rottitude.com

Compelling Reads

Suzanne @ Lavender Library

Shaz @ Shaz's Book Blog

Jody @ A Happy Spoonful

Chick Lit Uncovered

Chick Lit Club

Karan @ Hello Precious Bliss

Sheli @ Sheli Reads

Margaret @ Bleach House Library

Marlene @ Book Mama Blog

Sara @ Harlequin Junkie

Novelkicks

Fiona @ Fiona's Book reviews
Alba @ Lost in Chick Lit
Elizabeth @ Mungleville
Novelicious
Kim @ Kim the Bookworm
Chloe @ Chicklit Chloe
Marina @ Chick Library Cat
Chantelle @ Mama Mummy Mum
Amanda Moran @ One More page
Liz and Lisa @ Chicklit is not Dead
Tanya Phillips
Ella Pumpkin
Dizzy C's Little Book Blog
Lou Graham's Blog

And finally a thank you to you, the reader for buying this book. And to those readers who get in touch to say hello, thank you for supporting me, inspiring me, and making me smile. And most of all for making this writer's daily working life a little less lonely - and a lot more fun.

For Lesley and Cocoa McLoughlin, two special girls who put the sparkle in Christmas!

Chapter 1

It's Beginning to Look a Lot Like Christmas!

Sam

'I want a white Christmas... I'm thinking ski chalet chic and showbiz sparkle...'

I nodded in agreement. That's all you could do with my sister. She was standing in her hallway by a twenty foot Norwegian Pine, dressed from head to toe in Yves Saint Laurent accessorised with a Chanel-lipsticked smile.

'It's exactly like the one in Trafalgar Square,' she said in her posh voice.

'Only hers is bigger than the one in Trafalgar Square,' Gabe, her landscaper, piped up beside me. I smiled, he apparently found her as amusing as I did.

'Darling... let me ask you something,' she said, ignoring him, looking at me over her Chanel bifocals. 'Do you think it would be too much to put the dog in a onesie?'

I looked at her; 'Seriously Tamsin? Yes.'

'But it's a hand-made designer polar bear onesie... it's Italian!'

'Italian? Oh why didn't you say? No, I can't see the problem putting a big brown dog in a white costume for Christmas, especially if it's handmade and Italian.'

She nodded, oblivious to my sarcasm – or choosing to ignore it – and began squirting room perfume everywhere – it smelt of fake Christmas.

'The season in a bottle,' she smiled coyly.

'The season in my *face*,' I said, wafting the air. 'God, Tamsin, it's lethal that stuff.'

'It just says... *Christmas* to me,' she closed her eyes and breathed deeply through elegant nostrils ... the epitome of designer style even my sister's nose was elegant. 'It takes you back doesn't it?' She looked at me and for a moment I saw a fleeting, unfathomable sadness in her eyes. Now wasn't the time to ask if she was okay, not with two interior designers, a landscaper, the cleaner and Tamsin's kids in attendance for her family Christmas card photo shoot.

'So I assume putting the dog in a polar bear costume is to do with your white Christmas theme?'

'Yes. Why?' she replied, already moving on to another item on her to-do list.

I shrugged. What could I say?

She rolled her eyes, 'Oh it probably offends your Green Peace, hippy dippy values to include my pet in the festive fun.'

'I'm not sure the dog would see it as "festive fun", but why ask me anyway? You'll do what you want to do.' A determined woman, I knew Tamsin was quite prepared to rugby tackle the huge dog into his polar bear costume for the sake of her white wonderland theme whether he wanted it or not.

My sister always embraced Christmas. And this year she was even more stressed and obsessive than ever, not least today as she was 'dressing the house' for the family Christmas card photo shoot. She called it her 'little pre-Christmas tease', and this year it was all about transforming her 18th century converted rectory into an Aspen ski lodge.

'I don't know why you can't buy a box of mixed cards from Marks and Spencer and send them out like everyone else does,' I sighed.

'That's exactly why,' she hissed, 'because everyone else does.'

She marched past me into her designer kitchen where I followed to unload the mini mince pies I'd made. She stood against the counter top, clad in diamonds, perfectly groomed, smelling very French and fretting about her 'Christmas colours and concepts'.

'I know you think I'm silly, and it may have escaped your attention but Horatio's a chocolate Labrador,' she sighed.

'I noticed.'

She gazed ahead like she had the weight of the world on her shoulders. 'He won't look good against a white backdrop. I just wish when we'd told the kids they could have a pet I'd fought harder for a white Persian cat instead.'

'Mmm it's tricky, but if he isn't going to match your interior there's nothing else for it. You're going to have to send him to the kennels for the whole of December,' I said with a straight face. 'I mean something like that could ruin the season for everyone.'

'Mmmm, that's not a bad idea,' she acknowledged absently.

'I was joking,' I sighed, but she was miles away, no doubt lost in St Moritz glitz.

Tamsin's Christmases were perfect, down to where exactly the turkey was raised (we're talking a postcode) for the dinner, to the exact hue of each eye-wateringly expensive bauble on the tree.

Even when the kids were little there were no dancing Santas or multi-coloured fairy lights, just a tailored tree that children weren't allowed to decorate or touch. This was accompanied by perfectly placed Christmas floral arrangements, wreaths on most doors and swags in the accent colour of the season. My sister's relentless pursuit of the best Christmas began almost a year in advance and themes and shades were tenaciously nailed down six months before.

Fortunately I was merely 'backstage staff' in Tamsin's life and able to dip in and out of the Angel-Smith family's festive activities. Our family name was Angel, Tamsin's husband's was Smith so they'd hyphenated their surnames. I wish I could say this was Tamsin's stand against paternalistic social power, and a rejection of outdated social constructs - but it wasn't - it was just desperate social climbing because she thought it sounded posh.

So luckily I was merely an onlooker, but I felt for my niece and nephew who, at nineteen and twenty-one, came home from their respective universities to be manhandled into animal onesies and 'Christmassed up'. My brother-in-law Simon, Tamsin's husband of twenty years, was never around and when he did turn up was always late and never really engaged with what was going on.

'No one seems to be taking this seriously,' Tamsin snapped, in between barking orders at children, the dog and Mrs J, the cleaner – who'd wandered in around 1992 and never left. I wasn't quite sure how Mrs J found time to do the cleaning, what with reading tea leaves and Tarot cards and giving an often uncomfortable running commentary on what was going on in the house. This was invariably followed by her unique brand of advice and a Q and A debriefing with everyone in the village. Tamsin was horrified when complete strangers approached her in the street and discussed in detail the most intimate aspects of her life. When the vicar had asked Tamsin if she was still getting 'hot flashes' and a low libido it looked like Mrs J was finally for the high jump.

'That's it. She's done it this time, discussing my perimenopause with the vicar – in depth if you please. I feel like I'm starring in my own reality show,' she'd complained. But despite her brittle exterior and the vicar's apparent intimate knowledge of her hormones, Tamsin didn't have the heart to let her go. 'That woman's a pain in the bum but she's the salt of the earth,' she'd say with a fond smile.

Right now Mrs J was standing, hands on hips, surveying the scene before her.

'Oh Mrs J, there you are. Now, would you be kind enough to wipe the dog's paws, he's about to be photographed, it's bad enough he's brown he doesn't have to be dirty too.'

'Dog racist,' proclaimed Hermione, my beautiful niece. She'd wandered into the kitchen and was now on autopilot peering into the fridge. 'Anything to eat?'

'No,' Tamsin snapped, 'not until the photograph's been taken.'

Hermione rolled her eyes and tried to slope off but Tamsin was on her. 'So please spend the next few minutes doing something useful... like getting the dog into his onesie.'

Hermione scowled and picked up the dog outfit between finger and thumb making a half-hearted attempt to catch poor Horatio who was now hiding under the coffee table.

I'd made the mince pies (which Tamsin refused to call mince pies using an unpronounceable French name for them instead) and all I wanted to do was deliver them and leave. But as always I'd become embroiled in what my sister referred to as 'creative chaos'.

'Don't leave the mince pies in the oven longer than a few minutes,' I warned.

'Can't you stay and take care of them, sweetie?'

'No I have to pick Jacob up from the childminder.'

'Oh Sam, she won't mind having him a few more minutes, he's so delicious... let's have a quick sherry,' she said, grabbing the bottle. 'We can talk about the Christmas confections you're creating for my festive soiree.' I declined a drink as I was driving but she poured herself one anyway. 'I don't know what Heddon and Hall are up to in there,' she said, referring to her interior designers, whose camp and unbridled enthusiasm for Christmas equalled my sister's. 'I've left them to it – I can't bear to have one more conversation about swags, balls or fucking garlands.' The posh voice made way for the broad Manchester accent – which it often did when we were alone and she'd had a couple of sherries.

I smiled at her outburst.

'Oh our Sam, why do I do it? Every year it's the same. I decorate, organise the photograph, while I'm planning the Christmas drinks, the party...the bloody nibbles.'

'Yeah,' I added. 'Nibbles? What the fuck are nibbles anyway? Just fancy crisps.'

'Now now...that's enough,' she started. Drinks and nibbles were sacred to Tamsin, like communion bread and wine.

'You can't possibly enjoy Christmas, you've turned it into a career,' I continued, 'and all your "friends" are just competitive couples trying to outdo each other, from who has the best canapés to who has the biggest balls – and I mean that in every sense.'

Tamsin pursed her lips disapprovingly. 'Trust you to bring balls into it. How's Richard by the way?'

'He's fine,' I said, 'still handsome, still likes it and wants to put a ring on it.'

'Well, you could do worse... I'd get a ring on it before he finds someone else he wants to put his ring on... that came out wrong, but you know what I mean.'

'I know, but it's not about Richard, it's about me – you know that. I don't think anyone can ever take the place of Steve.'

She nodded. 'I know, but that's not what Richard's asking for. He's not trying to take the place of anyone he just wants to be with you... and I don't like to think of you alone.'

'I'm not. I've got my beautiful son and my precious memories.'

It was silent for a moment and Tamsin put down her glass. 'I don't want you to spend another Christmas feeling low and wondering what might have been, Sam,' she said, looking at me with a sad expression on her face.

'Don't worry, I'm determined to make the best of things and try and move forward. I feel more positive than I have for years and I really want to enjoy Christmas this year.

'Yes love, you have to embrace Christmas for Jacob's sake, I mean he's six, he wants to get excited about Santa – he doesn't want his Mummy sobbing all Christmas Eve.'

I felt uncomfortable, and guilty. I still thought about him, but hadn't actually cried over Steve for quite a while now. Perhaps time had finally begun to anaesthetise some of the pain?

'I wonder what Christmas carnage the boys are creating in my living room?' Tamsin said, sensing my unhappiness and changing the subject. She glanced towards the living room where Heddon and Hall, Tamsin's interior designers, were embarking on her winter wonderland of impossible feats and ridiculous demands. This 'photo shoot' was the preamble to her annual 'event of the season', the Christmas party held three weeks later. Always perfectly managed, smoothly executed, lavished with as much preparation and money as Elton John's Oscar's after-party, it was, she insisted '*thee* event of the season'. My sister loved Christmas and had to squeeze every cinnamon and clove scented ounce from it – but the irony wasn't lost on me. Tamsin spent so much time and money attempting to 'capture the Christmas moment' that what she actually captured was high-pitched anxiety and hair-on-end trauma. My sister wanted her kids to have everything she'd never had, and I got that, but somewhere along the way I felt it had lost its meaning and joy for all of them.

Looking at her now, all stress and self-importance, it was hard to imagine her having a laugh and letting her hair down. As her sister, I knew Tamsin had the capacity for 'fun,' it was just executing it that was a problem for her.

'Tam, do you really think it's worth all the stress? There are better things to spend money on, surely?'

'Oh I know it's meaningless and my head tells me there are children dying of hunger when I'm spending all that money on a few decorations,' she said, taking a large glug of sherry. 'So I buy more baubles, write a cheque to Oxfam and have another fuckin drink.' She was now full-on Northern accent, all the clipped tones and long vowels disappeared in a puff of sherry.

'Ok love, just write that cheque, get through December and worry about global hunger in January – you've got canapés to think about,' I laughed.

'Yeah, well you can laugh, but imagine if my party didn't go ahead?' she said aghast.

'Oh stop, that's too horrific to contemplate,' I joked, but she nodded like I meant it.

'I'm not like you, Sam. I can't throw a few mince pies in the oven, put me feet up and call it Christmas.'

'Thanks!'

'Oh you know what I mean. You just let Christmas happen, you were never one for big Christmas events and parties... even before.'

I nodded, and it hung there a few seconds until Tamsin moved on – as she often did when faced with something less than perfect. So she put on her posh voice again, despite the alcohol, and increased it by ten decibels.

'This year I want glittery, celeb-drenched glamour... my soiree will be the swirling centre of Cheshire's social scene,' she half-joked.

'And you're hoping to achieve that in three weeks with a box of expensive baubles and two inebriated old queens?' I said, but she just gazed ahead. Perhaps she was suddenly too overcome with her Christmas plans to respond? Her phone tinkled and she checked her messages; 'Great, Simon's working late again... today of all days. He knew it was Christmas family photograph day.'

I rolled my eyes and made a sarcastic comment as she read out his latest lame excuse for not being there for her.

'There's always something to do late at the office, isn't there?' I said sarcastically.

'Yes – as you know, Simon is very conscientious and never clocks off,' she shot me a look.

I could have made more remarks, but left it, the mood she was in it was probably best not to pursue that one.

Tamsin poured herself another sherry. 'Oh dear, I was hoping Simon would be home to get the dog into his onesie. That dog will do anything for Simon, last year he let him suspend him from the roof by his back legs for our charity performance of Peter Pan.'

'Yeah, but he wasn't the best Tinkerbell I've ever seen. The dress was lovely but those big brown paws...they were a bit...'

'What?'

'Butch? Brown...?' I offered.

'God, you two are gender stereotyping him now,' Hermione piped up from behind her iPad. She wandered in and leaned on the kitchen island, looking up at Tamsin with feigned disapproval. 'Ma... get a grip, wasn't dressing him up as a dog tranny enough for you last year? Does poor Horatio have to suffer further mortification and be dressed as another *species* this Christmas?'

'Yes he does. That dog lives in the lap of luxury and he'll earn his keep, Hermione.'

She pronounced her daughter's name 'Hermiuney' and I smiled again on hearing the forgotten flat vowels of the working class Manchester girl that once was. This was the girl Tamsin had locked away a long time ago – she rarely made an appearance in these leafy Cheshire lanes lined with £2m plus homes. Tamsin looked at me, and I knew what she was thinking, but there was no way I was grappling Horatio's huge chocolate thighs into tight-fitting white fur – Christmas or not.

She sighed, climbing down off the kitchen stool, propelled by sherry, and landing rather abruptly. 'Cum on, our Sam, let's see how far the boys have got with me Winter Wonderland,' she said, swaying slightly into the living room.

Heddon was whipping around the place like the sugar plum fairy as Hall draped the tree with giant white satin bows. Meanwhile Gabe, who'd been hanging around since October, was sitting on her Paris chair eating Monster Munch and flicking through *Vogue*.

She huffed when she saw him and after unsuccessfully attempting to dress the dog herself she demanded Gabe help her. He was understandably reluctant to get involved but my sister was determined he would do as she requested. After Horatio was dressed, Gabe said something to her and she wafted him away embarrassed. Then she rushed over to Heddon and Hall who were clambering up trees and along pelmets in the pursuit of Christmas style.

Peter Heddon and Orlando Hall decorated Tamsin's homes every season. She'd fly them out to her holiday home in France each summer, the apartment in Miami every January and they'd style all her other 'events' throughout the year here in leafy Cheshire. Today they were getting 'White Christmas ready' and to say they were on a Christmas high would be an understatement.

'Oh that wreath's not working... and the glitter to white ratio is all wrong,' Tamsin was wringing her hands – a storm was brewing and I just didn't have time for one of her dramas over the technicalities of a wreath gone wrong. There were plenty of people on hand to support her and I needed to return to the real world where people cooked their kids' teas, put a wash on and didn't obsess about 'glitter ratios' or dress their dogs up as polar bears.

I sometimes wondered what it was that Tamsin was looking for. To me, it seemed she had a perfect life; a husband, two great kids, plenty of money and several homes dotted around the world. Yet my sister was always searching for the next high and Christmas just seemed to bring out the worst in her. For example, a Christmas turkey was apparently 'out' this year and she was desperately trying to get her hands on an organic goose. I mean that literally – she would have chased the right goose and caught it herself if she thought it would look good on her table – or 'table-scape' as she called it.

Along with her Christmas goose, Tamsin also chose 'the right' friends. Wrought from a shared love of materialism, multiple homes and absent husbands, her friendships were with women who'd been spoilt by money. They spent their days in the spa, shopping in town or eating leafy lunches in glamorous restaurants. These women talked only of the next dinner party, their newest designer dress, who their husband's latest mistress was – and more importantly, where the mistress got her nails done.

I suppose they were all seeking fulfilment in their own way, too, but recently I'd begun to think my sister might need more than this. She'd seemed agitated and I worried there were things about her life she wasn't telling me. Only a few days previously she'd announced over a glass of Chardonnay that she wasn't sure about her future. 'I sometimes feel like I'm in the wrong life, one I don't deserve and I feel like I'm on a treadmill, only as good as my last lunch, my last dinner party – I wonder where I'll be ten years from now,' she'd said.

I was surprised at her honesty. 'Tamsin, stop looking over your shoulder to see who's coming up behind you,' I'd said. 'Life isn't about who throws the best dinner party,' though I suspected in her world it probably was. 'Stop judging yourself against everyone else – there'll always be someone more stylish, more wealthy, more accomplished than you...'

'Who? Where?' she said. 'I'll hunt that bitch down.' She was joking, but I couldn't help but feel that a little part of her meant it, because personal perfection and being the best had always mattered so much to her.

When we were kids we'd loved to try and catch snowflakes in our hands, twirling around with our arms outstretched just waiting for one to land. From an early age I was aware that the delicate snowflakes would melt as soon as they landed on our warm palms. But Tamsin, who was six years older than me, never quite seemed to comprehend this and she'd lunge for them, screaming in surprise, almost tearful, as they disappeared at her touch.

It seemed to me that she'd been trying to catch and keep those snowflakes all her life. She would grasp at things, ideas and people and like a snowflake, she wanted to touch them, possess them, keep them in the moment - but just like when we were children, they always melted in her hand and she was left with nothing.

The photo shoot was a perfect example of Tamsin's futile 'snowflake chasing'. She was desperate to get the best shot, to seem like the perfect family having the perfect Christmas. She wanted so much to present this image to her friends that she made everyone – including herself – stressed and miserable in the process.

I put my jacket on, stage one of my escape from the madness.

'Oh I don't know how we're going to get this photo done,' she was stressing.

'Why do you need to even take a photograph? Why not just *live* it, you don't have to record it for others to see you're a happy family,' I said, fastening my jacket. But she'd grabbed a passing Hermione and was virtually holding her down whilst applying glittery eyeliner to her lids and made some enigmatic remark about even though we were sisters I didn't really know her.

I hadn't the time or the inclination to start bickering. 'I'm going now – those fish fingers won't grill themselves,' I smiled.

'Nicole Scherzinger's personal trainer says eat nothing white after 6 p.m.,' Hermione added mock-earnestly.

'Oh no... how's that going to fit in with your white Christmas?' I asked. My niece snorted, we often teased Tamsin, who was usually a sport about these things.

'Close your eyes Hermione, and close your mouth Sam... I'm not such a pedant that I will make everyone eat white food,' then she winked at me. 'But now I come to think of it... you'd look pretty in my winter wonderland eating only egg whites Hermione.'

'Ha... Ma you're so random. One man's LOL is another man's WTF.'

'I'm not quite sure what she just said,' Tamsin looked at me, puzzled.

I shrugged, 'Nor me. I'm getting off now guys...'

'No. You can't, Jesus is here... I heard him at the door.'

I'd had enough of Tamsin and her Christmas circus, and Jesus' arrival was like the second coming – literally. In any other household, the announcement that Jesus had arrived may raise a few eyebrows, but not in my sister's insane universe. Jesus was the appointed photographer, who also happened to be an old friend of Tamsin's and like all her friends wasn't quite what he seemed. He was small, dark and brooding with a morose manner and a faux accent – and I really didn't have time for that pantomime today. I had to tackle the oncoming snow and collect Jacob from the childminder before the weather set in.

'Come on, just say hello to Jesus, we'll do the "switch on" and you can get off,' she smiled. Tamsin always got her own way, particularly with weaker mortals like me, so I agreed, and as Jesus whipped out his camera and started snapping, Tamsin walked up the central staircase in the main hallway. It was a beautiful wide staircase with wrought iron banisters sweeping downwards in a curve. Tamsin loved playing the film star and as she slowly walked down the stairs like Gloria Swanson, Jesus was shouting 'oh yes, go baby go...' like he was in the throes of sexual abandon. He was winding himself in and around the banister, his camera strap now almost choking him, but he carried on snapping and 'yes baby'-ing.

'God help us if Jesus gets his Nikon caught in that wrought iron,' I whispered to Gabe, who was watching the whole scene open-mouthed.

'Jesus, he's gonna hang himself... and as for him...' he sighed nodding his head toward the spectacle of Heddon dancing around the fireplace with a bale of baubles and white fur.

I rolled my eyes, it was complete madness, but as I watched Tamsin make her descent, I softened. She seemed so happy, smiling like a little girl – this was all she wanted, to be loved, for someone to say you are okay, fabulous even, and don't let anyone tell you any different. Tamsin was my big sister and even though I was now thirty-six years old she still bossed me around and called me every day to see if I was okay. She could be stroppy and stressy and annoyed the hell out of me with her bloody onesies and twenty foot Christmas tree, but as she waltzed and sashayed her way down my heart went out to her.

'You go girl,' I shouted loudly from the foot of the stairs while clapping, almost drowning out Jesus' cries of photographic ecstasy. She blushed and smiled, pretending it was all a huge joke, but I knew she loved the clicking camera and the applause. I also knew she didn't get any attention like this from her husband anymore.

'Fabulous,' I called as the lights were switched on and the room glowed with 'Christmasness'. I blew her a kiss and hugged Hermione whose eye make-up had been abandoned for Tamsin's Christmas lights switch on. As everyone made loud noises of approval, the door chimed.

'That must be Simon. He managed to get away from work early after all. He knew how important this was for me,' she practically chirped. Thank God, Simon's appearance would take up all of Tamsin's attention and I could be ruthless and use his arrival as my escape. Mrs J was now answering the door and I slipped quietly into the hall so I could leave while Tamsin greeted him. But as I walked down the hall I could see Mrs J was having a conversation with someone that wasn't Simon. She was asking whoever it was to wait on the doorstep, but someone was pushing past her and coming in. I watched open-mouthed as two huge bald guys asked her to step aside and began banging snow off their feet on the mat.

'Tamsin, they won't wait on the step,' Mrs J was shouting. I couldn't possibly imagine what these men were here for, perhaps my sister had hired yet more 'staff' for her festive decorating?

Tamsin suddenly appeared, a string of tinsel round her shoulders, a half-smile on her face.

'They're bailiffs... say they've got a possession warrant,' Mrs J announced. 'They've come for the house.'

Chapter 2
Balls, Bailiffs and Jesus
Tamsin

An Aspen ski lodge was this year's theme… a flutter of snowflakes, a taste of St Moritz glitz and a little sprinkle of film star glamour for Christmas? That's all I wanted. And how wonderful if my husband had been there to share it with me, but Simon called to say he'd be late, apparently Japan were on the phone.

'What the whole of Japan?' Sam asked me when I told her. She was the queen of sarcasm our Sam, 'sarcastic Sam,' Mrs J always called her and as my sister had never really been a fan of my husband, he was often at the blunt end of her tongue.

Anyway, I ignored her – she always said I was over the top at Christmas, she didn't understand how competitive it was on Chantray Lane. She had no idea of the work, the sheer toil involved in lists and mood boards and instructing staff to do exactly what you wanted them to do. Our Sam thought if she put up a chocolate advent calendar and a paper streamer that was the season 'done', and that's where we differed. I tried not to be too hurt that Simon wouldn't be there, but it would be yet another happy family Christmas card with my husband photo-shopped into the picture. As Sam had rather peevishly pointed out the previous year, 'I don't know why you're so bothered, he's been photo-shopped into your lives for years... he never gets involved.'

I pushed this comment about Simon from my mind and concentrated on my designers Peter Heddon and Orlando Hall who were currently straddling various balustrades and screaming with laughter. I made a mental note not to serve mulled wine next year until their swags and bespoke Christmas window-scapes were properly in place. I just hoped the frosty wreaths, crystal snowflakes and fur baubles would survive their jaunty mood.

I was immersing myself in the sheer madness and magic of Christmas preparation when I spotted Hermione and Hugo lounging all over the new white sofas.

'Will you both please get off my winter white seating it's not for sitting on! And why hasn't anyone dressed the dog?' I yelled.

I snatched the gorgeous, hand-sewn polar bear outfit from my son, who was aimlessly wandering around making half-hearted attempts to force Horatio's leg into it.

'I have to do everything around here,' I snapped, wrestling Horatio to the floor, at which point Gabe, my landscaper, looked up from the magazine he was clearly engrossed in.

'What's going on here then?' he said, in faux shock-horror like he'd caught me in a compromising position with my dog. How rude, I thought – I hadn't asked the same of him when he was leafing through my *Vogue* and eating vile onion snacks not five minutes earlier.

I was cross now. 'Gabe, can you please put down my Vogue and hold Horatio down – I need brute strength for this one,' I huffed.

'You are kidding me?' he was smiling, not moving.

'No. This is not a time for joking, please grab his paws and push.'

At this point I was forced to straddle Horatio, which can't have been pretty, but he was always very good-natured about these things. Gabe stepped forward and I have to say was surprisingly gentle and I was vaguely impressed by the way he firmly but calmly held Horatio, who was somewhat reluctant to be a polar bear. Despite complaining, it took Gabe only a few minutes to gently ease the dog into his costume.

'I'm not happy about this, Tammy,' he said, as over familiar and opinionated as ever.

'I'm not doing it to make *you* happy – it's for the photo,' I replied, still straddling the dog.

'You look like one of them hunters in the Arctic,' he laughed. 'Ha, like you've just killed a polar bear,' he was now laughing openly at me, which made me feel quite ridiculous.

Hermione laughed from the sidelines and I grimaced because Sam had said only that week that I needed to be more of a sport and laugh at myself sometimes. But when my daughter started taking shots on her iPhone enough was enough. 'Stop that Hermione I will not be the subject of some "my mad mother post" again on your sodding Facebook page.'

'I wouldn't waste this on FB, ma,' she huffed. 'This is pixel gold for my instagram... I may even tweet this shit it's so funny.'

I gave her a look, which she didn't get because she was too busy sending a picture of her dog-straddling mad mother around the bloody world wide web. I sent up a silent prayer that the women of Chantray Lane weren't witnessing this online spectacle as it happened.

'Can someone please help me up?' I yelled feeling abandoned for the hundredth time that day. I was wearing a tight skirt and it wasn't going to be easy, ladylike or even possible to stand up without losing what little dignity I had left. My legs were splayed, my forehead was damp and Horatio was beginning to whimper.

Gabe (who was still laughing) reached down and took hold of my hand to help me up. I was surprised at the gesture and when I lurched up and landed against him, even more surprised to discover how hard his chest felt. Just at that moment Hugo wandered back in.

'My mum and Gabe doing it standing up? Gross. I have to unsee that,' he groaned.

'Gabe and I were dressing Horatio as you full well know,' I answered a little breathlessly, straightening myself and ordering Horatio into the kitchen. Gabe sat back on the chair smiling and watching me cross the room, which I found extremely irritating. I must have blushed. He made me feel very foolish, and not for the first time I wished I'd never booked him to help with my Christmas decor.

'Now, I need you to think, Klosters, in Switzerland... the swish ski resort?" I said, determined to engage him and make him move his arse to do some work now the dog was dressed. But he looked at me blankly and stared at the dog who was wandering around the room. I'll admit Horatio was walking strangely and probably wanted to pee but there was no way I was taking off that onesie – he only had to wear the outfit for an hour.

'Tammy. You can't let your dog walk round like that,' Gabe whined.

'For God's sake, you don't hear Mariah Carey's dogs whimpering. They are delighted to be on her Christmas cards every year,' I said. 'They pant and pose with their little paws up AND they were there when she gave birth to the twins... that dog should count himself lucky he wasn't around when Hugo was born.'

'Blood bath,' commented Mrs J from behind the sofa.

'Thank you Mrs J... I don't think we need to go into it.' I turned back to Gabe who was looking me up and down, with his mouth open, no doubt imagining me in the throes of a horrific labour. Nice.

'Gabe,' I said, almost clicking my fingers to get him off the labour ward and back in the present. 'Haven't you got stuff to do?'

He nodded doubtfully.

'I'm looking forward to film star glamour and Christmas sparkle on the slopes... and as Heddon and Hall seem a little "tired and emotional", perhaps you can support them?' I glanced at Heddon who was hanging by a glittery thread from the chandelier in the hall. I was hoping for literal support from Gabe as I didn't want Heddon to fall and leave blood on my winter white wool Berber.

Gabe was looking at me vacantly, spinning a £100 wreath around in his hands.

'So, think about it from a design perspective' I trilled, suddenly worried about the ratio of glitter to winter white in the wreath he was holding.

'Think Richard and Liz in their heyday.'

'Don't you mean Richard and Judy?' he monotoned... which said it all really.

I looked at him and he looked straight back at me, defiance and humour mingling in a very disturbing cocktail.

Then he leaned towards me, his lips close to my ear, and his breath warm on my skin.

'You be Judy and I'll be Richard,' he whispered.

'What a horrific thought,' I said, batting him away, but couldn't stop the shiver running the length of my spine.

'Go on Tammy... you know you want to,' he whispered, his breath tickling my neck as he leaned in even closer.

'Stop that,' I said as I pushed him away playfully. He was so very naughty I had to smile. I moved away and turned back to see a twinkle in his eye.

After organising Heddon and Hall I noticed Hermione's make-up needed touching up so I grabbed some glitzy eye liner in silver. It was all over the catwalk that season and I was just transforming her eyes when Jesus arrived.

❄ ❄ ❄

'Dahling, I run from the airport, your weather she's so damned fucking cold,' he muttered as I embraced him. Jesus, the photographer, was an old friend who'd taken photos for mine and Simon's property company in the early days when we were poor and struggling. Our star had risen over the years, but Jesus' had gone stratospheric. He now jetted around the world snapping film stars and rockers in close-up half-naked sepia, before showcasing in stark white galleries in LA.

Dark, brooding and gorgeous he positively smouldered and I couldn't help but flirt – his presence seemed to tease out the young, vital woman I had been when we'd first met.

'Are we black and white this year, Jesus?' I asked, batting my eyelashes.

'No. I want you in full, glorious fucking colour,' he spat, without eye contact.

I loved Jesus, with his gloomy face, filthy mouth and faux depression. Of course he hadn't always been a morose South American with a chip on his shoulder, his name had once been Jeffrey and he hailed from Chorlton. He'd been quite jolly in his Jeffrey days, always eager to please and smiley but that's the problem when you're nice, it's seen as a weakness and people take advantage. It was only when he changed his name, developed a foreign accent and anger issues, the fashion world sat up and took notice. He called himself Jesus after some footballer, but as he'd only read the name and hadn't actually heard it spoken he didn't realise it was pronounced hezuus. By the time he found out, it was too late – he'd already announced (and mispronounced) his global entrance. Consequently, Jesus' actions and whereabouts had always been a huge joke in our family, if a little sacrilegious. Simon would say 'Is Jesus sleeping with that supermodel?' and delight in making jokes about the second coming. We'd laugh for hours, the possibilities for Jesus' whereabouts and actions being endless and hilarious.

I poured him a mulled wine as he unpacked his equipment. I felt akin to Jesus. We were both born pleasers from the wrong side of the tracks who had somehow reinvented ourselves. I often wondered if he felt like me, like an intruder in his own glamorous life.

Now our celebrity photographer had arrived we were ready and I marched to the top of my beautiful stairs, which were the reason we'd bought the old rectory house fifteen years earlier. The stairs came down into the centre of the open plan hallway and sitting room, sweeping in a dramatic curve. I would often sashay down them one step at a time, feeling very Bette Davis. In fact, some days I had been so bloody bored of shopping and lunching I'd stay home and go up and down my spectacular stairs again and again perfecting my walk. Arriving at the bottom I'd stand, hand on hip, and say, 'Fasten your seatbelts, it's going to be a bumpy night.' I loved doing that but stopped when Mrs J asked me why I kept talking to myself at the bottom of the stairs. I'd had no idea she was there, the woman was like someone from bloody MI5.

Surveying the scene from the top of my fabulous stair-scape, I could almost taste Christmas. The air sparkled, glittering snowy white feathers glinted with diamanté on the giant tree and I had to hold my breath at the Christmas my interior design geniuses and a calming white colour palette had created.

Jesus stood at the bottom of the stairs, Nikon in hand, a sardonic, but admiring smile on his face. 'Go baby,' he said. And I obliged.

'Boys, you are my angels – I am in Heddon and Hall heaven,' I announced in my best Bette Davis voice, wishing I had a glitzy cigarette holder to wave for effect.

'You are an outrageous tyrant, but we love you,' screamed Heddon, glugging the last dregs of his mulled wine before climbing the balustrade and hurling white fur and spangles in a delicious, if impromptu Christmas swag.

'Brace yourself gorgeous one,' sighed Hall, the younger of the two. 'I'm about to mount the main fireplace, light the Christmas lights and within minutes, my darling, you will be immersed in your own, sparkling, white Christmas-scape.'

I heard Gabe say 'Jesus' under his breath, and he wasn't addressing my photographer. I gave him a withering look. He didn't fit in – I'd only employed him for his muscle and he had no finesse. He just didn't appreciate our mutual adoration, camp affectation and love of all things gorgeous. He'd have to go.

I wasn't going to allow the butch, obtuse Gabe to impair my evening, so I began my walk down the stairs, each important step bringing me a little nearer to Christmas.

Heddon and Hall screamed and clapped as I swished and shimmied, camping it up just for them. Even Jesus had a little twinkle in his eye as he climbed the filigree banister to get me in my best light, while Sam shouted, 'Go girl.' How I loved being the star of my own Christmas show.

'Jesus, I'm ready for my close-up,' I said, breathlessly looking down his lens and abandoning Bette for an over-the-top Gloria Swanson.

As I reached the bottom, my kids were giggling and blowing kisses and I blew them back as Gabe stepped in and reached out a hand to walk me to my seat. I was touched, but I wished he'd washed his hands first, one didn't like to contemplate where they'd been, but as most of the wives on Chantray Lane had been recipients of his services, one could hazard a guess. I tried not to dwell on Gabe's sexual proclivities and personal hygiene as he led me to my seat next to Hermione and Hugo. I held my breath; the air shimmered with expectation as Hall leaned behind the fireplace pressed the switch, and flooded the room with fairy lights.

The whole room glittered, the tree shone and icy white baubles caught a million wintry rainbows in their facets. I was moved to tears by my own Winter Wonderland – and this was only early December and only Phase One. Everyone ooed and aahed and shrieked (Heddon) and sobbed (Hall) and swore (Jesus). And just as we began the ritual hugging, the Christmas doorbell chime set off. Simon. I was delighted, he'd left work early after all – he knew today was special and I felt warm, fuzzy and grateful all at once. Mrs J shuffled off to get the door and I turned in my seat smiling in anticipation of his arrival. But when Mrs J came back into the room, hands on hips, there was no Simon, just two big, rough men. I had never seen them before, but it was quite clear these two hadn't turned up for the official launch of my St Moritz-inspired winter wonderland.

'Who...?' was all I could say.

'They're bailiffs... say they've got a possessive warrant,' Mrs J said. 'They've come for the house.

It took several seconds for me to compose myself. I was frozen to the seat and all I could think was how apt that I should sit there like an ice statue in my own winter wonderland. When I tried to stand up, my legs buckled and I fell to the ground, face deep in pure wool, wall-to-wall designer carpet. After a few minutes, I came round, but remained on the floor, gazing upwards, hoping it was all a bad dream and that I'd wake soon. Sam and Gabe were above me, discussing what to do – he was offering mouth to mouth or something equally sinister, but I put my hand in the air before he got any ideas. The thought of his Monster-munch-scented breath lurching towards my lips made me want to heave, which I promptly did – all over my winter white flooring. Of course Heddon and Hall were now in full throttle, screaming, running around in a complete frenzy demanding hot water and towels.

'She's been sick, she's not given birth,' Sam said rudely, while wiping my face with what looked like one of my very expensive linen napkins, which caused me to pass out again.

Within seconds I was back, having been slapped in the face by a now hysterical Heddon, who was being comforted by Hall.

I felt woozy, and with everyone's blurred face in mine, I turned away. My eyes alighted on the Christmas tree, still magnificent, smothered in a million fairy lights and snowy white baubles... had I dreamt these last few minutes? The smell of Norwegian Pine danced in the air, but however hard I tried to pretend it was a nightmare and I was now back in my own winter wonderland, I was dragged into reality by two balding bailiffs standing over me, impatiently.

'I don't understand... it's all a big mistake... isn't it?' I felt a tear fall down my cheek.

'No,' the fatter and lesser tattooed gentleman answered gruffly. 'Ask your husband, he knows all about it, he's been in receipt of a Warrant of Possession for several weeks now.'

'Simon knows about this?' I looked at them.

The fatter one nodded. 'He's known for weeks.'

'Well you'll need to speak to my husband then and he isn't here is he. I don't know anything about it. So would you please leave...'

'You can't ask them to leave,' Sam said gently. 'They have a Notice of Eviction, Tam...'

'Okay... okay,' I couldn't think straight, I had no idea what a warrant of possession or a notice of eviction was, but they both sounded terrible – and not something one would associate with Chantray Lane. 'Well, if you won't leave, let's keep this civil and discuss what exactly is going on,' I said. 'Mrs J, mulled wine for everyone please,' I called. I was feigning the 'good hostess' trick, but really I needed alcohol in order to bring myself round, comprehend what had just happened and try to deal with it.

'It's not a bloody drinks party, Tamsin. This is serious,' Sam snapped from my side. I pulled away from her and addressed the men.

'Please don't do anything rash just yet – I'm sure we can sort this out. My husband will be home any minute, just sit down over there... no, not on the white sofas,' I cringed in horror at the very thought of these men's no doubt grubby backsides on my perfect seating. 'Use those dining chairs, and let's talk,' I said, with what little authority I could muster from my semi-prostrate position on the floor.

They both looked at each other and I saw a glance pass between them.

'No point talkin, you haven't been payin yer bills. You don't need to give out fancy wine to find that out,' Gabe said, rudely, as he and Sam helped me to my feet.

'Oh I'm so sorry. I should have spoken to you first, Gabe – after all, you seem to know exactly what's happening,' I snapped. 'I'm offerin these men a drink because I might be about to be repossessed – but I wasn't brought up in the fuckin gutter!' I'd raised my voice and dropped my g and shortened my u and my hand flew to my mouth, horrified at my own outburst. Heddon and Hall gasped and everyone stood open-mouthed, even Hermione looked surprised, and it took a lot to shock my daughter.

'Sorry,' I muttered, sitting down, supported by Sam. 'I just thought we all could do with a drink.' Well, I certainly could.

'You'll be offering them a mince pie next,' Gabe said, more gently this time, but just as annoying.

I didn't dignify his comment with an answer. Looking at their broken noses and tattooed knuckles, a Patisserie a la Joyeux Noelle definitely wasn't on their 'to-do' list.

'So we are in financial trouble?' I nodded, making it sound vaguely like a question, in the vain hope that the shorter bailiff (with a disturbingly naked lady tattoo on his arm) would say 'no' and this whole nightmare would be over and I'd be back to my unspoilt winter wonderland where the only thing I had to worry about was Horatio not spoiling his onesie.

He didn't say no. He just flexed his forearm which made the lady's breasts move.

'Financial trouble? You could say that, love. You haven't paid your mortgage for over a year and your husband's neglected to make contact with the bank with regards these repayments.'

'Oh... I see,' I tried to appear unfazed by this, aware I had an audience and suddenly feeling very embarrassed. My brain was working ten to the dozen, hadn't paid the mortgage for over a year, what on earth? I had no idea how this had happened, Simon was in charge of finances and he'd given no sign anything was wrong if anything he'd been working more. He was always working late into the evening and recently had even worked weekends, so I had no reason to question our finances.

This was the dirty washing my Nan always warned me about – don't let anyone else see it, keep your business to yourself. Heddon and Hall were standing with Mrs J, mouths agape, and Jesus was glaring out from jet-lagged eyes and about two years' worth of unwashed dyed black hair. It was like they were watching a cliff-hanger episode of Coronation Street. I wanted to die.

I should have known something was wrong – Simon had been even more stressed and grumpy of late, but I couldn't put my finger on it. I'd thought he might be having an affair, a mid-life crisis, but I never thought it would be anything like this.

I called him, sure this was all a big mistake, but it went straight to answerphone. This wasn't like Simon, he always kept his phone on, never wanting to lose business.

I tried again and with the phone to my ear just kept looking at Sam and Gabe and Heddon and Hall. My eyes moved from one to the next seeking some kind of answer... and rested on Sam, who looked as shell-shocked as I was. 'What do I do?'

Sam said we could stay with her for now and she asked the bailiffs basic questions I couldn't even utter like 'do they have to leave now?' And to my temporary relief, as the court order had been served, we didn't have to move out for two weeks. 'Small mercies,' I muttered, meeting no one's eyes.

Hermione and Hugo said nothing – which was distressing in itself to see my two kids in shock. This whole scenario was mortifying, and as I looked at the people around me, all I could see was pity on their faces.

'Where the hell is Simon?' I kept saying over and over again. We'd been lucky with our property business, starting up during the property boom, buying to let, beginning with flats and ending up with large office blocks, penthouse apartments. Our hard work and good luck along with Simon's business flair and contacts had got us here, but it looked like our luck and his talent for business might have just run out.

I was at a complete loss, and I kept asking Sam what I should do – a complete role reversal for us. Sam had to collect Jacob but suggested we all pack some stuff and stay with her, but I had to stay to see Simon, so she agreed she'd be back first thing and we'd work out what to do. I told everyone else it was all a huge mistake and to go home because I was absolutely fine and Simon had texted to say he was sorting it. He hadn't. I lied because I was embarrassed and worried and didn't know which way to turn and I didn't need people watching me in my anguish.

Once they'd all gone and the kids (who were still in shock) were in their rooms packing, I poured another dry sherry into a crystal flute and took my seat at the kitchen bar. My mouth was dry and I was numb, but slipped into autopilot – I raised the pale liquid under the light. 'Cheers,' I said to no one and took a long drink. The dry, spicy warmth filled my chest and tasted vaguely of Christmas as it went down, filling me with warmth but adding to the burn of worry in my stomach. Where was Simon?

I gazed around in the silence at my beautiful kitchen and took another big sip. We'd bought the sherry on our last visit to Spain and enjoyed it, along with amazing views, at a stunning bar set high in the mountains. It was the finest sherry in the region, served chilled, bone dry and brought to life by a dish of salted almonds at our table in the sunshine. It had been a good summer, I thought, then remembered how the following day Simon had been called away to deal with a problem at work. As he packed,

I'd asked if someone else could deal with the problem, but he shook his head, kissed me on the cheek and went, leaving me alone in our luxury hotel bedroom with stunning sea views and our own pool. I remember feeling terribly guilty, imagining how many people would envy me this – yet I'd never been so unhappy or so alone in my life. Like now.

I'd imagined all our troubles were behind us. Those rumours about him and a woman at his gym were as ridiculous as all the other silly stories about our marriage being a joke. As Simon had said, it was just nasty stuff put around by jealous people. Was it too much for others to believe we had all this money and a happy marriage too? It was like we weren't allowed both, and I was determined to prove that not only was it allowed – but that we had it! It wasn't a lie, I was happy and our marriage had survived the bumps on the road of life. I'd decided recently that fretting about Simon's whereabouts and our future was doing me more harm than good and I was going to put all my fears and insecurities behind me and celebrate by making this Christmas even better than the last. From the tree to the food to the music and our annual party, I'd planned to work hard and make it the best. I loved my husband and wanted to make him proud of me... of us. But at this stage it seemed I didn't even have a home to live in, let alone a house to hold a party.

'I don't know why you waste money every year having so-called charity events, you should give it all to charity instead,' Sam had whined when I'd told her my plans for Christmas. 'A carol service? A thirty-strong choir in the garden?' she'd said like

I was planning to build a bloody motorway through the front lawn.

'It is for charity... you don't begrudge those poor starving little children!' I'd said.

'Not at all. But the cost of putting a carol service on in the first place will cost a fortune. Why don't you have a small family Christmas and just donate the money directly to the charity instead of killing the fatted calf for those poor starving little children?'

'Who do you think I am? Bob Geldof?' I'd snapped.

'No – but I don't know who *you* think you are. Your front garden isn't St Paul's Cathedral on Christmas Eve,' she'd snapped back. She was always better than me in arguments was our Sam.

And here I was, no parties, no carol singers, no bloody lawn for that matter. I was just a crumpled heap, leaning on my island in my clotted cream designer kitchen, drinking last summer's sherry and wondering what the hell was going to happen next.

Sam hadn't got a clue. She thought my life was easy, like it was all just one lovely long lunch, but it was a constant battle. My social circle was highly competitive and if you weren't struggling to keep your husband, you were competing with kids' school results, party kudos and charity functions. I lived in a place where footballers' wives mixed with regional TV royalty, and since the Salford influx from the BBC, we were positively awash with new money and WAG glamour. Everyone wanted theirs to be the glitziest evening, the sunniest garden party, the finest charity lunch.

Christmas was the most punishing. Every year it was the same, you had to have the best location, the finest food and the glitziest baubles on the biggest tree. It was relentless and fickle, you were only as good as your last Christmas canapé - and quite honestly, though I hadn't admitted it to anyone, the mere thought of another round of bloody Christmas balls (in every sense of the word) filled me with dread. My friends would have been amazed to hear it didn't make me happy. I gave nothing away – and people marvelled at my Christmases, which had a different theme every year. Once my 'Victorian Christmas' was in a double-page feature in *Cheshire Life*. 'A bewitching Victorian-themed Christmas in the £2m home bedecked with vintage baubles and filled with a boisterous family and tinkling laughter,' it read. The reality had been a little different. Simon had been working late at the office – again! And so I'd 'borrowed' Mrs J's son for the shoot and told him to keep his back to the camera. I remember sitting there with the journalist while the photographer snapped away, thinking how it summed up my life. Everything was fake, from the feigned festive joy to the caring, present husband.

But this year I really hoped things might be different.

I'd seen less and less of Simon in recent months which he'd put down to pressure of work, but I knew it was more than that. Only the night before the bailiffs arrived I'd found him hidden in his study having a hushed conversation on the phone. He quickly clicked the phone off as I walked in and refused to tell me who he'd been speaking to. I'd had an uneasy feeling deep in the pit of my stomach and stormed straight back to our bedroom. I'd grabbed my bespoke pillows and gone to one of the spare rooms. But I couldn't sleep and on discovering the *Vogue* December issue I'd pored over the festive gloss, turning the pages of a lavish turkey dinner, champagne served in crystal and a perfect model wife and mother presiding over it all. Despite my own faked Christmases of a photo-shopped husband and borrowed children, I couldn't help myself and part of me still bought into the dream. I wanted to be that perfectly groomed, smooth-haired woman in her glitzy top and black velvet trousers. She was laughing, her mouth open showing perfect teeth with effortless glamour. She wasn't insecure in her marriage and stressed about the festive season, she was comfortable with herself and sure of her husband. Those glossed lips were saying, 'I am the best wife and mother, I make perfect canapés, cook the most golden goose and after all that I will still have enough love and libido left to delight my husband in the bedroom.'

I'd Googled the glitzy top the woman was wearing and bought it there and then, thinking if I wore that top on Christmas Day, Simon might love me again.

Simon. I finished my sherry. Yes – Simon was bound to arrive soon, or call. It was all so sordid and unseemly and things like this didn't happen to people like us. Oh how we'd laugh at the blundering bailiffs who probably hadn't even read the correct address. The paper they'd handed me was lying on the counter top, I reached for it and my eyes skimmed along the page looking for the wrong road, the incorrect house name (we didn't have a number – you're no one with a house number). But there it was 'The Rectory, Chantray Lane.'

My eyes filled with tears as my brain began to adjust to the possibility that this might just be happening... to people like us.

Chapter 3

Christmas Roses and Champagne Truffles

Sam

Before the bailiffs arrived I'd been keen to escape Tamsin's theatrical Christmas madness. I was looking forward to taking Jacob home to tea and cinnamon toast in front of our little open fire. We'd snuggle up, watching the glittering, silent snow outside and when he was in bed asleep I would start baking for the morning. This was my life now – and since Steve had died I'd been desperately trying to keep everything on track for both me and Jacob. I hadn't always succeeded, but thanks to Tamsin, who'd been my safety net – I was finally getting there. But looking at Tamsin sobbing by the beautiful Christmas tree while two guys hammered signs on the outside doors I realised I had to be her safety net now.

Like everyone else, my first thought was that this was all a big mistake – but when Tamsin couldn't get hold of Simon, we all realised this was very real.

'What am I going to do?' she was pleading, looking over at me for an answer. I couldn't speak, I had always been the one asking Tamsin what I should do – this was the first time she'd ever asked me.

I gave it a few seconds to take everything in, then took a deep breath and went outside with Hugo to talk to the two men. My nephew was shaken, but wanted to get to the bottom of it all and I linked him as we both walked out into the freezing cold evening. Once outside we asked for details and the bailiffs confirmed that that not only was the house being repossessed but their company was in receivership, too. What made the whole thing horribly worse was that Simon had seen this coming – and had disappeared. I wasn't surprised. I'd never really taken to Simon he was all about how things looked and how much everything cost. Tamsin always seemed so bloody grateful to have him, she refused to see anything bad in him at all and I felt she made excuses for him. I remember once going for dinner and he was bragging about their new home in France. One of the guests remarked that they too had a house in the same region and I watched his face change – he was suddenly so angry that he wasn't the only one with a house there. 'Yes, but yours is one of those little places near the river,' he said. 'Infested with rats those places, wouldn't touch them myself.'

'Oh Simon, don't be so mean, Anouska's French farmhouse is beautiful,' Tamsin had cajoled. She feigned a light laugh and I noticed her hand discreetly slip under the table to touch his knee, a pacifying gesture she'd thought no one would notice.

'What?' he said and everyone stiffened, waiting for the Tamsin-baiting to begin.

'And what the hell would you know about French property, Tamsin? All you ever do is shop!' he said, looking around the table for someone to laugh, join him in his bullying. But everyone looked away and Phaedra asked Tamsin for the pâté recipe to try and move the conversation on.

The rest of the evening was unpleasant. Simon's mood had darkened and there was no way back. Tamsin had asked me to make Bûche de Noël for dessert (chocolate log to everyone else, but Tamsin thought a French name made it more posh) and I think she hoped it would save the night. But even my festive chocolate log couldn't disperse the cloud of uneasiness hanging over the table. And when Simon threw his fork down in horror because it was 'dry and bitter', I could have pushed the log down his throat.

Sometimes Tamsin let it slip that he'd upset her, but mostly she kept it from me – probably worried I might confront him. I noticed the dynamic quite early on in their relationship and later when Steve and I visited together he'd picked up on it too. I did broach it with her once or twice, but she was furious with me for pointing it out. Tamsin seemed to be constantly treading on eggshells, trying to keep Simon, the pressure cooker, from boiling over. There were times I dearly wanted to step in but knew it would affect mine and Tamsin's relationship if I got involved because she loved him and typically wanted to deny anything negative about her husband or her marriage. I was torn between feeling protective of her and being angry with her for constantly trying to pretend everything was wonderful and constantly placating him, making him even worse.

That night when the bailiffs had left, Tamsin was in pieces. She'd texted and called various friends and colleagues who apparently knew nothing about Simon's whereabouts.

'Where is he?' she cried, through hiccoughing sobs. Pale and shaking, my sister's whole life had just been pulled from under her and, like the rest of us, she could barely take it in.

'What am I going to do?' again, that question. My heart flinched, she was looking to me, but I felt useless and helpless. I shook my head and I saw the fear in her eyes, the desperation and disappointment of a shattered life, and felt so helpless.

The first person I would call in a mess like this would be Tamsin and so, without her guidance, I hadn't a clue. 'It's obviously some horrific mistake and Simon will turn up in the next few hours and sort it,' I said, unconvinced. I put my arm around her and she nodded. 'Why don't you all come back to mine until he gets in touch?'

'I can't leave here,' she said, panic rising in her voice. 'He'll come home. What if he's trying to contact me...?'

'He'll call your mobile.'

'No... he may turn up, I'm not going anywhere until I make sure he's okay, Sam.'

I hated leaving her like this, but after a couple of hours of shock and tears she seemed exhausted and still convinced Simon would come home later that night. I wasn't so sure.

Driving home, I tried to put everything to the back of my mind and chat to Jacob. My heart wasn't really in it, but I wanted to pretend to both my son and myself that everything was okay.

'We're going to be so busy this Christmas at the bakery,' I said, as much for my own comfort as his. The White Angel Bakery had been open for almost twelve months and this would be my first proper Christmas in business. Ironically, for the first time in five years, I'd actually been looking forward to Christmas rather than dreading it, but now that had all changed, in an instant. Funny how your life can be going in one direction, future mapped out, happy, content – then suddenly everything you know and love is ripped away in seconds.

I pulled the car up to the kerb as we arrived home, it was now evening and The White Angel Bakery was waiting like a twinkly fairy sitting in the snow. It seemed to be covered in icing sugar, glittering under the streetlamps, and I caught my breath at the sight. My heart filled with warmth and comfort at the lights glowing inside, welcoming me back to safety and sparkle. In the window were the cakes I'd baked earlier that day; snowy white frosted cupcakes, pure white macarons with a scarlet cranberry filling and a beautiful Christmas cake, covered in a blanket of white icing. It was stacked with white champagne truffles and dotted with tiny white Christmas roses. How different everything had been less than eight hours before when I'd carefully placed those sugar roses on top.

'Our bakery is like an angel, Mummy,' Jacob said, his eyes shining.

'Yeah... I reckon she's our angel,' I sighed, and we both stood for a few seconds in the snow just staring.

'Is Daddy an angel now?'

I looked down at him. We didn't talk about Steve enough; I found it too painful.

'Yeah... Daddy's our angel, he's up there watching over us,' I said, looking up into the snow-heavy night sky, my throat burning with the threat of tears.

I stroked Jacob's head and he smiled. He seemed pleased and grabbed my hand with his sturdy little gloved one.

'Come on,' I said, trying to be 'happy', trying desperately not to think for a few minutes about Tamsin or Steve. I had to concentrate on my son, he needed me too.

'Come on Jacob, I'll race you,' I suddenly yelled and we both shot through the snow up the side path to the little flat above the bakery, laughing and panting as we landed at the door.

Once inside I couldn't help it, I phoned to check on Tamsin. She sounded a little spaced out and I wasn't sure if it was shock or sherry, but she said she'd be okay.

'Come over first thing,' she said. 'If Simon doesn't come back, I'm not staying here on my own. I don't care if I've got two weeks grace, I'm not sitting here waiting for them to come and throw me out. Those bastards have left a big medieval sign on the window saying something about my chattels and announcing to the whole of Chantray Lane what has happened... I am mortified.'

'Oh Tam that's awful, I can collect you now if you like?' I offered, hating to think of them all there. I knew what the residents of Chantray Lane were like and I doubted anyone would turn up to offer any kind of comfort, but they would all read that bailiff sign with relish.

She continued to insist she was fine. 'I won't hear of you coming out at night in this. It's snowing again – look after my nephew, he needs you too, I'll see you tomorrow.'

I put down the phone and half-smiled. Despite her bluster and 'posh lady of the manor' act, Tamsin was all heart and in her hour of need still considered me and Jacob. I sometimes felt unworthy of her – she'd always supported me, throughout my childhood she'd been there. And after Steve's death she'd held me in her arms and let me cry until I had no more tears left.

We were such different people, my sister and I; she was obsessive, materialistic, she cared how things looked, what people thought and she had this need to belong. I found that quite heartbreaking, because underneath the brittle, designer-clad exterior she was as vulnerable as a child. Tamsin's caring nature could be a little claustrophobic for me and I'd seen the bakery as my stab at independence. It was my chance to build a future for me and Jacob. After tonight's drama at The Rectory it was clear we had some heartache ahead but whatever happened I had to keep focussed on my own life too. If I was going to be of any use to Tamsin I needed to keep things together, especially the bakery. If business continued the way it had been we were in for a very successful first year, but only if I could keep things on track.

I'd always been the barefoot younger sister to Tamsin's soaring stiletto success – but I was proud of what *I* was achieving and that I could be there for my sister. Jacob and I sat by the fire toasting bread on our forks, and as the toast turned crispy golden, I wondered if perhaps this was finally my chance to be there for Tamsin?

Sitting with mugs of cocoa and our toast now browned, I dragged my thoughts away from her plight temporarily to give Jacob some attention. Tamsin was there, as always, lodged inside my brain, just behind my new recipe for Christmas cake and to the left of a vague worry about paying the latest electricity bill. But Jacob had spent too long watching me distracted – particularly at this time of year, and it was important to me to be with him and enjoy our time together. I asked him about his day, which seemed to consist mainly of playing with the childminder's cat.

'Mr Fluffy is cute,' he said, sipping his hot chocolate and licking milky foam from around his mouth.

'Yes, he's such a cuddly cat, isn't he?' I smiled, both hands round my mug in an attempt to warm them.

'Toby said I looked like a girl so Mr Fluffy got him for me.'

'Oh dear. That wasn't very nice of Toby,' I said. This wasn't the first time Jacob had hinted at problems with other kids – boys in particular. My son liked his hair long, just like his dad's used to be, and we both loved it. Steve had had his own unique style and would often wear whacky T-shirts and long shorts in the summer to work. He had been a teacher like me and his chemistry class had loved his lack of conformity. I could see so much of Steve in Jacob, who also liked his own style and didn't want to conform, even at the age of six.

'I played ball with Mr Fluffy,' Jacob was saying. 'He flew through the air like a big football.'

I smiled and swallowed my toast in one lump, horrified. 'You didn't hurt Mr Fluffy did you?'

'No, but he jumped on Callum because he said I looked like a girl.'

My heart twisted slightly, the thought of his friends laughing at him, mocking my little boy. It probably hurt me more than it hurt him.

'Do they make fun of your hair?' I asked.

He nodded again.

'But you like it long don't you?'

'Yes.'

'Ignore them. You don't want to look the same as everyone else do you?'

'No.'

'Okay.'

'I want to look like daddy.'

I smiled. 'Yes you do, and Mummy's proud of you... and so is Daddy.'

'Can he see my hair? From heaven?'

'Yes of course.' I felt a burning in the back of my throat, but cleared it pretending to be okay, strong for both of us.

He seemed okay with this and settled down to finish his toast.

I sighed, it was so hard being a single parent, worrying if I'd got things right and being the only one to have big life conversations with my son. I drank my chocolate, just wishing the other parents would keep their small-minded, prejudiced thoughts to themselves. I'd seen it first hand as a primary school teacher – kids picked on for being different, and I didn't want Jacob to conform just because of a few small-minded people.

'What do you remember about Daddy?' I asked Jacob.

He looked down, like he didn't want to talk about his dad because it would upset me.

'It's okay to talk about people who've died,' I explained. 'It's a way of keeping them with us... I know I get a bit upset sometimes when we talk about him, but that's okay too.'

He nodded, uncertainly. The fire was going down, so I stoked it up, added more fuel and pulled myself together.

I had a tough few weeks ahead leading up to Christmas and I had to stay strong. Until now I'd always had Tamsin to pull me through. We always stayed at Tamsin's on Christmas Eve and she spoiled Jacob something rotten with gifts, but as he had no grandparents and no dad I appreciated her giving him such a good Christmas. I had no enthusiasm for the festive season and just couldn't wait for it to be over – along with the memories of that knock on the door when the police had arrived.

'I know, let's rehearse your lines,' I said to Jacob, finishing my chocolate and collecting the cups and toast plates.

Jacob had two lines for his part as the donkey in the school Nativity play and he'd been delighted to be chosen. So as the snow came down outside, we rehearsed. I smiled and mouthed the lines as he said them, then nodded encouragingly as he improvised with a lisped 'neigh' and a nod.

We worked on this for a while until Richard called round and joined in with what he called 'nativity training sessions', but he and Jacob soon started talking football as usual. I didn't mind, it gave me chance to reflect on the Tamsin situation and consider the implications of what had happened. I couldn't say anything to Richard in front of Jacob, so I went into the kitchen to wash up and let my mind go over things.

Richard and I had been seeing each other on a casual basis for about a year. We had met at the school gate – his daughter played with Jacob and he was a single father going through a difficult divorce. Neither of us was ready for anything too heavy, so we were on the same page. He was warm and funny and he made me laugh, but recently he'd wanted more and I sometimes resented him trying to look after me (I had enough of that from Tamsin). I was fond of him, but a part of me was still struggling to let go of Steve.

I sometimes worried that perhaps I was looking for a father for Jacob rather than a partner for me. I could hear them playing football together in the living room and hearing the slamming of the ball against the wall followed by shouting and laughter made me smile. If everything was okay here, with Jacob, I could be strong and help my sister through this – she'd been there for me the night Steve died. I thought back to that night now in vivid Technicolor; when the police had appeared on the doorstep I'd thought it was Steve returning home. I'd run to the door to throw my arms round him and say I was sorry – but instead it had been the policewoman who was sorry. She was sorry to tell me that my husband had been killed. Just like that – not 'hello' or 'Happy Christmas'... just that. Enthusiastic roars of 'goal' intruded on my thoughts again and I sighed with relief – I had to stop torturing myself. In the past twelve months I'd found a wonderful man who loved me and my little boy. Perhaps now it was time to try and let Steve go...

Chapter 4

The Real Housewives of Chantray Lane

Tamsin

The following morning I had (without any sleep) managed to convince myself that it was all a horrific cock-up. Of course I wouldn't say the word 'cock-up' because that would be common, but I'd told the kids the bank had made a mistake and Simon must be delayed. Of course Sam wasn't so easy to convince.

'Delayed? Where – Australia?'

'Rude,' I snapped.

'He's done a runner,' added Mrs J from under the kitchen island.

Sam and I looked at each other.

'I don't keep her there you understand,' I said, 'she just appears in a puff of smoke.'

Sam laughed.

'So where is he? That hubby of yours?' came the voice again. Apparently she was cleaning the floor, but I suspected she'd just found a good vantage point for ear flapping.

'Look, I don't know where he is, but what I do know is he works hard. He's probably been working all night, he's pulled an all-nighter before.'

'Mmmm... that's what he calls it?' Mrs J muttered.

'Enough. That's my husband you're talking about.'

Mrs J didn't miss a trick, I once mentioned that Simon was very friendly with a woman at work and she'd pestered me for weeks about it. Asking if he was working, when he was working and who with until I suggested she ask him for a copy of his bloody work schedule. Now wasn't the time for her to be bad-mouthing Simon, though I have to say I was beginning to feel very angry with him myself. I was trying his phone every few minutes like an obsessed person, but it was permanently off. Where the hell was he?

Meanwhile, Sam had turned up at dawn and was trying to get me to pack, but how could I? My heart was breaking and I just kept thinking – if I wait another few minutes he'll be here, or he'll call and it will all be fine. But it was now 11 a.m., nineteen hours after the bailiffs had burst in – and still nothing from him.

'Coffee?' I asked her and she gave me a 'you should be packing' look.

'Tamsin, I can't hang around too long, love, I've left Richard running the bakery and he doesn't know his éclairs from his croquembouche.'

'Just a quick coffee?' I asked, feeling like a child.

She nodded and I put the kettle on. Suddenly I was asking my little sister for permission to make a cup of coffee – a lot had happened in the last 24 hours.

I opened my bag of coffee and breathed deeply, my rich roast Sumatra Wahana was like pure therapy. I remembered the first time I'd tasted it, in a little cafe in The Lakes. Just thinking about that holiday now made me want to cry, I grabbed a tissue and Sam immediately asked if I was okay.

'Oh I was just thinking... one of my best ever Christmases was when Simon and I spent an idyllic pre-children Christmas in a cottage in The Lake District,' I said, shaking coffee beans into the electric grinder. 'The cottage was almost falling down, no heating, a leaking toilet and frozen pipes, but each day we'd wrap up warm and wander the hills. We loved the snow, the fresh air, the nothingness, taking our pleasure from the peace and quiet and just being alone together.' I poured hot water onto the ground coffee, filling my nostrils with the nutty, soothing aroma of freshly ground beans. I took out two mugs while Sam slid into a seat at the kitchen table she was always a good listener. I suppose she had to be because I was a good talker.

'In the evenings we'd return to the cosy cottage and eat local cheese, a bottle of wine and sit by a roaring log fire,' I gazed ahead, remembering how life had been... how *we* had been. 'We had no money, a rented flat and little idea where our lives were going to take us. But we were happy, somehow – equal, you know?'

Sam looked puzzled. 'What do you mean?'

'Well, I know you think Simon can be a bit of a bully, but he isn't, it's just that over the years he sort of took charge. And as he became more successful I took a back seat and focussed more on the kids and home...'

'So you gave up helping out with the business and...'

'I didn't feel I could involve myself in the business anymore – it wasn't my arena... I lost my confidence.'

Sam looked angry. 'But you're a vibrant, intelligent woman with so much to give. You started that business with Simon, and once the kids were off your hands you could have gone back there to work, but he never let you do that. If you'd been in charge Tam we both know none of this would have happened – you'd have had much more of a grip on things than Simon had.'

She was right of course, but he'd cut me off years ago.

'I'd always planned to go back after the children were born but Simon put me off – he said it was all computerised now and I wouldn't have a clue. I didn't argue, it was easier to accept it and just stay at home...'

'Yes, but in doing that you lost confidence, made yourself very vulnerable and completely dependent on him financially,' Sam pointed out.

I had to agree. Simon would come home and scare me with stories about the young, go-getting women he worked with and I couldn't help but feel insignificant and worthless. Compared to these ballsy women with incredible knowledge and talent, I felt I had nothing to offer. But at home I could take control. That's why I always embraced occasions – especially Christmas, when I could showcase my talents, deck the halls and bring on the carol singers.

'That holiday in The Lakes was one of my happiest memories,' I sighed. 'I never felt the cold or was in the least worried about the fact our car kept giving up on the mountainous roads and we couldn't afford to eat out.' I smiled to myself. 'Who needed luxury cars and fancy restaurants when we had snowy mountains, lush forests and sex by the fire?' I plunged the cafetière and drips of strong, brown liquid escaped onto the perfect countertop and it dawned on me – we'd spent that holiday dreaming of our future. And we were the lucky ones... we got everything we'd wanted, but we lost each other along the way. We'd gone on to stay in five star hotels, swim in infinity pools and drink vintage champagne, but none of our holidays since had been as wonderful as the one in that little cottage with the leaking toilet.

Only a few days before, I'd suggested to Simon that we take a trip back to The Lakes and that run-down little cottage one day. 'We could revisit the past?' I'd said. But he wasn't interested. 'The past is the past Tamsin and who wants to freeze to death in an old cottage when there are perfectly good hotels?' I guess he'd moved on – and left me behind.

I'd never really talked to Sam about my marriage – I'd always protected her, tried to keep worry from her door. Even as a little kid I never really let her see what was going on and I'd continued to do that even as adults, especially after what she'd been through – I couldn't add to Sam's burden. Over the years, I'd become emotionally self-sufficient, or had I just pushed my worries to the back of my mind, folded them all up neatly and closed the drawer?

Of course it wasn't just my marriage that had been coming apart under the perfect roof of my perfect detached home with double garage, designer kitchen and tennis courts. My circle of friends on Chantray Lane were great fun, but I had never really been honest with them, never been able to tell them I'd been born in a council house, or that my Dad had been on the dole. The ladies of Chantray Lane weren't exactly known for their acceptance of others less fortunate (unless it was a Third World black tie charity event) and I dreaded being excluded. The school I'd attended was the one they spoke of in hushed tones, like it was some kind of borstal. It was the place they threatened their own kids with if they didn't work hard at their paid-for prep school. I would always blush when anyone mentioned it – and feigned deafness when anyone asked where I had been educated.

I sipped at my coffee, a warm, comforting caffeine embrace; 'I'll call the girls,' I sighed, 'I need to tell them before they drive past and see that bloody big poster in the window.' But Sam suggested I leave it for now.

'Talk to your friends once you know exactly what's going on. You know they will tell everyone so just keep it to yourself until you know what's happened to Simon.'

I nodded, she was right, my friends could be quite judgemental and I didn't want them calling Simon and hurling abuse down the phone at him on my behalf. Anouska, Phaedra and I all lived on the same road, known locally as 'Millionaire's Row,' and were all part of what we jokingly referred to as 'The Real Housewives of Chantray Lane.' We were all rich, all glamorous and all bosom buddies. Or so I thought.

'I bet Anouska's got Heddon and Hall over there now,' I said, over my steaming mug of coffee. 'They're probably straddling her balustrades as we speak.'

'Oh for God's sake Tamsin, that's the least of your worries,' Sam snapped.

Anouska lived in The Old School house and was rich, beautiful and freshly single due to her philandering husband's desire for younger flesh. She was also very competitive and each Christmas always tried to book Heddon and Hall before anyone else. They'd called in at Anouska's on their way to me and I reckon she put an extra snifter in their mulled cranberry juice to inebriate them in the hope they would inadvertently sabotage my Festive interior.

Thinking about this, I suddenly remembered Mrs J's tea leaf reading prediction and felt a shiver run through me. I grabbed Sam's hand.

'Oh My God,' I gasped.

'What? What is it Tam...' she looked genuinely scared, and well she might be.

'Bugger me,' I said, forgetting my clipped tones and posh vowels. 'On Wednesday, Mrs J peered into the remains of my Darjeeling and announced in a very dark voice that "Big changes are coming. Vultures are circling."' I said, shaking my head.

'Yeah. I was here. She also said she could see a map of Antarctica, and the face of a clown, but then decided it was the reflection of her own face,' Sam rolled her eyes. 'Honestly Tamsin you've got to stop with the spirits and the tarots and stuff, Mrs J hasn't got a bloody clue.'

'What cheek!' came a voice from the other side of the kitchen. Mrs J was now emptying cupboards and popped her head out.

'Oh Mrs J, I hadn't even realised you were still in the room,' I said. I swear the woman was SAS trained and used silent stealth to gain intelligence on me.

'I have got a clue Sam Angel ... didn't I tell you who would win X Factor this year, Tamsin? I bet Psychic Sally couldn't even tell you that.'

'Yes you did... she did,' I nodded to Sam in confirmation, 'and he wasn't the favourite, even Simon Cowell was shocked.'

'Well, if Simon Cowell had me workin for 'im he'd know who was goin to win and he wouldn't take on all them daft acts,' she continued, her voice now coming from inside the cupboard.

'Anyway, as I was saying,' I rolled my eyes to Sam who was trying not to laugh. 'I looked into my cup at the tea leaves too and unlike Mrs J couldn't see any vultures, clowns or X Factor winners... but after only a few seconds I swear I saw Anouska staring back at me. There she was, bold as brass among the debris of Darjeeling,' I whispered, going very cold. 'And I have just realised why – it was a premonition, she's going to try and make hers the best party, the best canapés... photograph. Photograph! Oh God. I need to speak to Jesus...'

'You mean to pray?'

'No. To check he isn't in Anouska's sitting room papping those little fairy children of hers like bloody Disney child stars while my life goes down the toilet,' I hissed, iPhone to my cheek.

Fortunately Jesus was as loyal as ever; 'I never betray you and go to the other side,' he said in that lovely Portuguese accent.

'Thank God there's still one man I can rely on,' I sighed putting down my phone.

'If Jesus is the only man you can rely on then you're truly lost,' Sam sighed.

I feared she might be right.

Chapter 5

Designer Shoes and Profanely Priced Face Creams

Sam

Tamsin was understandably sad when I arrived the morning after the night before. She was all over the place, shouting about Anouska stealing Heddon and Hall and Jesus for Christmas – it was as though she hadn't taken it in, that this wasn't her life any more. I said that she had to think of her life as pre-bailiffs and post-bailiffs – and that everything was different now.

After several cups of coffee and some encouraging clichés from me she still wasn't budging, so I suggested we pack her stuff together. I wanted her to have the possessions she loved and needed with her. I didn't care that my van was small and my flat was tiny, I just didn't want Tamsin to lose any more of her life than she had to. If that meant bringing all the family photos and every precious memento she treasured, then so be it.

'So, what's precious that we need to pack?' I asked, guiding her out of the kitchen like she was a little old lady suffering from dementia.

'My jewellery's worth a fortune... and my art,' she muttered, looking around helplessly.

'Yes but is it of value to *you?* I don't care how much it's worth we just need to make sure we get the stuff that matters... that's precious to you and the kids.'

The bailiffs had said the repossession order was for the house and cars only... these were now owned by the bank. The furniture, clothes, jewellery and computers still belonged to the family and were therefore moveable, but there was only so much we could take that day. 'We can come back tomorrow and get more, we'll hire a big van and move it all... you will be able to keep your things,' I said gently, 'but for now just bring the precious stuff,' I repeated, watching Tamsin gaze longingly at the stunning white Christmas decorations.

I ushered her through to the main sitting room. 'My winter white seating,' she said, lunging towards it like it was the crown jewels.

My heart sank, there was no way I could fit three white leather sofas in my van or my flat. 'Perhaps we'll leave those until we can organise a removal van?' I suggested. 'Let's just take the personal stuff for now. We'll start in the bedroom.'

I guided her up the fabulous staircase, expecting her to stamp her feet and refuse to go along with me, but she followed like a lamb. I was unsure of this bowed Tamsin who showed weakness and vulnerability, this was the side Simon must see, I thought. I was used to her being there, fighting our corner, acid-tongued and demanding; I kept taking sidelong glances wondering if the real Tamsin was still in there.

We reached the bedroom; I'd forgotten how beautiful it was. The bed throw was pure, baby-blue mohair, the walls a pale gold with several beautiful paintings. Her dressing table looked like the perfume counter at Harrods, and I wondered at the cost of all her designer candles dotted around the room – they were probably worth more than my second-hand van!

We were both standing in the doorway, it was as though she was scared to go in.

'So what do you need to take?' I asked again, rallying her.

'Well... I need my diamond bracelet... and the platinum ring, it's worth a fortune...'

'Okay,' I said calmly. I didn't point out that the word I'd used was 'need' and no one 'needed' a diamond bracelet or platinum ring that wasn't a wedding ring. I let it go – jewellery wouldn't take up any space and if it made her happy.

'What about photos, stuff from your wedding, the kids' first shoes – all those things?'

She looked at me blankly; 'Oh... yes...'

'And your quilt? Pillows? A warm dressing gown?'

'Don't you have quilts in your guest room?' she asked, incredulous.

'Tamsin, I don't even have a guest room.'

'Oh I'm sorry – I forgot. Everyone has a guest room.'

'No they don't. Now what else do you need?'

'I have to have my creams and serums, I will die without them.'

'No you won't.'

'I will, I'm over forty – my skin will dry up and I'll be like a wizened old husk in about two days. You have no idea how miraculous they are.'

I picked one up and saw the price on the base of the jar – I almost fainted – it would have to be 'miraculous' at £200 plus a pot.

Tamsin was wandering around aimlessly, clutching at a silk robe which probably cost what I paid for a month's rent on the bakery.

'Do you have anything warmer?' I asked.

'It's Agent Provocateur.'

'Does that mean it's warm?'

'No.'

'Well then it's no use where you're going.'

'I'm going to your flat, not the bloody Antarctic,' she snapped, the old Tamsin coming through strong. I was almost relieved.

'No but I can't afford to have the heating on all day and night like you do.'

'But it's winter. It's freezing, how on earth do you and Jacob cope?'

'We put a jumper on, welcome to the real world love,' I sighed.

She clearly didn't want to envisage the horror that awaited her back at my flat it was all a little too real for our Tamsin. So she busied herself around the room.

'I need this too,' she said, reaching up and trying to take down one of the huge artworks.

'You don't really "need" it, do you? Besides, it won't fit anywhere. Tamsin you just need your mementoes, warm clothes, towels and bedding for now.'

I stomped into the bathroom and grabbed a whole pile of towels. They were thick and fluffy and in every shade of grey to match the Italian bathroom.

'You can't take those to your place,' she said, horrified.

'Why, are they too good for me?'

'No, but your bathroom's avocado, the grey will look positively ludicrous.'

'I'll take my chances. If people want to come and have a laugh at my "ludicrous" bathroom they're welcome,' I snapped. 'Now get a bloody move on.'

'I refuse to go anywhere without this,' she yelled from her dressing room. I bit my lip, held my breath and stormed in, dreading what she was pitching for.

'No. No. No,' I said, shaking my head and my finger at her.

'But I can't go anywhere without them.' She was pointing at a whole wall of shoe boxes. Each box was labelled and the designer shoes (of which there must have been 200 pairs) were all colour and season co-ordinated.

'You don't need all those shoes,' I gasped. A couple of pairs will be plenty.'

'A *couple* of pairs? Are you mad? Well, I'm not leaving here without them,' she stood, arms folded, the vulnerable little lady from ten minutes before now gone in a puff of smoke and bluster.

'Tamsin, don't forget you also "need" all your designer gowns too. I mean, you never know when I'm going to throw an impromptu drinks party in my bijou flat above the bakery,' I said sarcastically. For a moment she looked at me quizzically, she never quite got my humour. 'No, Tamsin, I won't be throwing any impromptu parties, just pack your jumpers and jeans and let's get out of here.'

It transpired, to my horror, that Tamsin didn't actually possess a pair of jeans because she apparently 'never had cause to wear them'. I sighed and wandered through into the main bedroom before I lost my patience. I had to remember what she was going through, but watching her pile up boxes and boxes of shoes and designer gear she wasn't going to wear was a test. 'I'm going to start downstairs,' I said, leaving a pile of empty bin bags on the bed. 'You can bring from here what you can carry and no more.'

I went downstairs and into the dining room where a huge contemporary white sideboard filled one wall. I got down on my knees, opened the doors and inside were rows and rows of boxes, all different shapes and sizes and all labelled. How very Tamsin, I thought with a smile – she was so organised, not like me who shoved everything in draws and cupboards only to fall out every time they were opened.

I wondered if this was yet more stuff Tamsin 'needed' or could some of it be thrown away? We had nowhere to store any of it, the way things were going there wouldn't even be room for me and Jacob once Tamsin and her shoes moved in. Looking through quickly, there were boxes filled with birthday and Christmas cards she'd liked and bought and never sent. Boxes filled with glassware, some china and a lot of cutlery – all labelled, all very expensive. Then I came across a box labelled 'Xmas Trinkets', and as she already had enough 'Xmas Trinkets' for the next hundred years getting rid of the box may be a good kick start to a declutter. I pulled it out from under other boxes and opened it up. I couldn't quite make out what was in there at first, it seemed to be mainly stuffed with old, yellowing newspapers, but once I'd delved deeper, I opened up some of the now crispy balls of paper to find a glass owl. I held it up to the light, remembering how every Christmas we would hang it on Nan and Granddad's tree. I delved into the newspapers, finding more old Christmas ornaments from my grandparent's home. Then I found the little wooden rocking horse, and my favourite as a child, the blue Cinderella slipper. I wondered why she'd kept them, because Tamsin would never use them on her own tree. They weren't fashionable or beautiful enough, but as I opened each one it took me straight back to that cosy little terraced house on Hyacinth Street. I shook the lovely snow dome, noticing a faint crack across the glass as the snow storm erupted; I discovered baubles I'd long forgotten and a fairy that had once stood on top of the tree. I smiled, Tamsin and I had made that fairy together from paper and foil. It was a lovely Christmas memory, a little sparkle in the darkness of everything that was happening around us. I put each decoration back carefully in its paper tomb. They'd obviously been put away one Christmas and never been out of the box since.

I explored further in the huge cabinet and, lo and behold, there was my grandparents' dusty old tree. 'It's meant to be,' I said under my breath. I put the box and the tree in the pile of things to go back to my place; this would be the first year since Steve had died that we would have a tree. Jacob would love it.

I wandered into the kitchen and my eyes filled with tears as my sister's great loss hit me. This room had been her pride and joy. Tamsin had loved being in this kitchen where she'd been the star of her own show. Another family would sit here now, someone else would drink wine on her island, cook unpronounceable French meals on her Aga and fill the air with the fragrance of fresh coffee.

I stood there for ages until Heddon and Hall appeared in the doorway and I was filled with such gratitude I hugged them both. 'Thank you so much for coming, it will mean a lot to her.'

'She's a wonderful woman and has been very good to us over the years, we owe her,' Heddon said. 'I'll go and give her a hand.'

Orlando put his arm around me. 'She's got bags and bags of stuff,' he said, nodding in the direction of the sitting room. 'Are you in that little white van with cakes all over it?'

I nodded. At this point Gabe appeared, he was covered in snow, stamping his boots on the Amtico flooring while Mrs J's voice chastised him, saying something about 'her ladyship's disapproval'. I had to smile – Gabe shrugged and carried on; he didn't give a toss.

'I can take a lot of the stuff in my truck,' he said, like a knight on a charger. He was big and broad and dependable and I could see why the housewives of Chantray Lane all had the hots for him. If he wasn't so unkempt and didn't smell so strongly of Monster Munch I'd have fancied him myself, he definitely had something. I wasn't alone in my thoughts either, glancing at Orlando who was licking his lips and looking Gabe up and down.

Gabe rubbed his big hands together. 'I'll load it up. Come on Orlando let's get humping,' he said over his shoulder.

Orlando shuddered with delight and raised a perfect HD brow. 'I'm coming, you big brute,' he called after Gabe, then as he was leaving, winked at me and whispered, 'every cloud and all that.'

'Tamsin's paid a fortune for Christmas decorations we haven't even used yet,' said Heddon, who wandered back into the kitchen clutching a white hankie to one tearful eye. 'We had merely scratched the surface last night with our switch-on it was only Phase One of Project Christmas. There is a stunning, white, life-size reindeer, a collection of exquisite angels... giant snowflakes, a veritable landscape of ENORMOUS baubles... and...' he was clearly quite upset.

'I'm not sure I can fit all that into my van,' I sighed, resting my head on my hands on the worktop.

'Don't even think about it, my lovely, Orlando and I will put it all in the spare downstairs room here, it's fine for the next fortnight. If it's still here after that, we'll store it in our shop until she needs it.'

I thanked him and as Gabe, Orlando and the kids began loading things onto his truck, I packed Tamsin's designer clothes. I was stuffing hundreds of pairs of colour-and-season-co-ordinated shoes into my van when I felt someone tapping my shoulder – it was Tamsin.

'Sam... please don't put November in July's pile. Can you imagine the chaos and confusion that will cause?'

'Carnage,' I said, pushing her into the van and slamming the door.

Heddon rushed to the passenger side and hugged Tamsin, before rushing round to me in the driver seat. I wound my window down and he clutched emotionally at my shoulder; 'That woman is a bloody saint... she's moving me to tears,' he gasped.

'Mmm me too,' I said under my breath before setting off through the late afternoon snow.

Hugo and Hermione hitched a ride with Gabe and I took Tamsin, who didn't utter a word all the way to mine. On arrival we helped her inside and I told Richard what had happened while we moved furniture in the flat upstairs to make room for everything.

'Will you be able to live with her?' he whispered, his brow furrowing.

'Yeah... well, no.'

'You're the most easy-going person I know, but she'll drive you up the wall. Why don't you and Jacob move in with me, and Tamsin can stay here?'

'Thank you, but no, Richard,' I smiled. He asked me to live with him on a daily basis, and it was now becoming a bit of a joke between us. I cared about Richard and there were days when

I thought it would be nice to live together with Jacob, just the three of us in out own home. But I couldn't allow another man into my life – what if I lost him like I had Steve?

Richard shrugged. 'Oh well. You can't blame a man for seeing a chink of opportunity and giving it another go,' he said.

'You know how I feel.'

'I do,' he enveloped me in his arms and it felt good. After all the chaos of the last couple of days he was my safe harbour and he understood me so well, which made it even harder to say no to him.

'It's not just me, it's about Jacob too. We're both still healing,' I said, but then we heard people coming up the stairs and I pulled away. Richard went downstairs to help Gabe unload while I explained to a very excited Jacob (who'd just been delivered from his friend's house after tea) that his auntie and cousins were doing a sleepover. I tried to make Tamsin and the kids comfortable and kept telling them it was all a big mistake and it would be over soon. And while I was saying it I was really thinking what the hell is going to happen to them? I couldn't imagine a life where Tamsin wasn't rich and didn't live in a big house in a life of utter luxury. My sister oozed money and glamour, breathing in designer labels and French perfume – her whole life was spent worshipping at the altar of money – it was her religion. How would she survive in any other life?

I suggested Tamsin lie on my bed and I'd bring her some tea. The kids both had sleeping bags on the living room floor, but said they'd stay with friends if this 'homelessness' went on more than one night. 'It's not fair on you, Auntie Sam,' Hermione said. She was tearful, but brushed everything off with 'it's going to be fine, it's all fine,' just like her mum. Hugo was older and more independent from the family, he'd been at university for two years (unlike his sister who had only left home for university three months before) and apart from the financial implications, his life wouldn't be affected as much.

I went downstairs and opened the front door where Richard and Gabe were still standing by his truck, they'd unloaded lots of stuff and filled the upstairs with it, but there was still so much more.

'It's a good job I'm not a tidy person, I'd be driven mad with all those shoes and clothes lying around. We're going to have to climb into my little rooms.'

'Is she okay?' Richard asked. I shrugged.

'Shame, she loved that house,' Gabe sighed, lighting a roll-up.

That was an understatement, but then Gabe seemed to be king of those, nothing seemed to faze him. I considered myself to be laid-back, but even I was amazed at his calmness and ability to just go with the flow. The rest of us were all traumatised and Tamsin's stress was infectious, but he was immune, just leaning against his truck taking a long, slow drag of his cigarette.

'She'll be fine. She's a tough lady,' he said, breathing a lungful of smoke and blowing it slowly out into the cold air.

He was right, but at the moment she was definitely a little wonky. I was glad to be there for her in her moment of need – especially as none of her so-called friends had turned up. Mind you I'd met all her friends and there wasn't one who would be happy to hurl bin bags onto a truck on a freezing cold morning in December. I almost smiled at the thought of that 'up herself' Anouska with her highlighted hair and always perfectly made up face. She was so thin she'd break if you handed her a filled bin liner.

'I just hope Tamsin's hubby hasn't done anything stupid,' Gabe said, flicking his fag ash on the ground. I wrapped my cardigan around me, it was freezing cold, but I wanted to talk. 'Do you mean...?'

'I dunno. People do stupid stuff when they can't see a way out.'

'Simon's too egotistical,' Richard suddenly said into the smoke and the steam from our breaths. I had to agree, Richard had, along with me suffered a few of Tamsin's dinner parties in the year we'd been together and said Simon seemed to look down on everyone. My brother-in-law was an ambitious man – he wanted to be the best and have the best – nothing was ever quite good enough for him. I think Tamsin felt at times that she wasn't good enough for him either. I worried their relationship fed into her low self-esteem, because despite the bluster and the money and the talk – she was incredibly insecure.

'Well, I just hope he's still in one piece – ego or not,' Gabe sighed, looking at Richard and taking another long curl of smoke.

As a reformed smoker I always wanted a cigarette and I couldn't watch a second longer and asked Gabe for a fag. Richard looked at me with vague disapproval and I ignored him. I was a grown-up and I would smoke if I wanted to. No one controlled me – I'd had enough disapproval from Tamsin for a lifetime and I was damned if I was going to be made to feel guilty about having a cigarette.

Gabe rolled me one and I took it between my thumb and forefinger, breathing it in slowly, relishing the warm, soothing hit at the back of my throat.

We were all standing there contemplating unloading another black bin liner from Tamsin's life when she appeared in the doorway, hair on end.

'My Gaggia!' she shrieked.

We all looked at her bemused.

'Your whattia?' Gabe joked, still leaning nonchalantly against his truck, his eyes half-closed through smoke.

'My coffee maker... I left it behind.'

He smiled, gave a nod and slowly stubbing out his cigarette with his boot, climbed in the truck and drove off.

Richard and I both looked at her.

'What? I may not have a home, a car or a husband... but I'm damned if I'm going to drop my standards... is that a cigarette in your mouth, madam?' she asked. I felt fourteen again and was about to tell her to piss off but she went back inside.

'Ha, you're in trouble,' Richard laughed.

'I feel for her and I know she's hurting. But I want to kill her and it's only Day One,' I said.

'Well, I can't stay around watching this comedy unfold. You have sanctuary in the form of keys to my place if you change your mind,' he smiled.

I wrapped my arms around him. There was nothing I would have loved more than to take Jacob and go over to his place there and then. My heart wanted to snuggle down on his comfy old sofa and sleep in his big bed, but my head kept saying no.

I waved him off and once inside put the kettle on and made Tamsin some tea to calm her down until her Gaggia arrived.

'I wonder if Simon's okay?' I said. I felt I should at least broach the possibility that he might be distressed somewhere and contemplating taking his own life.

'He's fine. I heard from the accountant when you went downstairs, didn't want to say in front of the kids... the coward took his passport and is heading for the only home we have left – in France.'

Chapter 6

Gabe, the Gaggia and Ghosts of Christmas Past

Tamsin

It was one of those wintry afternoons when we left The Rectory and headed for Sam's place. It was as though everywhere had been painted in grey watercolours, and pulling out onto the main road, the cars and houses and trees all merged into one. I couldn't look back at the house, and tried to look in front of me, my head held high. Everything had changed. My life wasn't the same and the man I loved wasn't who I thought he was – everything had dissolved like snowflakes landing on a warm hand. It had taken all morning to pack our stuff and Sam had been very annoying and bossy about what she thought I should take. I mean how could I possibly leave my collection of shoes behind? So by the time we'd argued about what should stay and go, we arrived at the bakery in a wintry dusk, the snow being the only source of light in the grey-white. Sam turned off the engine and we sat for a little while – the bakery looked almost ethereal glowing in the middle of the square – like an angel waiting for me. I had to give it to our Sam, she'd made The White Angel Bakery into something very special.

I got out of the car, almost ran inside and it welcomed me in. It looked like a sweet gingerbread house glittering from the inside, filled with bright, cinnamon warmth. It was only early December, but fairy lights were twinkling, the smell of Christmas baking filled the air, and I felt warm and safe for the first time in ages.

❄ ❄ ❄

All I wanted was my stuff, a hot drink and a good cry on my own, but within seconds, I realised to my sheer horror – I had forgotten my Gaggia. I simply couldn't live without it and the fact I'd left behind something so vital was a testament to my fragility and disorientation. I was devastated and despatched Gabe immediately to go and fetch it. Meanwhile Sam made some strange supermarket tea in an attempt to make me feel better – but it upset me even more. I thought she knew I only ever drank Darjeeling.

We sat together in Sam's tiny living room and drank the vile brew. Surprisingly, she asked if I thought Simon was okay, and I told her about the phone call I'd taken earlier from the accountant. I explained that whilst everyone had been unpacking, I'd lay down on Sam's bed, trying to stop my head spinning. What on earth was going on? How were we all going to live together? Then my phone rang. At first I thought, hoped, it was Simon, to clear all this up and tell me it was after all a mistake and everything was now sorted, Christmas was back on and I could go home. But it wasn't it was David Harris the accountant, who told me just how bad everything was and that Simon had known and was now in France.

'He's left us to the wolves,' I said to Sam.

Better men, with bigger companies than Simon, had gone to the wall in the current financial climate... and in itself that wasn't a shock. But his abandonment of us was like a betrayal, the worst betrayal.

'What happened to sticking together through thick and thin? And if he didn't care about me – what about the children?'

Sam shook her head. Then she said; 'He's always been... quite self-preserving though hasn't he Tam?'

I was about to tell her she was wrong – my husband was perfect, but then I remembered, I didn't have to defend him anymore. For years I'd pretended he was different, that he wasn't selfish, self-obsessed and bullish – I'd said he was hard-working, distracted and proud of his own achievements, but I'd been lying to myself.

'Yes, you're right,' I sighed. 'Self-preserving is a good way to describe Simon. Once, we were on holiday on one of Rosalind's yachts and I fell overboard. I'd had a little too much vino and one minute I was Voguing on the poop deck to Madonna, the next I was inspecting the ocean floor at close range. As you know, I can't swim and fortunately all the men leaped in immediately to rescue me. And when they dragged me out of the water sobbing and coughing up all kinds of canapé and sea urchin, I looked to see where Simon was.'

Sam looked at me. 'Where was he?'

'He was bloody waving from the lower deck, a glass of champagne in one hand and Rebecca Hartley-Brewer in the other. Later on I asked him why he hadn't dived in to save me and he said, "Oh darling, I had my Armani shirt on and it's dry-clean only."'

Sam gasped.

'At the time I thought it was a perfectly acceptable reason to watch your wife drown, but it's stayed with me... Is it my fault?' I asked suddenly. I'd spent so much of my childhood taking on blame and responsibility, I'd carried it on into adulthood.

'No, and don't you dare suggest it is,' Sam admonished, like the school teacher she had once been. I wrapped my cashmere shawl around me and thought about how different my childhood had been from what came later – but had it really?

Feeling the warm, pure white cashmere, like loving arms around me, the magical softness against my face, I was suddenly seven years old, sitting safe on Santa's knee listing my Christmas desires. It never occurred to me then that the whole point of asking Santa for presents was to ultimately receive them on Christmas day. I never got to own any of the items on my list and, until I was much older, assumed no one else did either. Once or twice I was given some gifts on Christmas Day that I was able to keep, but often they'd disappeared to the pawn shop the day after Boxing Day. Visiting Father Christmas was never about the presents for me – it was about the safety, the cosiness of snuggling up to the red coat. I loved his impossibly thick, snow white beard, the soft, kind eyes. When Sam and I were kids, Lewis's department store, fifth floor, was where Christmas lived all December. Sam and I loved it there so much we would get the bus into town, often being thrown off if we were caught, because we never had the fare, and would have to walk the four miles home. The department store was a free playground of space hoppers, dolls in boxes and Chopper bikes in flame orange. Sam and I would wander through that wonderland caressing and longing for the baby doll that cried real tears, the red roller skates, the toy post office with paper money, real envelopes and perforated stamps. One year Sam fell in love with a bright blue oven and stared longingly at it every time we visited the store. I told her it would burn her fingers if she touched it and she believed me. She never got to find out, and I never got to wipe the baby doll's real tears or ride on those roller skates. I smiled, imagining myself as a little girl in Lewis's department store asking for that baby doll off Santa. He was big and whiskery like my Dad, but that's where the similarity ended. The man in the red coat with the white beard was softly spoken and gentle, he smelt of burnt candles, cedar wood and cinnamon, and I was safe on Santa's knee.

Simon had been softly spoken and gentle too when we'd met. He was my rescuer – I married him to escape my father and my childhood, and for twenty four years, I'd thought his love and our money had kept me safe.

Simon had taken me away from the pain and the poverty and by his side I'd been able to fly – but now I realised we'd been in a hot air balloon bobbing along on nothing but air. And in the end he hadn't loved me enough to stick around. Perhaps he wasn't so different from my father after all?

Sam was threatening to make another cup of vile tea, so I asked for something stronger and she produced a bottle of wine and two glasses. I pointed out it was New World wine, which wasn't ideal, but she said it was all she had, and it had to be better than her disgusting tea.

'You might have to get used to cheap plonk, love,' she said, pouring two large glasses. We talked for a while, and halfway through the bottle I began to relax.

Looking around the tiny flat it wasn't all I'd have to get used to – I felt like I was in a cave, it was so dark and small with no window-scapes and just one sofa! I hadn't been for a while – I often popped into the bakery to order something fabulous for a coffee morning or a dinner party, but I'd rarely been upstairs. I had to admit though despite its complete lack of colour-co-ordination, artwork or style – I felt surprisingly at home.

Sam and I talked for a while, drank a little wine and halfway through the bottle I began to relax.

'It wasn't a happy marriage, Sam,' I said out loud, like I was hearing it for myself the first time.

She nodded, she didn't seem surprised.

'After the children were born, Simon abandoned me emotionally. Oh, he continued to provide and paid lip service to our marriage with sex once a fortnight and a weekend away at anniversaries, but that was all.'

'I reckon you filled up the gap he'd left by spending money,' she said, emptying the dregs of the bottle equally into our glasses.

'Yes, but it could have been worse, it could have been drink or drugs or – God forbid – food.' I shuddered, pulling the sparkling cashmere throw around me, contemplating the sheer vulgarity of excess weight.

'Tamsin. Don't be so shallow, it doesn't matter about a few extra pounds...'

'Oh that's where you're wrong. Imagine the scenes if I'd allowed myself to become addicted to food? No designer clothes, no front row at fashion shows, other women sniggering behind manicured hands at my burgeoning hips.'

Sam shook her head in disbelief. 'Oh yes, it would have been absolutely terrible, dahling!'

'Don't laugh at me, Sam,' I said, seriously. I sometimes felt Sam didn't understand me, and my life was a joke to her.

She put her hand out to me and held mine. 'I'm not laughing at you love... I just think your idea of what's important in life is different from mine.'

'I must sound so shallow and superficial to you. I know you're a much better role model than I am, you're a woman who lives by her own rules and you aren't influenced by others – I must be weak, Sam.'

She shook her head vigorously.

'You'll hate me for saying this,' I went on, 'but I'd wanted to look good, stay slim and young for Simon. In the early days he'd always seemed so proud to have me on his arm, but then he changed and didn't seem to "see" me anymore. I'd come downstairs in something sexy and fabulous and I'd have to ask him what he thought – he'd never volunteer it – and if pushed he'd say "You look nice." Nice?'

But now my world had shifted on its axis and I was beginning to see it wasn't me – it was him. Perhaps the friends who'd laughed behind their hands as he reeled off his list of possessions and achievements had a point? They'd seen the ruthless Simon I'd chosen to ignore. When your heart is broken by your daddy as a little girl, you can't put yourself through it all again, so you lie to yourself to make your husband your hero.

I hated him for what he'd done. I thought he was strong, but strength wasn't running away – it was staying and fighting, standing your ground and facing the consequences. Heroes didn't abandon their families.

❄ ❄ ❄

That first morning at Sam's, I woke up and reached for Simon, then I remembered, and my heart clanged shut. Eventually I climbed out of bed, dressed, donned my dark glasses and went down into the bakery to see Sam. She was busy serving customers, this was her world and I was the intruder and completely out of place in black Prada trousers and YSL blouse. I needn't have bothered with dark glasses because Mrs J spotted me from across the shop and announced my arrival to all and sundry. So much for discretion.

'Oh here she is... here's our Tamsin. Are you alright, love? I was just saying,' she gestured to a couple of ladies drinking coffee, 'after what's happened, you'll be cooking your own teas from now on...' To my abject horror, these women were nodding, she'd clearly filled them in on everything. 'Nice stews, big pea soups, that's what you need, none of that fancy schmancy stuff... you need to build yourself up, I've always thought you was too skinny.'

Great, so Mrs J was now 'helping' at the bakery and keen to educate me in the culinary delights I had in store as a homeless, moneyless person. I really didn't need her to go on and on... but she did, and at the risk of a migraine (the vibrant green image of 'big pea soup' lodged in my head and stomach), I grimaced, turned round and went straight back upstairs.

I made myself some coffee (thanking God for Gaggia and Gabe) and tried to read one of the magazines I'd packed. Leafing through Cheshire Life I felt a stabbing pain at the sight of Anouska in scarlet draped around a Nordic pine Christmas Tree like an anorexic Red Riding Hood. I couldn't bear to turn the page and threw it to the floor, it was all so painful. Last year it was me with my Nordic pine splashed across the society pages. How I hated being out of the loop, stuck in the flat above the bakery – I wanted to go home and get ready for the season but had to keep reminding myself it wasn't mine any more. The kids had already gone to their friends' houses where there were spare rooms, flat screen TVs and plenty of light and heat. It was freezing in Sam's flat and I was just glad I'd packed my cashmere shawl – I gathered it around me as I sipped my coffee. Pure Sumatra Wahana, one of the few luxuries I had left in the world, and who knew how long for? I sipped sparingly at the rich roast of my old life and turned on the TV. One of those awful trailer trash daytime things sprang up – where people accuse strangers of being the father of one of their ten kids. A rotund man was arguing with the host about how much he drank and how he didn't beat his wife – and my insides shrivelled. The air was blue and the man was spitting at his wife as he spoke: his face scarlet with burst blood vessels, beer and rage, her face pale with the kind of fear only a woman in her situation knows. I couldn't watch any more so turned it off, wishing it were that easy to turn off my memories. The red faces, the spittle of anger, the hurt, all the damage. In adulthood, money had soothed me, cocooned me in perfumed interiors and luxury fabrics. I had wrapped myself in love and cashmere... but had I ever been really happy?

I suddenly remembered it was Tuesday. Anouska, Phaedra and I always lunched at Puccini's on a Tuesday. Oh how wonderful to have pumpkin ravioli again, I suddenly longed for the crunch of garlic croutons in rich, hot minestrone, and my mouth watered at the prospect of a liberal sprinkling of tangy Parmesan. The girls must have been wondering where I was and why I hadn't yet turned up for our usual pre-lunch Prosecco. Recalling the delicious prickle of those cold bubbles, I dug my phone out of my handbag surprised to see there were no missed calls or texts so called Phaedra. She would be so upset when I told her what had happened she'd insist on collecting me and paying for my lunch herself. It rang out for a while, but she didn't answer, she must have been late and missed the pre-lunch Prosecco. Yes she would still be driving to the restaurant – so I texted her. She'd get back to me when she arrived. In the meantime I called Anouska. I was slightly more reluctant to speak to Anouska; I had an uneasy feeling she might get a little thrill from my total devastation, but her phone kept ringing out too. She'd be straight on the phone when she saw my missed call so I made some more coffee and checked my phone. Surely they had arrived at the restaurant by now? I sent them both another text and settled down to watch This Morning and a lovely item on Christmas Cocktails. I wrote down some of the recipes thinking how cranberry juice and champagne would be fabulous to serve at my Christmas charity supper for Alcoholics Anonymous. Then I remembered – I wasn't hosting any charity Christmas suppers this year. I was the charity now.

I tried to make contact with the outside world by calling a couple of other friends who didn't pick up either. A man came on This Morning talking about money and I opened my purse and found a ten pound note. I wondered if I could still use any of my debit or credit cards. I called the bank – the answer was no.

I surfed the few channels Sam's TV had (honestly it was like being back in the bloody 70s – no satellite, no Freeview – it was an outrage – I honestly don't know how she survived).

I called Phaedra again, but there was obviously no signal.

Then Cash in the Attic came on and it had a lovely Christmas flavour with old tree decorations and a super wooden rocking horse. I thought about selling some antiques, but everything I owned was either at The Rectory or in black bin liners and it would take weeks to work out what was where – there was no way Sam would have labelled anything! I sat there among the bags of my life, Phaedra and Anouska still hadn't returned my calls, and only then did it finally dawn on me… I was the new Mimi.

Mimi was the woman in our social circle that we avoided. She may have been rich and beautiful, but she was from the wrong side of the tracks – and unlike me had never tried to hide it, so had never been accepted. None of 'The Real Housewives of Chantray Lane' felt she was worthy and we never invited her to any of our soirées or deigned to attend any of hers. 'NLU' Anouska had said of Mimi. I must have looked puzzled when she said this because she explained; 'Not Like Us, darling,' then she giggled, and I'd giggled too at Mimi's exclusion, which had made me feel more included. But it looked like I was the outsider now – I was 'NLU'.

I texted Simon – I wasn't sure how long my phone would remain connected and figured it would be cheaper to text the bastard. By 4 p.m. I had left several messages on his phone which started with polite requests for him to call me, and – I'm ashamed to say – descended into a tirade of unladylike abuse.

I wandered downstairs to talk to Sam. She was busy kneading dough, the bakery was quiet, the snow was falling more heavily and inside felt warm and cosy. I leaned against the kitchen worktops watching her work as she pummelled at the unrelenting olive-studded dough. Behind her on a shelf was a stunning white chocolate Christmas cake, and I felt a festive rush walking towards it, pure and white, stacked with truffles and Christmas roses, with just a suggestion of glitter. Then I realised it must have been meant for me.

'You can still have it,' she said, reading my mind.

'I wouldn't dream of it, sweetie. I can't pay for it for a start.'

'It was a gift,' she sighed. 'I was going to surprise you before your Christmas soirée, make it the centrepiece – you know?'

I nodded. I felt like the little girl that Santa forgot. It was stunning and would easily have served the sixty guests I would have been expecting... how I wished it was still mine.

'Don't sell it though – I don't want Anouska getting her hands on it – or God forbid, Mimi ordering it and adding something tasteless and purple to the top,' I added.

Sam rolled her eyes and threw herself back into the dough, giving it an unnecessarily hard punch. I almost felt it myself!

My biggest fear had always been a return to the way life had been as a child. No food on the table, no money for the electricity meter, and Dad, drunk. Christmas Eve had always been the worst... Mum and Dad would come home very late, we'd be in bed and then it would start. I'd lie upstairs listening to them. It began with just a monotone background noise of bickering and bitterness, spiking gradually until both their voices were fighting to be heard, to beat the other down. Then came the smashing of crockery, the yelling, the screams and the thumping of Mum's head against a wall or a table, followed by the worst sound of all... silence. It was the silence I dreaded the most – it was like a knife in my heart. Sometimes, if I was feeling brave, I'd go downstairs and open the kitchen door, I'd hold my breath and close my eyes, unable to face what I knew was waiting. Mum lying on the floor, or staggering to get up, pretending she'd fallen, Dad glowering in the corner. 'Just banged my head, love, I'm a silly billy.' But we both knew the truth.

He knew I knew and as I'd help mum onto her feet he'd spit some insult at me, 'You're just like her... nothing.' And that's when I decided to prove him wrong, I hated him with such rage, such anger it ate away at me night after night. Once, when I couldn't take it anymore I'd tried to wake Sam, I couldn't bear the burden alone and wanted to share it with his perfect child, who believed he was the perfect father. 'Can you hear him, downstairs?' I asked.

'Who father Christmas... is that his reindeers I can hear, Tamsin?' she'd said, sleepy eyed while the thumping continued. I looked at her for a while, wondering whether to tell her what was going on, but didn't have the heart and just nodded. 'Yeah... it's Father Christmas and his reindeers,' I whispered. 'Now go back to sleep.' She'd had no idea – and I'd never told her, and I'd kept the truth from her ever since.

Two children, sisters in the same house, the same family – both with very different childhoods, and very different memories. I remembered my father as a man who drank too much and was emotionally and physically cruel to his wife and eldest daughter. Our mother was a weak person, who'd been ruled by her own father and when faced with the same life as an adult had also turned to drink. I felt like the observer, the only sane person in a mad, beat-up world of drink and anger. I didn't resent Sam because she'd had it easier – but I did resent the fact that I was alone and had no one to tell. I'd spent years trying to make up for my childhood, make a better life for myself and Christmas was my chance to create some sparkle, some magic to erase the past. I worked hard and if I'm honest I'd never really achieved the kind of Christmas I dreamed of. And now there was no chance of a decent Christmas ever again - I was back to right where I started, with nothing.

I dragged my mind away from it all. Sam was still beating up the dough like an angry wrestler and I figured we were both a bit stressed. 'Come on, let's have a cup of delicious, fresh coffee,' I said, heading upstairs to my Gaggia and sticking two fingers up to my past.

Chapter 7

The Tea, the Tarot and a Film Star Lost in Suburbia

Sam

Poor Tamsin was really out of her comfort zone at my place. Everyone stared at her emerging from above in designer clothes and huge sunglasses – well it was the middle of December! I was busy serving, but noticed as everyone in the bakery turned round. Looking like a film star lost in suburbia, she stopped in the doorway and peered around (for the paparazzi?). She seemed stiff and awkward, like an alien lost in another world, and swept back upstairs with just a nod to Mrs J who I'd invited to work at the bakery as she now had no work with Tamsin. Mrs J tried to engage her in conversation, but Tamsin wanted to escape and diva-like swept back upstairs. I had to smile – there had always been a touch of Gloria Swanson about my sister. Even when we were kids she used to watch old black and white films on the TV and pretend she was Bette Davis or Joan Crawford.

I sometimes marvelled at how our lives were so radically different. My days were spent baking, serving in the shop and looking after Jacob and I was beginning to feel like I'd finally found myself. Just when my sister's life was falling apart.

Where once my sister would spend her days 'doing lunch,' with friends at overpriced bistros and a spot of retail therapy she now spent her days wandering around upstairs, drinking her special ground coffee and watching Jeremy Kyle and Loose Women on a loop.

After her third day of DNA results, menopausal humour and overpriced caffeine she looked very pale. I asked if she was okay and she'd nodded, lethargically... clearly the caffeine wasn't working.

'I wish I knew what was going to happen to me,' she sighed. This wasn't like Tamsin, life didn't 'happen' to her, she 'happened' to it.

'Don't be down, just take a few days to come round and make some decisions. None of us know what's round the corner... even Mrs J, despite her skill with the tea and the tarot.' I giggled and reminded her of a reading she'd had from Mrs J after which she hadn't been able to sleep for weeks because of the cards that came up for her.

'Mmmm that death card was a knife through my heart,' she nodded vigorously.

I smiled, remembering the late night phone calls, the will, the emails filled with music playlists and internet links with glossy shots of preferred canapés to be served at her funeral. There was also a detailed email about the red Gucci shift dress she wanted to be dressed in - along with her favourite Louboutins in red ('not black darling no one wears black to funerals anymore').

Tamsin was miles away. 'But on her last reading, she'd said, "Big changes are coming. Vultures are circling." Mrs J may be more psychic than we thought. I might get her to do another reading... knowledge is power at a time like this.'

'I thought I was supposed to be the hippy dippy one,' I said, trying to lift her mood.

She took my hand and squeezed it. 'I don't know what I'd do without you Sam, hippy dippy or not... suddenly my whole world has come crashing down and there you are my lifeboat in the wreckage.'

'Yes I 'm here for you and I think one of the keys to this is keeping everything as normal as possible, which reminds me, I'd promised Jacob we could put the tree up tonight.' I hadn't, but I thought it would take her mind off things – even though she would baulk at the dusty old tree and unfashionable baubles. I knew my sister though, and before long she'd be dictating what went where and how we should put the lights on – I never thought I'd say it, but I wanted the old Tamsin back.

I rushed into the bedroom and pulled out the cardboard box I'd found at her house.

'I hope you don't mind me rescuing these,' I said, plonking the box in the middle of the room, 'they're from Nan and Granddad's.'

'No, I don't mind. God I thought I'd thrown that lot out years ago...'

'It seemed a shame to leave them in a cupboard – all these lovely memories,' I said, feeling a frisson for Christmas I hadn't felt in years. 'Come and see, Jacob... we're decorating our Christmas tree,' I called. He was delirious with excitement at this and was soon head down in the box, discovering the Christmas treasures. The old tree was wrapped in bin liners and as I peeled them off, half the tinsel 'pine needles' came away with them. This didn't seem to bother Jacob, who shrieked with delight as the tree was slowly unfurled. It was so rickety and old and frail, I suddenly felt a wave of nostalgia for Christmas past and my lovely grandparents who'd always been so caring.

We dragged everything through into the living room, together turning the box upside down and shaking all the glittery Christmas detritus onto the carpet.

'Oh, I'm not sure you should be using this old stuff... it's so dusty,' Tamsin complained, but couldn't help herself and was soon on her knees looking through the baubles and tinsel with us.

Once I'd secured the tree in the corner of the room, Jacob and I dived into the box, rummaging through the treasure it contained.

I picked up the glass owl. 'I often wondered as a child the significance of owls at Christmas,' I laughed to Tamsin, who was gazing at the snow dome. She reached for it and held it in both hands, caressing it gently, looking into it like it was a crystal ball.

'Are you okay, love? Is all this a bit much for you?' I asked. Perhaps it had been a bit tactless of me to dress the tree when she was going through so much turmoil. I knew how much she loved her Christmases at The Rectory and this one would be quite different.

'No... it's fine. I was just remembering this,' she held the dome up to the light, there were tears in her eyes. I put my hand on her shoulder, 'Let's put it on the mantelpiece like we used to at home?' I suggested, but she didn't want to.

'It'll look better over there, near the lamp,' she said and placed it over on the bookshelf, which couldn't have been further from the mantelpiece.

'What's this?' Jacob held a scarlet and gold Japanese fan, a remnant from one of Tamsin's themed Christmases from a couple of years before. I looked over at her to remind her of the madness of Mrs J in fancy dress serving up dim sum platters in black kohl and blue kimono. But Tamsin was miles away again, now holding a white glass angel with a broken wing and looking like she was about to burst into tears. I let her have her space and time to think while I concentrated on Jacob.

I showed Jacob how to waft the oriental fan, making him giggle, and within seconds he was back searching for more treasures, almost disappearing into the box.

'Mummy, look at this – a beautiful lady,' he said, emerging from the box waving a paper fairy in the air. 'Can Auntie Tamsin keep this fairy? I think she'll like it.'

He got up, and clumsily staggering over the baubles and tinsel, he held out the fairy, looking intently at Tamsin's face.

'Don't cry Auntie Tam... Father Christmas is coming soon.'

She gently took the paper fairy from his hands and drew him close, hugging him and kissing his cheeks.

'Ew... you made me wet with your cry,' he said, coming over all tough guy for a second. Then he bent down putting both hands on his chubby little knees and looked right into her face.

'It's okay, Auntie Tam... you can do a sleepover with us all the time, you don't need a house.'

I bit my lip and my heart melted at my little boy's kindness. 'That may or may not be what you want to hear just now,' I smiled.

'It's just what I want to hear,' she said, hugging Jacob once more, burying her face in his neck for a long time.

'Can Horatio sleep over too?' he said. Jacob loved that dog, but there wouldn't have been room for him at the flat so one of Richard's friends had taken him for now.

'One day, when we're all back in our own homes and Horatio's home too, you can come and sleep over with him, how about that?' she said.

Jacob nodded enthusiastically, and extricating himself from Tamsin's hug, she passed the fairy back to me.

'We might need to give her a makeover,' I laughed, looking at the fairy who seemed every bit as unloved and dishevelled as my sister.

Her silver foil crown was askew (the fairy's, not Tamsin's) and looking at the scribbled-on eyes, the yellow wool hair and the bent wings took me straight back to my nana's kitchen. It had been freezing cold and Tamsin and I were sitting by the oven for warmth, while Nana buttered toast and made mugs of steaming tea. It didn't matter how cold it was outside, it was always warm and safe in that kitchen. And there was always something cooking on the stove or in the oven. Fruit pies, soups, mashed potatoes, all the comfort food I loved now had been fed to me there, forever associating it with warmth and happiness.

I remembered sitting at the kitchen table drawing the fairy really carefully, while Tamsin waited to cut it out with the scissors. I was about Jacob's age and she would have been about twelve, old enough to be allowed to be in charge of the scissors. How I admired the way she cut the shape of that fairy – I longed to be an almost-teenager like Tamsin. My big sister knew stuff and had lots of friends... one of them had even been to Spain on her holidays; they were so sophisticated and grown up. I loved my sister, she was so clever and I remembered as she cut out the fairy she'd made her 'talk' in an American accent. I recall roaring with laughter as the paper cut-out stomped up and down the table saying, 'Happy Holidays' and whistling carols.

'Mummy, let's put the lights on,' Jacob lisped excitedly, dragging me back into the present. As we finished the tree together, I worried Tamsin would be secretly horrified, there was no sense of style or theme or colour scheme.

'I hope this isn't making you feel worse,' I laughed. 'It must be causing all kinds of feng shui problems for you, Tamsin.'

She smiled and walked over to the tree. Putting one arm around Jacob, she surveyed our Christmas mash-up and then placed a glitzy little angel on one of the branches. She'd been holding it in her hands as we'd dressed the tree – I wondered why she'd been looking at it so long.

'I don't remember that,' I said, puzzled.

'I do, I thought she'd gone a long time ago – she's a brooch really, but I think she belongs here.'

'Oh... was it yours, Tam?'

She nodded.

We all stood and gazed at the spectacular tree, laden with lights and memories. It was a cocktail of everything Christmas should be, crazy messy, uncoordinated and fun. I felt a rush of happiness, almost childlike at the sight of our little tree – I'd been so caught up in Jacob's exuberance I hadn't thought about how I felt. Yet here I was feeling a sense of happiness I'd long buried.

Jacob clapped his hands. 'Yeah... I think we all deserve a big round of applause,' I said, joining him.

'Hang on a minute,' Tamsin said, one finger in the air. She reached in and moved Cinderella's glass slipper up a branch and fluffed the feathers of a glittery bird then looked at us both.

'NOW we can clap.'

Tamsin Angel was gradually coming back into the building.

Chapter 8
A Christmas Snow Storm

Tamsin

Seeing that snow dome had taken me straight back there, to the place we lived when I was six. Mum had placed it on the mantelpiece that Christmas Eve – she was still taking part in life then, we even had a tree that Christmas. I stood for ages turning the snow globe upside down, creating my own little wonderland of swirling snow, waiting for each snowflake to land and finally reveal the polar bear and the little igloo. I imagined what it would be like to live in a place like that, so pure and white and perfect. I remember Dad coming in with the tree and a bottle of sherry. It was Christmas Eve and he was in a great mood, shouting Ho Ho Ho and singing loudly. I giggled (with relief) and when he laughed too and ruffled my hair I felt such complete happiness. But as always my joy was edged in fear. As a young child I couldn't comprehend the mix of my father's emotions, and always walked carefully on the tightrope between his incredible highs and punishing lows.

His jokes and teasing and tickling could change with a look; a smile could turn into a smack across the mouth just from a word or cup in the wrong place, a meal or moment that didn't suit. And it was always down to the drink.

That Christmas Eve, with the winter wonderland dome on the mantelpiece I dared to hope we would have a happy Christmas. And when he told me I must sing 'Oh Little Town of Bethlehem' and he would teach me the words, I was delighted. Always desperate to please him, keep him calm, keep Christmas happy, I nervously repeated each line he gave me. Once or twice the words were wrong or muddled and I waited for the blow, but when nothing happened, I carried on, becoming more and more confident with each note. He'd told Mum things would be different now the new baby was here and I thought perhaps the terrible screaming and hurting was over. I didn't see the significance of the opened sherry bottle he was swigging from and when he tired of my singing I gathered all my courage and took the snow dome down from the mantelpiece. I walked towards him on my six-year-old legs, smiling, wanting to share this wonderful white world with him. We would look together into a world where snow and ice and polar bears lived all year long – the dome would cast its magic spell and make him so happy he'd never hurt us again.

But as I got closer, the tone of his voice was already changing, escalating, calling Mum 'an idiot', and as he lunged to grab her by the hair, I knew the spell was broken. I saw the red-rimmed eyes, the angry mouth, and heard my mother's screams as he grabbed her and I was inadvertently knocked to the ground. I landed in the mantelpiece, clutching my little snow-dome world to my chest to keep it safe. I didn't feel the pain in my forehead as it crashed onto the stone fireplace, but I felt the pain as the snow dome bounced from my arms. Later, when Mum put a cold compress on my forehead and put me to bed, I kept the snow dome under my pillow. It was cracked from its fall, and so was I – but we had both survived him. I must have taken it to my grandparents' for safekeeping, away from him and it had found its way into Nan's old Christmas trinket box. And seeing it there at Sam's, running my fingers along the fine crack creeping around the glass, I was reminded that however far you go, the scars don't always heal.

I wanted to cry and rage against my father, against Simon and against my mother's inability to protect me. I had trusted these people to love me and care for me and they had all let me down. I breathed deeply, as my therapist had instructed, and counted to twenty, then Jacob was holding that bloody paper fairy with its tin-foil crown and bent cardboard wings, handing it to me like he was giving me his heart. I wish I'd thrown all the decorations out years ago, it was just an unhappy reminder of the past, but for some reason I'd kept them. What Sam clearly didn't remember was on the day we made that fairy in Nan's kitchen, our dad had arrived unexpectedly and demanded he take us back home. Nan had tried to placate him, suggesting he leave us with them for the night, but he was drunk and looking for an argument and screamed at her, pushing her around the kitchen. In the end

Granddad called the police and Dad was bundled into a police car; I remember watching from the front bedroom window as it drove off down the road and being confused and surprised at my own feelings. He scared me and I was relieved he was leaving, he couldn't hurt us tonight – but he was still my dad and he looked so vulnerable in the back of that car, I cried for him.

I tried not to be dragged back into the past because it didn't help to dwell on the negative memories – but losing everything had forced me to confront things I'd never faced before.

I discovered the diamanté angel brooch in the bottom of the decoration box, it was embedded with glitter dust and I hadn't recognised it at first. But then I remembered, it was a Christmas gift from my dad when I was about ten years old. I'd loved that little angel, but when it went missing after Christmas I'd assumed Dad had pawned it like everything else. Like the snow dome I'd taken the brooch to my grandparents' as it was the only place anything was safe – the only place I ever truly felt safe. But she'd survived – just like I had, and somehow in all the darkness, that little diamante angel had given me hope. I wasn't the frightened little girl any more, I was a strong woman with two beautiful kids and somewhere out there was a future for me. I wasn't quite sure what that future held, but it was going to be very different from my past.

❄ ❄ ❄

The morning after the Christmas tree was decorated – Simon called. I'd just had a bath and was wondering how Sam's skin seemed so soft with no bath oils or gels. She never had a massage or a facial and I told myself that when all this was over I would take us both on a lovely spa weekend to thank her for everything. Then I remembered there was no 'when all this was over' because this was my life from now on and spa days wouldn't even figure anymore. Suddenly my phone rang and I heard the voice of the architect of my devastation on the other end.

'Tamsin... Tamsin... I don't know what to say.' He sounded like he was addressing an employee about a minor business issue.

'You could say "sorry I'm a selfish, cowardly tosser"?' I suggested. My anger overwhelmed me – a few days before I would have been so happy to hear his voice, to say let's sort this together and get back on track whatever that means – but now I resented him, I was filled with hurt and betrayal. Looking down my knuckles were white, my fists clenched, how could he leave us like this?

'I don't blame you for your anger... I just lost it. I didn't know which way to turn, I even thought about taking my own life, Tam.'

I doubted this was true – it was probably his way of gaining sympathy and wriggling out of everything – but this wasn't just about *his* life and *his* pain.

'What about your family? And what about the people that work for the company? Where do they stand in all this?'

'There's insurance, thank God, they will get payments, but obviously there's no work now, that's why I tried to keep everything going... for them and for you.'

'And you,' I said. 'Let's not forget you in all this, Simon.' He was king of his own little universe – the rest of us were simply accessories.

'You have no idea how I've suffered... I couldn't tell you because I wanted to protect you.'

'You wanted to protect *me*? But you hung me out to dry, you left without any warning, what did you think would happen?'

'Look... I came to France because there was this last ditch hope, I had to make a deal with a Parisian property agency... but...'

Again 'I' figured largely in his sentence. Why had I never faced up to the fact that this selfish man was my husband?

He was also an optimist, convinced his ship was coming in – which explains why, according to our accountant he drained the company of hundreds of thousands of pounds. He did it believing that he could make the money back – like a gambler he just kept throwing more money at it hoping it would eventually pay out, but of course it didn't.

'You should have told me! Before you sneaked off you could have said, "Tamsin we're in trouble, bolt the doors, the bailiffs are on their way, but I'm okay, I'm off to fucking France."' I started to cry, I didn't know if they were tears of hurt or rage, but I felt both.

'I knew you'd be devastated and I couldn't face you... or anyone else. Tam... you know how important it is to me, how I've struggled to get us where we were. You must remember how hard it was for me to break into that circle? The guys at the golf club,

The Rotary... you know how it feels. I wanted to be part of that world, like you did...'

I couldn't answer him. I was too angry and upset.

'Tamsin, can you imagine me having to tell them all at the golf club our house had been repossessed? Imagine having everyone know that I failed the business... lost everything?'

'I don't have to "imagine" anything,' I spoke calmly, regaining some control over my inner rage. 'I don't have to imagine being ripped from my home with nowhere to go. I don't have to imagine my friends blanking me and not returning my calls, because it really happened, Simon. It happened to me!' I looked down and my whole body was shaking.

He said nothing. What could he say?

'So what exactly are you planning to do, now?' I asked... and whereas a few days before I would have begged him to come home - I suddenly knew what I wanted from all this, my independence. I had to start getting my own life back on track, have some control over it rather than blindly believing in my husband as I had for years - but in order to do that I needed to know what his plans were.

'I... er... just need some time and space...' he said.

'Oh, YOU need some time and space? Well, *I* need time and space from you – for the rest of my life,' I snapped, 'and yes, me and the kids are homeless but fine, thanks for asking,' I added before slamming down the phone. I sat for a few moments numb and bruised and empty. Then I rushed into the kitchen and got the Gaggia on... it was my drug of choice and all I had left – I couldn't now go shopping at times of distress and a pre-lunch Prosecco was but a distant memory.

I sat on the sofa and sipped on my Sumatra Wahana but couldn't think straight – it was such a mess. I'd used money to make myself feel better and now I was going cold turkey. A new designer dress and a lovely bottle of perfume made me feel whole, it plastered over the wounds and as Phaedra always pointed out, 'nothing says 'love' like a new Chanel clutch bag.' I wondered who would love me now – because Chanel wasn't an option.

Later, Sam came up from the bakery. She was tired and covered in flour but seemed happy.

It struck me that I'd always appeared to be the successful sister – but Sam was the one with all the answers, she was the real success, in spite of what life had thrown at her.

'You are my little sister – but so much wiser than me,' I sighed. 'I was so easily seduced and in those early years I felt like a success. My shiny happy money-filled new life was like Christmas every day.' What I didn't tell her was that for a little while it had drowned out the noise of my mother's head thumping on the kitchen table.

But for now, I told myself, no more dwelling on the past. I would try to look forward, and though the present was pretty bleak I had to start to think about what was ahead for me and the kids. I had to regain my strength and my confidence – and what better way to do that than to put on a pair of my fabulous designer shoes – in scarlet.

Chapter 9
The Phone Call From Hell
Sam

It wasn't easy sharing our cramped little flat with my sister and as she became stronger over the next few days she became quite assertive again. She'd strut round in her designer stilettos, commenting on everything from how I cooked to how I spoke to Jacob to how I conducted my 'sexual liaison', as she referred to it, with Richard.

'Oh... you should make it more permanent with him, he's lovely,' she'd said. 'Don't keep saying no or he'll find someone else.'

And, 'Mmm I wouldn't put that pasta in now, I always wait until the water's boiling...'

Or, 'Oh, do you allow Jacob to watch TV after 7 p.m.?'

She'd also suggested on more than one occasion that I have Jacob's hair cut because, 'he isn't fitting in.' I was quick to point out to her, 'He doesn't want his hair cut – and who says he wants to fit in and become boring and small-minded like other people?'

She seemed to have missed the fact that his hair was reminiscent of Steve's and therefore this was about more than just a haircut. I was beginning to find her presence claustrophobic – every time I walked in the living room she was there watching TV or reading a magazine. She saw no one and refused to go anywhere and I worried she'd never move on. She'd heard nothing from any of her so-called friends who, in her time of need, hadn't even bothered to pick up – let alone take the trouble to call her. She was no use to them now she had no money, but even I was surprised at the speed they'd dropped her.

One evening her phone rang and she just ignored it. 'Why don't you pick up?' I said. 'It might be one of the girls.'

'It's not – it's bloody Mimi. She's been calling me for days. God, she just doesn't know when to give up.'

'Well, she might be nice to go for... a drink with?' I said, sounding like a mother suggesting her sulky teen start socialising. 'She's the one who's married to the football manager, isn't she?'

'Yes. She's also the one who pole dances. She slept her way to Chantray Lane and now expects to be accepted by the other wives. Ha.'

I sighed. It had been a long day, I was tired and quite frankly fed up of Tamsin's mountain of bin bags, pile of magazines, fancy shoes, face creams all over the bathroom and the incessant gobbling sound of her bloody Gaggia. This comment about being 'accepted' was the final straw.

'Well... you have something in common with Mimi, you've both been ostracized by the Stepford Wives,' I replied, which was a bit mean, but she was being so judgemental about Mimi it made me cross.

She went on the defensive immediately. 'The girls are giving me chance to settle in, and when I have, they'll call – people are embarrassed when things like this happen and don't know what to say…'

'Mimi isn't.'

She huffed and pretended to be engrossed in the previous July's edition of *Vanity Fair* that she'd 'rescued' from the house. I knew she wasn't really reading it – she wouldn't normally touch an out-of-date magazine.

'Of all the "wonderful" friends you had, isn't it funny how the only one who bothers to call you is the one you all treated so badly?' I said softly.

My sister gave herself to everything and her heart to everyone, but I think she'd been so obsessed with being part of the gang, she'd allowed herself to behave against her nature. I was amazed that she'd been so unkind about Mimi – despite her obvious flaws my sister was one of the kindest people I knew. I'd taken Steve's death so badly I'd had a minor breakdown, I hadn't slept or eaten for days and my body and mind had just collapsed and I was rushed to hospital. She'd been so supportive, despite sending in her flaky life coach Fifi who was so irritating she almost drove me to suicide. Anyway, Tam needed me now, I had to be there for her, however infuriating she might be. I was on the floor wrapping some of Jacob's presents and she was lying full length on the sofa pretending to be interested in an article about luxury swim wear... in the middle of December.

'That's so last summer,' I said, trying to bring her round.

'It's all I've got,' she snapped. 'Or had you forgotten?'

'So have you heard anything else from Simon?' I asked, trying to ease the tension in the room.

'Mmmm, he called this morning as a matter of fact.' She didn't look up.

'Really? Any news?'

'No. I already told him I wasn't speaking to him ever again, we're now talking through solicitors – when we can afford to get them.'

'So why did he call this morning?'

'To tell me to stop harassing his parents or they'd call the police.'

'What the...? To quote Hermione, WTF?'

'He said I had no right to leave abusive messages on his parents' home phone.'

'Did you?'

'Do I look like the kind of woman who would say "you fucking bastard you ruined my life" down my in-laws' telephone?'

'Mmmm no... so why do they think you said that?'

'Because apparently it came from my mobile...' she went back to her magazine, hoping I'd drop it. As if...

'Oh My God. It *was* you who called them, wasn't it?'

'No. Oh... yes okay, so it was me,' she snapped.

'Why, Tamsin?'

'I didn't do it deliberately. I'm not some psycho, I've always tried hard to get along with Simon's parents.'

'Which begs the question why you would leave abusive...?'

'Okay. I was angry after it all happened and when I couldn't get hold of him I called a few times and sent several texts.'

'Saying "you fucking bastard you ruined my life"?'

'Yeah and other stuff...'

'What?'

'About... oh it doesn't matter.'

'Oh it does, Tamsin, you have to tell me.'

'Okay... I may have said something about his manhood.'

'You're kidding me? Why would you talk to your husband's parents about his dick?'

'Don't be crude, Sam. I was under the impression I was texting him, but "Simon's Phone" and "Simon's Parents" are next to each other when you scroll down on my phone. I was upset, I didn't have my glasses on... and sent the texts to his parents' landline instead.'

'If you text to a landline a voice reads out the text when they pick up the phone, doesn't it?'

Tamsin nodded, her eyes closed. 'So I believe – apparently Marjory was beyond distressed to hear the British Telecom lady describe her only son's penis as "a nasty little maggot".'

I couldn't stop myself and burst out laughing. Tamsin was mortified, but even she had the glimmer of a smile across her face and eventually laughed with me.

'Will you call them to apologise?' I asked when I'd stopped laughing. 'Or will you be calling them with further penis updates?' I laughed again.

'It's gone beyond that – they are talking injunctions, Simon's trying to calm things his end.'

'Good luck with that,' I said.

We sat silently for a few seconds but I couldn't leave it.

'Maggot?'

'Nasty little maggot... get it right,' she giggled. 'I also said he'd never been good in bed; that I'd been responsible for my own orgasms since 1998; and when I shouted "yes, yes", it wasn't sexual relief, I had just been glad it was all over.'

I looked at her; 'And the BT lady told Marjory and Fred all this?'

'Apparently. Simon said he was hurt... that he'd have appreciated it if I'd told him.'

'Rather than calling his parents to give them the blow by blow account of your disappointing sex life?' I said.

She started laughing again. 'Oh I can see Marjory's face now, shuffling to the phone and picking it up, anxious to hear from Simon...' she was doubled over now.

'And instead it was the BT lady with a tirade of disgusting and graphic details about her son's sexual technique... or lack of,' I added, joining her in hysterical laughter. When we'd eventually calmed down, I carried on wrapping Jacob's presents and Tamsin resumed her in-depth study on swimwear, but every now and then she'd look up over her *Vogue* and say 'maggot' and we'd both fall about laughing all over again.

❄ ❄ ❄

So there were times when Tamsin and I really enjoyed each other's company and deep down, despite her brittle exterior, she could be very funny and we shared that sense of humour. But it wasn't all laughs – my sister was interfering, controlling, annoying, a snob and a drama queen. And her presence and lack of tact wasn't doing much for my relationship with Richard either. Our time together had always been limited (by me) to weekends and the odd week night – and I never wanted him to stay the whole night. I hadn't been ready – every time I thought about a potential future with Richard I saw Steve's face and the guilt overwhelmed me.

Before Tamsin had moved in Richard would sometimes spend the evening at the flat with Jacob and I, then later when Jacob was in bed we'd have time alone. Now our evenings were spent watching television with Tamsin. I'd wanted her to feel at home so didn't object when she said we all had to watch Mastermind and answer the questions – she was so competitive she'd shout her answers over ours. It seemed to cheer her up so I didn't mind, but felt torn trying to be a girlfriend to Richard and a sister to Tamsin. I achieved neither – and I never won Mastermind.

On a practical note, Richard and I couldn't be alone in my bedroom now either because I shared with Tamsin. It was early days, but I could see the situation becoming more difficult as time went on.

'Perhaps you and I could go out?' he suggested on the phone one day when we discussed the problem. 'If Tamsin's there she can keep an eye on Jacob and we could just go for a meal... it would be good to have some time on our own.'

I agreed it would be good to have some time alone and I also badly needed a break from my sister.

Tamsin was delighted to babysit and that evening when Richard turned up to collect me it felt like a proper date – which was lovely. We'd never really had a traditional 'courtship', as Tamsin called it, because we'd originally met through the kids. He'd started as a friend and then things had gone further, and though we missed out on the early frisson, we'd never had that 'first date' or awkwardness that comes with new relationships.

I thought about how this Christmas would be so different from the previous one. I had only just opened the bakery this time last year when I met Richard. I had literally bumped into him on the school run. I'd walked Jacob to school through the snow and slush, enjoying various en-route snowball fights and games where we slid along on our bottoms. When we arrived at the school there were no yummy mummies in perfect make-up and designer snow wear as there had been earlier in the week. I was at first relieved, as we were both wet through and those women made me feel stupid and ugly at the best of times. They'd gaze at me as I walked past them, catching each other's smoky eyes and looking in my direction, a glance at my wrist tattoo, a snigger at my ankle bracelets in the summer. I wasn't like them, they didn't understand me, and most people's reactions to something or someone they don't understand is to be scared. I had no desire to belong in their gang – and clearly the feeling was mutual, I just wished they didn't make me feel like I was 14 years old again.

Anyway, the absence of their perfectly made-up mean faces soon became clear as Jacob and I wandered to the school gates and saw the sign saying 'Closed today due to bad weather.'

It was a bit of snow for God's sake, why close the school? It wasn't going to kill anyone to walk through it. Besides, most of the shiny mummies around here drove the few yards from their homes to the school in massive cars which were more like armoured military patrol vehicles, all shiny black with a stylish capacity to cope in any war zone, siege, nuclear attack… or school run.

'Oh shit,' I sighed.

'Oh shit,' Jacob imitated, folding his chunky little arms in indignation at the 'stupid school'.

'You know what this means, don't you?' I said, in mock seriousness.

He nodded. He had no idea, but was going with it.

'We have to take our sledge on blackberry Hill,' I said, pretending despair, starting to walk and shaking my head, waiting for the inevitable reaction. The shrill screeching of pure delight this last statement produced echoed around the empty white stillness of the school playground and provoked an impromptu shrieking competition between the two of us. And I wondered why the yummy mummies hated me? Our screaming competition went on for some time until Jacob's shrieks were suddenly accompanied by a jumping up and down and running around in circles like a puppy dog who just saw his owner.

'Ella... Ella...' he'd yelled, pogoing through the snow and bounding up to a little person who had suddenly appeared in the otherwise deserted playground. 'Ella... Ella, it's me Jacob... I'm over here.' I couldn't see clearly because the snow was falling quite heavily now and Jacob was pulling on my hand and dragging me across to join Ella and what looked like her parent. My heart sank, I just couldn't do small talk with a perfect mummy. I braced myself, but as we approached I saw through the white blur this was no yummy mummy dressed in designer waterproofs and a 'cute' bobble hat. It was Ella's dad.

'I guess you guys did the same as us?' he said.

I could just about see his face through the swirling flakes as we got closer. I recognised him from parents' evening. I remembered chatting to him and his wife once, while waiting in the queue to see Mrs Robinson. And he'd just witnessed me having a shrieking competition with my son in the school playground. Great.

'We're going sledging on Blackberry Hill,' Jacob yelled in Ella's face.

'Jacob, just because it's snowing it doesn't mean everyone's gone deaf,' I laughed. I was now trying to redeem myself and sound like a responsible parent having just wailed like a banshee.

'Sledging sounds good,' Ella's Dad said as we all began walking away from the school in the same direction. 'Do you mind if we come along?'

'Yessss... Ella, you and your dad are coming sledging with us,' Jacob was still yelling in her face.

'Yay,' she yelled back into his... apparently snow deafness was a thing.

Anyway, that day as the kids sledged up and down the hill, Richard and I chatted and it turned out he was divorced, and it turned out I liked his smile. Later, when the kids insisted we both go downhill together on the sledge, it turned out I liked the way he held me. And, when Ella was safely home with her grandma and Jacob was in bed that evening… it turned out I liked the way he made love.

Tamsin of course had been horrified. 'Good grief, I know I said you have to move on love, but picking lone fathers up from the school gate?' she'd said, standing in her kitchen, hands on hips disapproval on face.

'Yeah, well why waste time with small talk? I carry my sex toys in a Perspex bag for the school run… you never know when you're going to spot a 'lone father.'

I told Richard (and Tamsin) from the beginning that I wasn't going to fall in love and wasn't looking for another husband… I'd had the best. I told Richard that no one could ever replace Steve for me or Jacob, and I didn't intend to marry again, which at first he was okay with.

However we'd now been together almost a year, and Richard was talking anniversary and future and I was talking casual and no commitment. That night we walked through the snowy square from the bakery to the restaurant, holding hands. It felt good to be out with Richard, like a proper date – his hand in the small of my back as we walked into the warm, garlic and tomato spiced air, his eyes on mine as we sat across the table from each other. I liked being with him, I liked how he made me feel about myself – and I liked how we were as a couple too. We chatted animatedly with each other and he made me laugh and I wondered if a future with Richard was possible after all?

We ordered pasta and red wine and talked about Christmas.

'I'll have Tamsin and the kids and Heddon and Hall are threatening to join us,' I laughed, 'so much for my planned little Christmas with Jacob.'

'I could help you?' he offered, suddenly seeing an opportunity to take our relationship up a notch by spending Christmas Day together. Ella was spending Christmas with his soon-to-be ex-wife and it would be the first Christmas Richard wasn't with her. I felt for him, I couldn't imagine not seeing Jacob on Christmas day, but Richard had lots of friends who had already asked him to spend the day with them - he wouldn't be alone.

'I don't mind sharing you with your sister and her friends. Jacob's my little mate... it would be good to spend some of it together and I can help out with the cooking.'

I worried it was too soon to bring him into the family, would it give Jacob the wrong idea too, that Richard was his new dad? Although Jacob had only been 1 when Steve died and had no memories of his father, I'd tried to speak about Steve when I could and show Jacob pictures. If someone new was going to come into his life, I needed to know that he would stay around. It was about so much more than just about Christmas lunch. I gazed across the restaurant trying to work out how to tell Richard that I was scared to say yes. Scared to take our relationship to the next level. What if it all fell apart again? Then I spotted

Tamsin's friend Phaedra. Her skinny, worked-out arms and fake tan stood out a mile in the middle of December. I thought of Tamsin sitting at home waiting for her call and was suddenly filled with rage.

'Excuse me a moment,' I said to Richard, standing up, dropping my napkin and heading to her table. Phaedra looked up as I approached and perhaps assuming I was going to the ladies she put her head down, pretending not to see me and no doubt hoping I wouldn't see her. This heightened my anger; how dare she abandon my sister at a time like this, how dare she not call or phone or even send a bloody note to ask how she is.

'Hi,' I said, loudly.

She blushed scarlet, even through the layers of make-up, and looked up from her plate of leaves.

'Oh... hi er Sam.'

She glanced at her dining companion and smirked, embarrassed. Her friend looked up, false lashes fluttering questioningly, matching fake tanned arms and a forkful of leaves suspended in surprise.

'My sister's okay, thanks for asking,' I stood over her, just glaring into her face.

'Oh... I was going to... call her... I.'

'Call her now, she's home alone, you have her number don't you?'

'Well I... it's not convenient.'

'Oh Phaedra, love, I can only imagine.' I said in mock concern. 'How rude of me to interrupt your meal and demand you spare a minute to call your friend, who's just lost everything she owned. I'm sure you've been so busy, you just couldn't fit it in. Where do the days go? What with the manicures, the shopping and those endless exhausting massages at the spa...'

'Look, now isn't the time for this. Speak to her husband he's the one who's run off with another woman and left her penniless... it's nothing to do with me.'

'It has everything to do with people like you, Phaedra,' I turned around and marched back to the table. Her comment about Simon having 'run off with another woman' had shaken me. What the hell did she mean by that? Had Simon cheated on Tamsin? Did she know and was keeping it from me?

Back at the table, I told a surprised Richard, who'd been able to see the encounter but not hear it, what had just happened.

'I wouldn't take comments like that too seriously,' he said. 'Simon had a reputation for being a bit of a player...'

'Did he? Really? I thought that was just Tamsin being paranoid.'

'Yeah but take what Phaedra said with a pinch of salt. Simon has a bit of a reputation, and people have put two and two together assuming he's run off with another woman.'

It made sense, and I didn't want to add to Tamsin's woes by telling her what Phaedra said – it probably wasn't true and would only make things worse.

'So, Christmas?' he said, again.

I groaned.

'It's only Christmas dinner – not the rest of your life, Sam, for God's sake,' he seemed a little angry and after my encounter with

Phaedra I didn't want to discuss turkey and sprouts with Richard. I suddenly didn't want to eat any more pasta. I just wanted to go home.

Yes, it was *only* Christmas dinner, and I was aware of that, but there were implications for me and Jacob. I know Richard felt I was over thinking it all, but now I had other stuff filling my head and I just wanted some space.

It was still early so I suggested we go back to mine. I couldn't stay in the same restaurant as that woman and if Richard and I were going to have another bloody argument about Christmas I didn't want an audience and an Italian soundtrack.

When we arrived back, the lights were out – perhaps Tamsin had finally got the message that Richard and I needed time alone and had gone to bed? Everything was deliciously quiet and calm, just as it had been before Tamsin had 'invaded' when Richard and I could sit alone in the living room with Jacob safely tucked up in bed. I began to relax, and putting Phaedra to the back of my mind I poured us both a glass of wine and we lay together on cushions by the dying embers of the fire. 'I do care about you,' I said into the semi-darkness.

'I know and I care about you too, a lot, but I don't want to spend the rest of my life alone. I can't wait forever, Sam.'

He hadn't talked like this before and I think all the stress over Tamsin had made us both a little edgy.

'I'm not asking you to wait forever. I just need some time,' I sighed, kissing him. He kissed me back, and by the twinkly lights of the tree I felt warm and Christmassy and I liked his arms around me. I realised that I'd missed the intimate closeness of him, and once we'd started kissing, we were soon naked, our flesh warm and touching from top to toe. Silently, I climbed on top of him, looking down into his handsome face, forgetting for a few minutes about Tamsin's troubles and all the baking I had to do. I stopped worrying about tomorrow and lost myself in him. His grey eyes flickered in the firelight. I ran my fingers along his chest and neck and leaned down to kiss his face. I could feel his slim, firm hips beneath me as his hands caressed me and though I wanted to groan with ecstasy I restrained myself. I pushed onto him, my knees on the rug, my face now touching his as I kissed his lips. We rocked backwards and forwards for a little while, and I sat up straight still moving, still feeling him inside me – God, it was good and getting better until... I became aware of a rustling behind me.

'Is that you, making that noise?' I whispered to Richard.

'Oh no it's only me, Tamsin... I'm not looking. I just need that copy of *Woman and Home*.'

I leaped off Richard and we both lay their naked and stunned.

'*Woman and Home*? Really?' I hissed at the silk-dressing-gowned figure now delving into the magazine rack completely unabashed.

'Well, quite. It's not my preferred reading material – but my subscription to *Vogue* has probably cancelled itself. One has to economise...' she sighed, locating the magazine and giving a little wave. 'Good evening Richard. I didn't see a thing,' she added as she left for the bedroom.

We both rolled over, turning to each other and suddenly laughing with embarrassment. I hid my face in his neck. I was hot with horror and stayed hidden for a few minutes, but one thing led to another and we were about to carry on where we'd left off when the bloody door opened again. This time I screamed as our naked bodies were flooded with light from the kitchen, which made Tamsin scream too.

'Oh you frightened me to death!' she had the cheek to say.

'Tamsin for Christ's sake don't just walk in...'

'I'm just popping into the kitchen, anyone fancy a Sumatra Wahana?'

'NO,' we both shouted, though Richard did add, 'thanks, er, Tamsin.'

I turned to see him lying there, both hands over his groin, a pained look on his face.

'Perhaps she'd like a quick round of Mastermind?' he sighed, clearly frustrated.

'Carry on... don't mind me, I'll just make my coffee and take it straight to the bedroom,' she trilled from the kitchen. But she'd have to walk back through the living room to reach the bedroom so any minute would be back in again. We lay there in silence, listening to the gobbling Gaggia and Tamsin singing a Christmas medley, and by the time she wandered back in with her steaming coffee and magazine, lust had fizzled into the air like a dying sparkler. We hadn't had many opportunities like this over recent days and once she'd settled back in the bedroom with her magazine we tried half-heartedly to continue where we left off. But after a while we both gave up. 'I'm sorry, I can't do this... not with that,' I gestured to the bedroom where she was now singing Celine Dion.

'I can't think why?' he sighed, sitting up and putting on his jumper.

'I know, I mean, most people would really want to get it on with Celine Dion reading her *Woman and Home* and singing "I will go on" in the next room, wouldn't they?'

'Coffee?' he asked.

'Instant please,' I said, 'I don't want any of her whacko Wahana stuff.' It was my own little act of rebellion to reject the Gaggia and refuse to drink what Tamsin called 'proper coffee'. So Richard put the kettle on in the kitchen, Celine sang in the bedroom and an indignant Jacob appeared round the door wanting to know 'why are you not in your pyjamas, Mummy?'

I took him back to bed and rubbed his forehead until he fell back to sleep.

When I wandered back into the living room, Richard was there holding out a mug of steaming coffee. I smiled and took it gratefully, as a wave of guilt ribboned through me.

I felt bad saying no to Richard coming round for Christmas, it would have been perfect. As he said, he would help with the cooking and I knew Jacob would love having him there, but that was part of it. As for me – I could see a future with Richard, he made me happy and I had fallen in love with him. But could I risk handing my heart to someone and risk losing them again as I had with Steve?

Chapter 10
Festive Frisson on Winter White Velvet
Tamsin

I couldn't take another day without my juicer and detox shakes. And my parched skin was crying out for the Amazonian elixir of Spa Rainforest Regenerating Serum. So I arranged with our solicitor and the bailiff people to go back to the house and collect the rest of my belongings.

Gabe kindly drove me to The Rectory as Sam was busy in the bakery. She said I could use her funny little beaten up van with pictures of cakes with wings on – but obviously I'd declined. 'Darling, I'd rather travel in Gabe's truck,' I laughed, 'and that's saying something!'

Driving through those snowy country lanes back to my old life, I glanced across at Gabe. It was ironic really, all my well-heeled friends had disappeared off the face of the earth when I needed them, but here he was, rough and ready Gabe with his unkempt hair and five o'clock shadow. He wasn't suave or sophisticated but he had a certain 'earthy' quality to him and glancing down at his workman jeans and big hands I felt a wave of something come over me. I asked him to turn down the heating in his truck, hoping that would help.

Perhaps Mrs J had been right when she'd said our guardian angels send us people when we need them, and they aren't always the ones we think they are. Gabe was turning out to be a godsend and to think I'd worried he wasn't pulling his weight. Just like Mrs J, who was helping me for nothing, he was giving up his free time to help me in my hour of need. I thought my guardian angel would be Phaedra, or Anouska – not this laid-back man in tight jeans and a white T-shirt (in winter!).

Funny to think when he first arrived I'd wanted him to leave. He seemed to spend his time sitting around, making things untidy and laughing in my face. My opening words to him (when first discussing my Christmas decor) were, 'Christmas ski lodge,' and he'd said, 'Where?' like it was behind the bloody sofa. I think he was being funny, but from the get-go I found him quite challenging – I hated sarcasm, I have enough of it from Sam.

During his interview for the job I asked him where he saw himself in five years and he said 'On a beach.' No ambition, no direction. He smoked in my bathrooms, swore in front of my guests and left empty Monster Munch packets everywhere. 'Gabe' I'd said after a week of high tar roll-ups, filthy language and onion snack wrappers, 'this is my home. How would you feel if I smoked, swore and left Monster Munch packets all over your sitting room floor?'

'Depends on what you were doing on my sitting room floor,' he said, staring at me with that challenging face followed by a wink, which made me blush. Anyway, my pep talk didn't make any difference, he continued to go his own sweet way, smoking, swearing and crunching rather inelegantly on onion flavoured snacks.

Heddon and Hall loved Gabe on sight and had been very excited when I introduced them. Well, he was all pecks and posture under his old T-shirts, with a hint of vulnerability and that kind of combo just drove the old queens wild. Gabe had dirty nails, a big hammer and erected an outhouse in ten minutes... and despite Heddon and Hall claiming to adore craftsmanship and design they could often be found admiring his 'work'. The spectacle of him hammering hard in a tight white T-shirt brought them running from all corners of the house. I'll admit there were times when I found myself mesmerised by him too, but not for long.

Sam said he was sexy, but as I pointed out, 'He's not sexy at eight o'clock in the morning when he's dropping ash and f words all over your designer kitchen.'

Glancing over at him now in his truck as we swept through snowy lanes I felt very lucky to have him around. He had turned out to be such a good friend, helping me move all my stuff – it had to be fate that I'd gone to all that trouble to find him. The previous year he'd worked for Anouska and I'd been very impressed with his hardcore landscaping – particularly his trellis-work. But when I asked her for his number she was very cagey. This was hardly surprising as rumour had it he'd erected more than her walled Mediterranean garden that winter. Sam said Anouska was jealous of me and would never give me Gabe's number, so I began my own investigation. I always enjoyed a challenge, so like all modern day detectives I started online. However, I hadn't really considered the full implications of Googling 'Gabe hardcore' on my son's laptop. I can't begin to describe the sexual spectacle served up before me on that screen. Within seconds I was deluged with male appendage and threesomes popping up all over the place – just as Hugo walked in.

'WTF?' were the three letters I was greeted with by my son.

'I'm looking for a man,' I said, flustered, pressing keys, and inadvertently making the panting sounds even louder.

'I can see your looking for a man, Ma,' he monotoned, just as another video appeared of a bearded gentleman proudly holding (and waggling!) his huge appendage. Gabe Hardcore, I presume?

'Oh... that's gross,' Hugo sighed without flinching, like it was a regular occurrence to walk in on his mother downloading hardcore pornography. He leaned in for a closer look, like I was waiting for his detailed critique. 'Shit, I wouldn't if I were you, ma – that's got A & E written all over it.'

'I have no intention... of anything like that... I want him doing stuff in the house.'

'I bet you do.'

I'd wafted Hugo aside while desperately trying to get the images off the screen, but the more keys I pressed the more disgusting, and possibly illegal, it became. While hitting keys and letting out the odd horrified yelp, I tried to explain exactly why I appeared to be watching an illegal sex act on his computer, but he just laughed. I was sure my son could end the whole tortuous episode with one click of the mouse but he was enjoying it all too much.

'I'm not angry with you, Ma... I'm just disappointed,' which is exactly what I'd said to him the previous week when I'd caught him smoking something earthy in his bedroom.

Anyway, when I'd finally removed all traces of anything sexual from the screen, I abandoned my internet investigation and plucked up the courage to call Mimi. I was reluctant to engage with her – after all she wasn't one of us, but I was desperate to book this apparently talented craftsman so kept it short and businesslike. Mimi seemed delighted to hear from me giving me his number straight away hinting that he was 'just fabulous to have.'

I was smiling to myself at this memory as we pulled up outside The Rectory. Then my heart sank. The house I'd loved so much looked unloved and deserted, no Christmas wreaths, no fairy-lit path, no outdoor tree resplendent near my oak front door – Sam always said it was bigger than the one outside Manchester Town Hall.

I sighed. 'Oh Gabe, it's hard to believe it's not mine any more. Just seeing it reminds me that this isn't a temporary situation... it's forever. I can't ever go back.'

He pulled on the handbrake and leaned both arms on the steering wheel. 'Everything in life is temporary, Tammy, you can't go back. Just keep movin forward...' he patted my arm and I felt a frisson between us. Was it a moment? Or had I just been starved of physical affection for so long it felt like one? I pushed unsavoury thoughts to the back of my mind as I saw Mrs J had just arrived, courtesy of husband Lawrence.

'She's so good,' I said to Gabe. 'God knows when I'll be able to pay her.'

He smiled. 'She likes being around you.'

'I can't think why,' I sighed.

'Some people are just good to be around... you know?' As he said this his eyes took on a soft, lingering gaze - I didn't know where to look.

I flushed and reached for the car door. What was he up to? Was he flirting or teasing? I was never quite sure with men – especially men like Gabe. And having only ever flirted with Simon (many years ago), I wasn't quite sure how to cope with this and what to take from it. I climbed out of the car, trying for sophistication, but three feet of snow in Jimmy Choos didn't make for the daintiest landing and I tried and failed to walk nicely, aware his eyes were on me. I made a mental note to buy a weatherproof coat and wellington boots so my legs wouldn't splay in the snow next time. I had to smile at the thought of me in wellies – who would ever have thought I'd even consider such a purchase? I only had smart day dresses and designer shoes, I'd never gone for casual, I loved glamour – like a magpie seeking all that glittered. So much for that – nothing was glittering in my world now.

We trooped to the front door, me on dodgy heels with a very heavy heart and Mrs J oblivious and insensitive to the emotional trauma I was suffering. Coming up beside me, she surveyed my former home and pointed out how 'if this isn't sold soon it will go to rack and ruin.'

I looked at Gabe, who almost seemed ready to catch me if I fell – or was that wishful thinking? He smiled at Mrs J. 'Hey Margaret, *you*'ll never go to rack and ruin, will you? You little minx!'

Mrs J positively glowed, and slapped him on the arm like a schoolgirl. I never knew her name was Margaret.

I put the key in the lock and it was a relief when the door opened, but walking in, it felt like somewhere else – an art gallery or a museum. The heating had of course been off, so it was cold, unlived in – but it wasn't just that, it was the stark contrast between this and the warm, vanilla-scented bakery with its cramped, cosy flat, where life was messy and ungroomed, but actually quite cosy. Walking through the linen-shaded rooms, where a cushion was strategically set, a vase positioned just so, it occurred to me this wasn't a place where people had lived. My house wasn't a home, it was a perfect composition of a life that had never really existed. Our 'happy family' life had been displayed like artwork on the walls, through photographs, paintings, choice of furniture – even the crockery. 'This is us' it screamed, 'I am artistic' 'I am happy,' 'we are a family.' But having lived in Sam's life for just over a week I realised mine wasn't real. It had all been just for show.

Mrs J went upstairs to collect all the bedding while Gabe walked round the house with me as I decided what to take. My plan was to have everything, but now I wasn't sure – apart from the photographs and the mementoes it was all meaningless.

Standing in that white space I was reminded of something Sam had said to me the day after the bailiffs came: I was in such a state at the time I could barely remember what she'd said, but it was something about only taking stuff from the house that was important to me. I hadn't understood at the time – weren't they one and the same? Surely if it was worth a lot of money, it was worth a lot to me? But wandering around here aimlessly I began to realise what she had meant – the real value is in the sentiment, the memory, the love that lives with 'stuff' not the price tag.

'I won't take it all,' I said to Gabe. He smiled, he'd probably always known how meaningless it all was – that's why he'd laughed at my silly demands. I tried not to think too deeply and pretended my change of plan was more practical. 'Sam's flat is very small and cramped now with all my stuff; we are banging into one another as it is... perhaps we'll just sell all this stuff.'

'You'd get a few quid for it,' he nodded slowly, taking it all in.

'Yes. And let's face it, Gabe, I need the money.'

I had to get some money together so I could rent my own place and give the kids a home again. They were both at university most of the time, but everyone needed somewhere to come home to and I'd seen a lovely Victorian detached for rent on Chantray Lane, but then at almost two grand a month I had to remind myself for the millionth time I didn't have that kind of money any more. It was hard to keep coming back to the cold hard fact that I had no cash. I wanted to move into my own place, have my own space in my new life but I needed the freedom my money had brought me.

'Are you okay? Gabe suddenly said as we wandered through the sitting room.

'Yes... considering. I just feel very alone,' I added. I didn't look into his eyes, though I could feel him looking at me. There was some chemistry between us, or at least on my part, and in my vulnerable state who knew what I was capable of?

He didn't answer, just kept looking at me. 'Shall I take these?' I asked, touching the forget-me-nots in the antique bowl by the window and trying hard not to think of *Lady Chatterley's Lover*.

'Yeah... is there anything else you want me to do?'

I looked up from the bowl of flowers into deep blue eyes. He was staring, waiting for my response. My heart was thudding, he'd batted the ball over to my court, and I could either take it or bat it back (I had never been very good at tennis and not quite sure this analogy works, but bear with me). I smiled while trying to suppress the rising fear in my throat at the thought that this man might, in his own way, be propositioning me. It had been such a long time. My sex life had been non-existent for a while. Simon seemed to have lost interest and consequently so had I. Remembering the rumours about Mimi, I glanced over at Gabe's broad shoulders, his laid-back stance, and imagined cold, hard trellis against my back. I gazed at him under my eyelashes, fingering the forget-me-nots seductively and trying to look like those women in porn videos, knowing in my heart I could never be as flexible.

Gabe had a twinkle in his eye and I could almost feel that hard trellis on my back, rough, calloused hands on my thighs. Where had all this come from? Gabe wasn't my type, he had no stocks and bonds, no career portfolio and no penthouse apartment – but he certainly had something. He turned away and wandered towards a white sofa where he sat down, slowly stretching his arms across the backrest, looking directly at me. He looked so inviting on my winter white sofa, I didn't even think about how he might make it dirty with his workman jeans. I didn't care. I walked towards him – in what I hoped was a sensual way and sat next to him on the sofa close enough to breathe him in. I reckon Gabe had pheromones only women could smell... musk and Monster Munch laced with high tar tobacco, yum. French perfume houses would pay a fortune for that, I thought, leaning towards him and trying not to let him see I was sniffing him. He leaned in towards me and our heads touched and in that moment I sparkled, like someone had just flicked a switch and fairy lights were twinkling in my chest.

I don't know what pheromones smell like, but if I had to name Gabe's smell I'd call it 'Dirty Delicious.' Blame his intoxicating scent, but I convinced myself that what I was about to do was right. I'd been so disappointed by Simon, I had to have my fragile faith in men restored, didn't I? I had to stamp out my husband's weakness and betrayal and the only way I could do that was by putting my hand firmly on Gabe's inner thigh. He didn't flinch and I leaned against him, keeping my hand on his thigh and putting my head on his shoulder. It felt good. He didn't stir for a few seconds then I felt his hand slide slowly behind my back.

'Gabe. I feel so empty,' I sighed, but before I could say any more his lips were on mine. It was clear that hardcore Gabe had been in this situation a thousand times and like any road well-travelled, he knew just what to do. He had very skilled hands and his lips were rough, not soft and wet like Simon's. Here was a real man. I tried to play hard to get and pretended to pull away, but thankfully he grabbed me firmly around the waist and pushed me back onto the cushions, his hands on my back, and moving downwards.

'We can't just do this. On the sofa,' I said, wanting him, but knowing this was dangerous, anyone could walk in. I turned my body round to try and clamber out from under him... who did he think I was? Mimi?

'I'm giving you a stress massage,' he said. 'How do you like it?' His voice was husky with desire, his hands all over me, moving up under my dress. This wasn't like my usual stress massage at the spa – and the hand movements were certainly not ayurvedic. He asked again if I was enjoying whatever it was he was doing.

I couldn't answer him, I was face deep in one of my Christian Lacroix 'Croisette' cushions with a hard (in every sense of the word) landscaper on top of me. And those cushions weren't meant for faces – all I could think was thank God I'd chosen the bougainvillea pink, at least the lipstick marks wouldn't show.

When Mimi had said Gabe was 'fabulous to have', I realised the rumours were true – she'd meant it literally.

I was just beginning to relax into the massage when I felt a cold draft around my buttocks. I was lying awkwardly on my stomach, trying to pull my knees up but concerned it might look to Gabe like I was offering him my bottom... which I most certainly wasn't. But Gabe was now busy hiking my Azzedine Alaïa up over my thighs. Yes, it was a stretch 100% wool dress, but I wasn't sure it was meant to be quite so stretched. I was thinking about how much it had cost, when my silk Janet Reger lingerie was tested for durability and expertly whipped down to my ankles. I was excited and a little scared, but this was just what I'd wanted, what I needed – to be desired again. Rampant workman-like passion and rushed foreplay had never been on my sexual 'to-do' list... but, my god, I realised what I'd been missing as Gabe breathed in my ear and manipulated my thighs. He kept telling me over and over again how 'hot' I was, but trust me, I wasn't 'hot' on any level. I was lying face down on winter white velvet with my Janet Regers round my ankles, my arse in the air and a mouthful of designer cushion. I was having trouble breathing, but despite my discomfort I suddenly realised how good being a little bit naughty could be. And how easy it was to lie back and think of Bohemia like my sister and Mimi did. I was just about to ask if we could adjust position because my panting wasn't about sexual arousal but near suffocation – when Gabe did something very skilled with his fingertips. I couldn't help myself. 'Oh God! Oh God that's so...' I shouted, loudly, just as the front door opened and Mrs J waddled in.

'Oh... oh God,' I said again partly in reaction to Mrs J and partly what Gabe was still doing. In my embarrassment I suddenly found the strength to heave myself up on to all fours, which apparently surprised and excited Gabe who was now so consumed with lust he was unaware we had an audience and was now detailing his next moves, audibly. 'Gabe!' I groaned. 'It doesn't... matter how HARD we try – we're never going to get this stain off... winter. White. Velvet... Oh God!'

He froze, suddenly getting the message, and there we were caught in flagrante like a Christmas sex tableau. For a few seconds we just stayed in this strange position - until I suddenly I pretended to notice Mrs J. 'Oh hi. Mrs J...' I feigned nonchalance, not easy from underneath a hardcore landscaper. 'Gabe and I are dealing with a very stubborn wine stain.' Still face down, I was rubbing at the non-existent stain on the sofa, but given her folded arms and lemon lips I doubt she was buying it. Looking us both up and down slowly, she continued to stand in shocked silence staring.

'What?' I said, looking up at her from the cushion, like she was the odd one and it was perfectly normal for the lady of the house to be wiping her sofa on all fours, bare bottom on view with the hardcore landscaper coming up the rear, so to speak.

'Gabe is providing the muscle. It's a tough stain' I added, making it all so much worse. I was pulling down my dress and muttered something about lifting it out of the way so I wouldn't get bleach on it.

'I use a Stain Devil myself,' she huffed and let it hang.

I heard her take the vacuum out of the cupboard and find a vantage point on the stairs where she could vacuum with aerial view of anything that may occur. I glanced at Gabe, now lounging on the other sofa with a big smile on his face.

'It's not funny,' I hissed. 'What we were doing... there... whatever it was will now be all over the bloody village.'

'We were only cleaning a "very stubborn wine stain",' he said in a posh voice – and a bad impersonation of me. 'Anyway, I thought you liked it, Tammy?'

'It was okay.' I said, feigning nonchalance and plumping up my Christian Lacroix cushions, which had taken quite a pounding.

'Okay? Just okay? We should go again then,' he was staring at me, teasing me, his hand reaching for me.

'No way, not again, not like that, there...' I said, batting him away and gesturing to the scene of the crime.

'So... somewhere else then? Do you want to get it on sometime?' he asked, rolling a cigarette.

'No,' I said a little too loudly, even though I did. A lot. 'Before I even consider "getting it on" with anybody, I like to be asked out first.'

'Okay, we can go out first if you want,' he was smiling and zipping himself up in front of me as I tugged my bra into place, just as the front door opened and in walked Hugo, Hermione, Sam and Jacob carrying pizza.

Hugo just stood there with his lip curled, the look on his face made me feel twelve years old. I shrugged apologetically, what could I say? The real tragedy was we now couldn't afford the cost of therapy to get my son over this one.

'We brought pizza, thought you guys would be hungry and we could have a moving party together,' Sam said, looking from me to Gabe before heading to the kitchen.

'Oh pizza, lovely,' I jumped up and began hugging everyone.

'What the fuck, Mum...' Hermione said as I went to put my arms around her.

'I've told you, stop bloody swearing Hermione, I'm only giving you a hug!'

She was looking down at my shoes, and when I followed her gaze I saw, to my abject horror, my silk pants were slung around my left ankle. For a moment we both looked down at my pants – and before she could say anything I quickly plucked them from my leg and brazened it out, putting on my best mummy smile and sweeping into the kitchen. 'Is everyone okay?' I asked, addressing Sam and the children, and trying not to blush while stuffing my pants in a drawer and watching Gabe under my eyelashes. There was definitely something about him, I thought, while trying to avoid Sam's stare.

'Are *you* okay, Tam?' she asked, a smile playing on her lips.

My sister was looking from me to Gabe, and I knew she'd put two and two together. A good-looking man, a vulnerable woman and a wayward pair of pants – it didn't take a detective to work out what she'd just walked in on. Sam caught my eye and my face flushed scarlet as I helped myself to a slice of Tuscan Temptation... while feeling like a Tuscan trollop.

Chapter 11
All is Calm, All is Bright
Sam

I worried how Tamsin would feel after visiting The Rectory and as I'd had to stop at the supermarket, she and the kids were already back at the bakery when I arrived. I opened the kitchen door, expecting to find her in floods of tears. But Hermione and Hugo were seated at the table studying their iPads and Tamsin was standing by her Italian espresso machine looking every inch the Stepford Wife in full make-up, fluffy white jumper and matching trousers. All was apparently calm, she was smiling and I couldn't decide whether it was genuine or she had actually lost it. Was she really making coffee or merely holding on to her Gaggia for support?

'You okay?' I asked uncertainly.

'I am fine and dandy,' she said, a phrase she often used when on the brink of a complete meltdown.

'Okay... so why don't you sit down and I'll make the coffee?' I said, wanting to move her away from the block of sharp knives tantalisingly close to her fingers.

'Nonsense,' she snapped. 'I'm making supper – an omelette.'

I sat down tentatively at the table and watched as my sister stirred eggs vigorously in a pan. I wasn't buying this bright and bubbly persona and as she handed me a plate of abused eggs I saw the wild eyes and knew I was right. Tamsin had gone from manic lover of life and people and things, to egg-destroying crazy lady. I smiled, taking the plate from her as she turned to make the coffee. I put a forkful to my mouth but it was truly inedible. 'Tam – it's kind of you... but I'm just not hungry, thanks anyway.'

'It's okay, I know I'm rubbish - eggs just don't work in the pan for me,' she smiled over her shoulder, pouring thick dark coffee from the machine. 'I'm not gifted with food like you are, Sam,' she glanced at the congealed egg and rolled her eyes, plonking two mugs of coffee onto the table she sat down.

The kids shuffled off as soon as she joined us. They hardly spent any time at the flat, there just wasn't the room but they all kept in touch and we just had to hope Tamsin could find somewhere for them all after Christmas.

'How do you feel?' I asked, dreading her response.

'I don't know... well, I do. I want to throttle Simon. I want to put a light over his head, ask him impossible questions and pull out each of his fingernails one by one. And then the other part of me wants to just book into a fabulous boutique hotel and spend a fortune on room service.'

'Yeah... but that's where you went wrong before. You both just threw money at everything,' I said, again gently so as not to rub salt in the wound. 'Talking of money... I know it's early days and you can stay here as long as you need to, but you might need to... earn some?'

'You're right, of course you are,' she began tapping her nails on the table, looking around for an escape. 'Me having to earn money,' she said, incredulously. 'I can't believe I'm in this situation, Sam. I checked our credit card bills this morning and we've been living totally off credit for over two years. I knew things were tight but Simon never objected to anything I bought, never said stop. Sam, Christmas is in two weeks and I haven't bought a single gift.'

In previous years Tamsin always spent a week each September ordering Christmas flowers and seasonal room perfume directly from Paris. These things were oxygen to her, if there was no 'shopping/holiday/luxury therapy' available she would have some form of superficial breakdown.

I gently pushed the omelette away, it was making me quite nauseous.

'No one's expecting you to buy gifts and make everything perfect again. This is life – you can't always find the thread, you can't always plan... sometimes shit just happens and you have to go with it,' I said, feeling like a crap Dr Phil.

'Yes, you just have to go with it,' she repeated. 'And on that note – I think I might be about to have a sexual adventure, Sam.'

Then she went on to tell me some confused story about Gabe the hard landscaper and how he'd been 'touching her' on the sofa.

'So. You and Gabe?' I said, I'd guessed something was going on earlier, when she'd greeted us with a red face and her pants round her ankles after 'packing' with Gabe.

'Well, if Mrs J hadn't appeared like the avenging angel from behind the balustrade who knows what might have happened on my winter white sofa,' and she actually blushed. I was intrigued I didn't think I'd ever seen Tamsin like this over a man before – even Simon.

I demanded more details but Tamsin was deliberately vague, trying to make what sounded like a sexual encounter into a refined affair involving a few giggles and a little footsie. Mind you, when a grown woman refers to her own vagina as 'my fairy', her vagueness around a sexual encounter on the sofa didn't surprise me.

Anyway, among the euphemisms, she mentioned Lady Chatterley and as Gabe was a sort of gardener, I got the message.

'Oh get over yourself, Tamsin. A good shag with a handsome guy isn't the worst thing you could do,' I said.

'I didn't.'

'I know... but what I'm saying is, you should.'

'Mmm, well, thank God Mrs J saved me from myself,' she sighed. 'I could have ended up going all the way. Things might have climaxed into a bodice-ripping session on my winter white sofa,' she said, her face flaming even more.

I laughed, she was definitely coming round to the idea and I was convinced a couple of hot nights with Gabe was just what she needed. I threw away the omelette, and rather than tackle the Gaggia, I made more tea and put a few mince pies on a plate... after all it was Christmas.

'I remember drinking tea and eating mince pies at Nan's,' I said, putting the plate in front of her. 'She'd start making them at the beginning of December and by Christmas Eve we must have eaten hundreds.'

Tamsin smiled. 'Yeah... Nan's mince pies were almost as good as yours.'

'You're very kind, but nothing tastes as good as when you're a kid, does it? Do you remember Nan's Christmas pudding, it was delicious... it was fudgy and sticky and sweet, it stuck to the roof of your mouth. And the rum sauce – you always pretended to be drunk,' I laughed.

'I had plenty of material to work with – especially round Christmas, Dad was permanently pickled,' she said, a touch of bitterness edging her voice.

'I can remember you loved pulling crackers at Christmas and you'd always scream the loudest when they cracked, and then you had to be the one to read all the jokes out,' I smiled.

'I'd almost forgotten that. We only have expensive crackers now. They are – were – exquisite and always matched the table. But they don't snap any more... not like they did then.'

'It's probably as well, your bloodcurdling screams wouldn't have been good at one of your posh Christmas dinner parties,' I said, trying to cheer her up and failing.

'What am I going to do, Sam?' she suddenly said, like the panic of her situation had been bubbling under but had just overwhelmed her like a huge wave.

'You'll be fine,' I sighed.

She reached out and held my hand. 'Just being here is enough.'

She was surrounded by her life in boxes, each one boasting a designer name, or a French champagne and there was even more stuff after her last visit to The Rectory. There was even a huge Fortnum's hamper which had once been filled with Christmas goodies and was now filled with Tamsin's pants and jumpers. Christmas past, I thought wistfully. And there she sat, amongst the wreckage of her former life, dressed in Balenciaga, sipping from a Villeroy and Bosch mug. I had to hand it to her – you could take the girl away from the glamour, but you couldn't take the glamour away from the girl.

'Tamsin... all this stuff, we need to do something about it. You can't stay like this, watching TV and sitting here with your boxes all day...'

'Mmm, a week ago I would have agreed. But I'm becoming rather fond of Jeremy Kyle and his guests... yesterday a woman who'd had a foursome with her sister's husband and his brother was pregnant... and hadn't a clue whose baby it was,' she laughed. 'Imagine?'

'Look Tam, you may need to change your mindset. I don't want to sound mean, but you have been used to just clicking your fingers, signing a cheque, swiping a credit card and making everything right. You don't have that any more – you are now just like the rest of us. You can't sit here all day hoping someone else is going to sort your life out for you.'

'That's right, rub it in. Rub salt in my weeping wound...' she started.

'Oh give Bette Davis a bloody rest, Tamsin. I'm fed up of your drama and feeling sorry for yourself because you might not see the pissing lavender in France next spring – welcome to my world!'

She looked at me. 'Why are you so angry with me?'

'I'm not angry with you. I just hate to see you wasting yourself and your life! You should be up and about, you need to shake it off, get on with it.'

'And you would know about that,' she bit.

'Ouch... my situation was quite different.'

'I'm sorry,' she sighed. 'I didn't mean that – but what else can I do? I have no friends... my home is gone...'

'Yes, I know and you will never get to swim in your Miami pool again... and you can't afford another Chanel handbag.'

'Sarcasm?' she asked.

I nodded.

'Look Tam... I need some help downstairs. Tomorrow I have several huge orders to deliver and I don't want to leave Mrs J alone in the shop. Last week I went out on deliveries and she set up an impromptu séance in the coffee area. Customers were queuing for cupcakes while she was summoning up the ghost of someone's dead mother.'

She nodded. 'Okay – so you're saying you want me to do the séance this time?'

I looked at her.

'Sarcasm. We can all do it you know,' she half-smiled.

'That's quite funny for you.'

She smiled at me. 'Okay so you want me to do the deliveries?'

'Please. That would be great.'

'And how will this take place?'

I wasn't quite sure what she meant and looked at her with a puzzled look. 'Take place? It's not an event...'

'I know, but what time will the driver arrive and what sort of establishments will we be visiting on the delivery trip? I have to know these things so I can dress accordingly.'

I sighed, it was going to be quite a steep learning curve.

'I'll go through it with you tomorrow,' I said, too exhausted to even go there.

'Good. I'll empty some bin bags tonight and find suitable outfits – if I have several to choose from I can decide once I know what's involved.'

'Yes – as long as you only wear designer stuff for deliveries. I'm thinking young European designer, slightly edgy but with a classy core,' I continued, sarcasm oozing from every pore.

'Exactly, we're on the same page,' she said, with no hint of irony. 'This has come at just the right time,' she added. 'I was going to offer myself up to The Jeremy Kyle Show, but I'll call and say I can't be in tomorrow's special; "homeless desperate woman in clinch with her gardener on the family sofa!" she roared, laughing at this. 'As if I would...' she looked at me. Did she want my approval?

'Tamsin it's only sex, it would do you good.'

'It might be "only sex" to you, but I find it hard to open up to someone.'

'I know.'

'I feel so angry all the time, Sam. I try not to think about it, but looking back Simon could be unkind, cruel even.'

'I kind of guessed it wasn't always easy with him,' I said.

'The more successful he became, the less worthy I felt and if there was lipstick on his collar or he smelt of a different perfume when he came home late from the office, I let it go. I felt I deserved to be hurt by him because I wasn't good enough. I never told anyone before, but I felt very vulnerable with Simon – and didn't feel I could confront him – if I said anything I worried he'd say something nasty or leave me.'

I was surprised at her 'confession,' and the fact she was beginning to finally see that perhaps her marriage and her previous life hadn't been so perfect after all.

'Domestic violence works on different levels,' I said.

'I know that. I'd been emotionally and physically hurt as a child, so for me it was my default position, "stupid Tamsin, give her a slap." So when Simon told me I was ugly, old, a waste of space, I accepted it – it was familiar, words I'd heard before, and in his way he hurt me as much as Dad did.'

'I don't understand, Tam...? What does this have to do with dad?' I was struggling to comprehend what she was telling me.

'Dad... his drinking.'

'Yeah. I heard Dad liked his whisky,' I sighed, 'he cleaned up his act after you'd left home though.'

'It was too late for me then. I don't know if you ever realised but it's like we lived in different houses growing up, and the only time our memories are in synch and we were both truly happy was when we were at Nan and Granddad's.'

I wasn't sure what she meant and would have liked to push her further but she was clearly upset. I thought of their little house on Hyacinth Street and I could see us now – me, Tam, Nan and Granddad toasting bread by the fire, eating homemade angel cake with hot milk.

'I can almost smell the warm cinnamon. Ooh and Christmas pudding with rum sauce, and Nan always made us a gingerbread house.

'Yeah,' she smiled, 'and candy canes and mince pies...'

'I can remember every nook and cranny of Nan's... but you know what's funny? I don't remember our own house as clearly.'

'Our house was different. It wasn't a happy place Sam,' she sighed. 'You must remember Dad had a temper?'

I nodded. 'He could be really grumpy sometimes and we had to stay out of his way,' I said.

'But when he'd had a drink, Sam, oh God it was awful. You were too young to remember, but he was… violent...'

I was shocked. What did she mean? I had vague childhood memories, the smell of whisky, the sound of tears, mum leaving for days on end, but I'd never questioned it. 'Mum's gone away,' Tamsin would tell me, and as long as she was there I was okay.

'What happened... when Dad was violent?' I didn't want to know, yet I had to know. I owed it to my sister to share it with her now. 'Tell me Tam.'

As a young child it hadn't computed, but I remember feeling fear and hearing noise and forcing myself to sleep.

'He hurt us... he hurt Mum mostly, but if I said the wrong thing at the wrong time or tried to step in front of Mum to stop him, he'd hurt me too.'

'Oh Tam I never knew. I remember stuff... blurred memories really. I was too little to comprehend... and I always felt safe because I had you. You kept me away from it didn't you?"

'I tried to. Mum had been so emotionally wrecked by him she had no voice, and she couldn't defend either of us. It was down to me. I tried to keep us all safe, but I was a little girl and I couldn't protect my own Mum.'

I just looked at her, it was like I was seeing my sister for the very first time.

'Oh Tam, I didn't know.'

'It was bad enough at the time – but these things shape you. After Dad I was a ready-made victim, just waiting for a man to come along and treat me as his whipping boy. Simon never physically hurt me, but speaking to me like dirt and putting me down in private and in public made him feel better about himself... just like Dad with Mum.'

I felt such sadness. I also felt guilty for all the times she'd suffered. 'I feel so bad Tamsin... I never really saw that side of Dad. Yes I know he had a terrible temper but...'

She half-smiled. 'The days after the beatings when Dad sobered up he would lavish love and affection on you... at least it meant you were safe. He'd never beat you, his precious little girl.'

I looked at her. I didn't know what to say, she'd carried this round with her all her life – it had even influenced the dynamics of her relationships, her marriage – and I'd never known. 'I'll be honest, Sam, there were times I was so jealous of you – the way he included you in everything, talked to you, laughed with you – he never did that with me.'

I had never really thought about Dad's relationship with Tamsin, I'd just assumed it was the same as mine was with him.

'If we did anything as a family... which was rare, it was always you and Dad and me and Mum. We'd walk ten paces behind you and you'd be there like his little Princess sitting on his shoulders, or linking arms with him and laughing.'

I remembered those times as well as my sister, but I never felt the undercurrents, I never saw that she was being excluded... that she was suffering.

'It explains why you left so soon, when Mum died. I feel guilty now, but when I had to look after Dad I resented you,' I said.

She seemed surprised.

'You were living your life. You never came to see us, you would send money, gifts... make the odd phone call, but I dealt with everything else... including his death.'

'Do you understand now why I had to leave?'

'Yes, I do and I'm so glad you've told me. At the time I felt abandoned, deserted... you were the one person I could rely on and you just walked out.'

'I'm so sorry Sam – by then I hated him. He'd ruined every moment, every childhood memory,' she was saying. 'When I think of our Dad I think of the Christmases where he'd just drink himself into oblivion. He'd spent all the money and there was no food, no gifts,' she stopped talking and looked at me. 'Once I dared to ask if Father Christmas had been,' she said, her chin trembling at the memory. 'And I was hurled across the room and made to spend Christmas day in the cupboard under the stairs. I'd asked the wrong question – Dad had pawned the few gifts Mum had bought us and spent the money on drink.'

I put my arm around her. I couldn't bear to hear this, but had to force myself to listen, to face the truth.

'One minute we'd be wrapping presents and dressing the tree, the next someone would be screaming, hurting, all because of him. And you know what's crazy? I'd have forgiven him everything for a taste of what he gave you... I just wanted a dad who loved me.'

I couldn't believe what she was telling me, but it was all beginning to make sense. The bruises, the tears, always the knife-edge tension tight like a drum... it hit you when you walked into our house. I'd never drunk whisky, yet the mere smell of it made me retch – and now I knew why. I desperately searched my head for good things to soothe my sister.

'Tam, he was your Dad, of course he loved you in his own way. I remember one Christmas being in the sweet shop with him and he bought a quarter of sugared almonds. "Our Tamsin loves sugared almonds," he'd said.'

She started to cry. 'Did he? I'm amazed... I still love sugared almonds, the kids buy them for me every Christmas. Thank you for telling me that... I needed to hear it, because over the years the bad stuff overpowers the good.'

'Yes... I know. Everyone deals with the past in their own way. I try and think of the good times with Steve and don't dwell on the painful memories. My way of coping is to suffocate the bad times with all the happy stuff.'

'Yeah... I like that. The other day, when we were dressing the tree and I found the diamanté angel I got upset.'

'I noticed. I assumed you were just crying because of everything that's happened with Simon and the money.'

'Well, that's never far from my tears, but it was something else that made me cry. Dad gave me that diamanté angel one Christmas. It was the only time he'd ever given me a gift, done something special just for me. I think he bought it from a man in a pub, or won it in a bet, and it was probably handed to me to ease his guilt – but that didn't matter and I can't tell you how happy it made me. Despite all the rows and the fear and the violence, I forgave him everything for thinking of me for just a moment. But then a few days after Christmas it went missing and I assumed he'd pawned it – which hurt more than any of the beatings. So when I found it there among the Christmas decorations the other night I felt like he was sending me a message, asking me to forgive him. Of course he wasn't – I'm spending too much time with Mrs J and her mad superstitions about bloody guardian angels and tea leaves.'

'No,' I said; 'you're right – you have to think like that. If you didn't you'd be driven mad... we have to believe there's good in everyone and try and forgive them.'

She nodded; 'I'd been so proud of that diamanté brooch I'd placed it on Nan's tree so everyone could see it – proof of my

Dad's love. It must have just been put away with all the other decorations. So he hadn't sold it after all. Just seeing it gave me a kind of hope... am I being silly?'

'No you're not,' I said gently, touching her arm. 'But perhaps it's a message – that it's time to forgive. He took away your childhood, don't let him have the rest.'

She smiled and patted my hand and we sat quietly together in silence, contemplating our pasts and our futures, with the leftovers of my sister's life in bin liners around us.

Chapter 12

Glittery Cookies and Christmas Clouds

Tamsin

'So, looks like we got 6 inches yesterday?' was Mrs J's opening remark the day after finding Gabe and I on the sofa.

'Mrs J, do you mind,' I snapped. 'Gabe and I were cleaning a red wine stain...'

She folded her arms and pursed her lips; 'I'm talking about the snow... we had 6 inches of it. Woke up to a complete white-out...'

'Oh, er, yes of course... snow... everywhere,' I added, turning a bougainvillea shade of pink.

Mrs J had just arrived to clean the bakery before it opened. Fortunately Sam was making tea in the kitchen or she'd have laughed loudly at my misunderstanding and confirmed Mrs J's suspicions that she'd walked in on a passionate encounter between Gabe and I.

Sam wandered in with the teas and I took a sip of the awful rust-coloured liquid.

'I would have preferred a fragrant Darjeeling,' I sighed.

'Would you? Well you're out of luck, it's a fragrant PG Tips,' Sam replied.

I pulled a face.

'Get used to it,' she said, giving Mrs J a big conspiratorial smile.

I had just taken a big gulp, but their pantomime faces amused me, like two old dears with their tight lips and their folded arms. 'You two look like twins,' I laughed, which caused me to cough, and before I knew it the Prada blouse I was wearing was covered in tea.

'You are a bloody mess, Tamsin,' Sam scolded. 'Get that shirt off and I'll steep it in some water.'

'This shirt is pure silk and can only be dry-cleaned,' I gasped.

'Well I'm afraid along with my cheap tea and coffee, your designer garb is going to have to rough it out in the washing machine with my Primark blouses,' she said.

I sipped some more vile tea, knowing I'd never get used to a brew like this. 'The day I enjoy this tea is the day I say goodbye to my cultured palate, which has taken many years and thousands of pounds in fabulous restaurants to develop,' I sighed, both hands around the mug for warmth.

'Oh stop whingeing and go and get another designer outfit on for deliveries,' Sam said. 'And make sure it's fabulous... my customers expect pure glamour from my delivery men.'

As if I'd ever wear anything that wasn't pure glamour. When I'd agreed to step into the breach, save the day and do a bakery delivery, I assumed I would be in a PR capacity. I had no idea I'd be the tradesman, driving the awful shuddering little van through the mean streets of Cheshire, but what could I do?

I helped Sam fill boxes with her tipsy cupcakes laced with rum and we carefully packed the gorgeous white snowflake cookies, their sparkly topping catching the light and reminding me once more of the festive season. 'Who said you can't save the world with the right shade of macaron?' I smiled, holding up a scarlet cranberry disc, sandwiched with salty pistachio buttercream. 'I reckon this baby could be just what the world is looking for – I'll email the White House,' I giggled. 'Am I being sarcastic?'

'A little,' Sam smiled. 'And it was actually quite amusing.'

I was pleased. I could be funny too?

'Mallows and meringues,' she said. 'They are the next big thing. What do you think?' She handed me a clementine and clove mallow. I bit into the squidgy white fluff. It tasted of a million Christmases rolled into one, a whiff of cinnamon, a suggestion of cloves and the sweet warmth of orange and ginger. 'Oh Sam, it's wonderful... like a cloud filled with Christmas.'

Sam liked that description and said she'd label them, 'Christmas Clouds.'

I tried another, forgetting about my promise to myself to lose 6lbs for Christmas. It didn't matter now anyway – I didn't have to fit into a party dress – I wasn't going to any parties. I didn't have a perfect Christmas to plan or a canapé to fill, I was just going to be here with Sam working flat out at the bakery. It wasn't what I'd planned but it was better than being on the streets.

Sam asking me to help out had actually united us and lifted my spirits – being in the bakery was like being home. That morning I'd woken at dawn, put on my delivery outfit and felt good for the first time in ages – it was like I'd re-entered civilization. The first thing I did when I went downstairs was put all the lights on and I wandered outside in the freezing snow. The air tingled with cold and I wrapped my now shabby cashmere shawl around my shoulders and stared at the bakery from the outside. It was like a beacon of Christmas hope twinkling in the darkness, reminding me of those little shops we sometimes used to visit with Nan around Christmas time. There were the big department stores, but also independent little cafes and groceries that didn't have a homogenised corporate logo on the door. The White Angel Bakery was like stepping back in time, something from a Victorian Christmas card standing in the snow with its shimmering lights and windows of cake. Glittery cookies, white, sparkly cupcakes and several Christmas cakes adorned the window. I could almost taste the icing, crisp and sweet and snowy around a centrepiece Christmas cake.

Once back inside I turned the ovens on and made everything perfect for when Sam came downstairs. I'd seen how hard my sister worked and I wanted to do something for her and to let her know I was there to help. Once she'd finished the cakes and we'd packed them all in boxes lovely Richard called by and helped me to load the van with my sugary orders.

'Have you tried those cookies?' he asked as we put the final box onto the van.

'No. I had a mallow this morning, delicious, but I try not to eat anything Sam makes, I would be the size of a small car if I did.'

He laughed and I was pleased I'd amused him. Little things were beginning to mean more to me these days. In Sam's world if people laughed at what you said it was because they thought you were funny – not because you had something they might want.

Eventually the van was packed and Sam gave me vague instructions about driving it. Honestly I don't know how she coped, no heated seats, no iPod station for music, no integral sat nav, in fact no sat nav full stop. 'But how will I know where I'm going?' I asked through chattering teeth, it was below zero and I was wearing black jersey loungewear, I thought it would be warm yet elegant, and one had to consider one's dignity when climbing in and out of a van. I couldn't find my Ugg boots so had resorted to the previous season's Jimmy Choo scarlet kitten heel. Sam had laughed, but I defended my selection and pointed out, 'If you can't wear red shoes with heels at Christmas, darling, when can you?'

However as my foot hit the accelerator and the van set off at high speed with lurching movements I hoped I wasn't going to live to regret my festive footwear of choice.

I set off, driving on ice, bumping over snow and losing track of which gear I was in. The van was old and rusty and just not what I had been used to and what made it worse was the so-called heater – which every now and then blasted freezing cold air in my face. I sang a few Christmas songs to keep me warm, and tried to stay cheerful – after all it was only my first day on the job – things were bound to get better, weren't they?

Chapter 13

It's the Most Wonderful Time of the Year

Sam

I watched Tamsin kangaroo off the bakery forecourt into a sea of oncoming, slow-moving traffic and almost died. It was still dark, but snowy and the morning rush hour in our area had started. I'm sure as she pulled away I saw her pull down the mirror and apply lipstick, almost causing a seventeen car pile-up... but as she skidded out of danger almost leap-frogging several other cars, I had to go back inside.

That morning Jacob and I walked to school with Richard and Ella. Within minutes, one of the yummy mummies was chatting with Richard, and once Jacob had gone to his classroom I wandered over. No one had any idea that Richard and I were seeing each other, and as I approached, she completely blanked me as the yummy mummies always did. She was batting her eyelashes, touching Richard's arm every now and then, clearly interested in him. He was an attractive man and the school playground was full of bored housewives looking for available males to take back to their lairs after the school run. Watching this woman leave her hand on Richard's arm a second too long and caress her own neck as she spoke to him, I felt a sting of jealousy. And for the first time, I wondered if I could have more than just a casual relationship with Richard. But always the fear was there in the back of my mind – could I do that to me and Jacob? What if it all went wrong Richard left? Could I live with a man again and make another little family only to risk losing him?

Eventually I wandered over to them. The woman clearly felt I was interrupting, looked me up and down and then turned with her back to me to block me out. The body language was all there and if it hadn't been so cold I reckon she'd have stripped and laid down on the gravel, but Richard seemed oblivious.

'Stacey... this is Sam,' Richard started, and she threw me a glance over her shoulder and an almost inaudible 'hi,' before turning back to him. I felt humiliated and walked off.

'Hold on... where are you going?' Richard called, catching me up.

'I don't have all day to wait for you,' I said as he panted and puffed and caught me up.

He discreetly caught my hand in his - and the feeling of his warm glove around my cold bare hand was so comforting I melted slightly felt an urge to kiss him - but resisted. We didn't show our affection in public because I didn't want it to affect Jacob and Ella at school. If the other parents knew we were an item, then the kids would too, and if things didn't work out it would make it all the more difficult for everyone.

We wandered back, chatting and laughing, away from the playground without the yummy mummies lurking, I felt free and being with Richard felt good. But arriving at the bakery I was delighted, and concerned, to see a small queue had formed, with Mrs J behind the counter trying to handle it alone.

'Do you want any help?' Richard asked. 'I can serve if you like?'

I knew Mrs J could handle it – as long as no one from the afterlife distracted her. The previous morning I'd come back from the school run to find her ignoring the queue of customers to do an impromptu Q and A with deceased members of the Coronation Street cast. Consequently, I was keen to have extra support which was why I'd asked Tamsin to help – and I liked having Richard around. In fact, I'd started to miss him on the nights he stayed home, which certainly hadn't been part of my plan to keep things casual.

So Richard helped Mrs J take the money and serve people while I replenished the stock and laid out more loaves and cakes. Most people had turned up to buy emergency bread because they hadn't been able to get to the supermarket due to the snow-blocked roads. And this was working for the White Angel Bakery – because along with the bread, they were buying cakes, cookies and Christmas gingerbread.

When Mrs J had to leave to 'get our Lawrence's dinner' at noon, Tamsin arrived, slipped off her kitten heels and got behind the counter with Richard. I had been expecting a panicked call from her all morning to ask where somewhere was or who was going to help her carry boxes, but she'd done it all. 'So everything's delivered?' I asked, surprised. She nodded coolly; 'Of course, what did you expect? Now if you don't mind I have customers,' she gestured to the waiting hordes. I blew her a kiss, my sister was quite amazing when she wanted to be. She and Richard were brilliant, chatting away and serving quickly and efficiently. I smiled as I heard Tamsin describing the gingerbread as 'sublime' and waxing lyrical about the savoury plaits until they were all sold. Her glitzy black top was covered in bread crumbs and cake dust and by three pm we had sold all the bread and far more cakes and cookies than I'd ever expect to sell on a snowy Wednesday in December. The door was jingling constantly and at one point I looked up from a tray of steaming Mediterranean bread to see Richard serving a group of yummy mummies at the table... all four of them watching intently as he went through the menu... and, I noticed, caressing their necks as he described each and every cake. Tamsin looked over at me and winked, 'I told you, love – get in there before someone else does,' she said, taking the tray of bread from my hands.

Later, Tamsin went to collect Jacob while Richard and I cleared up.

'I sometimes wonder if I'm not interesting enough for you,' he looked up from the table he was wiping.

I shook my head. Where was this coming from?

'I do have a past,' he smiled. 'I used to paint,' he leaned back on the counter, staring ahead. 'I never had the courage to try and make a living from it like you did with this place.'

'Wow... you never said.'

'I sold a few to a gallery once, just watercolours, not big and daring art. I'm no Damien Hirst.'

'I'm glad to hear it. I have a problem with art – well some art. It comes from having a sister who would have paid a million pounds for a toenail if someone had told her it was art,' I laugh.

'Ah... you can laugh, but the right toenail…' he smiled.

'So if you don't create bizarre installations of your unmade bed or the odd toenail what do you paint?' I asked.

'I just paint what I like, I wanted to paint you and Jacob and Ella walking home from school in the snow yesterday.'

My heart melted. He reached out to me, slipping his arm round my waist.

He laughed. 'When we walked back here and I saw the window filled with Christmas cupcakes I wanted to paint that too... I think you've inspired me.'

'Ah... I'm touched.

'...and when you're naked... I want to paint you.'

'Oh God – weirdo – and he knows where I live,' I rolled my eyes.

'I'd like to paint you... now, laughing like that,' he said.

'Naked?'

'Yes, preferably,' he had a glint in his eye and he pulled me closer.

'There you are!' Mrs J appeared in the doorway.' What's going on in here with you two mooning over each other?' she said, starting to polish the glass counter. Honestly it was starting to feel like Central Station with Tamsin or Mrs J popping up at the most inopportune moments.

Richard said hello to Mrs J then said he'd better get off. I think he found some of the ladies in my life a little too forceful - they intruded with force and said what they thought – loudly. 'There was no mooning, Mrs J,' I curled my lip. 'Richard and I were just having a rare and quiet moment,' I said pointedly, when he'd gone.

'Whatever – just don't let that sister of yours know you're entertaining gentlemen callers during office hours, she's worried you'll relapse.'

'Relapse into what? Prostitution?'

'Ooh Sam, you've got a filthy mouth, it's shocking,' she said, putting the chairs on the tables so she could give the floor 'a good do'.

I smiled, she worked hard at the bakery, cleaning and stepping behind the counter when necessary and was as reliable as clockwork. She also never, ever failed to pass judgement on what I was doing. It was annoying and often humiliating – but I had to smile, because somewhere underneath that perm and those tight, disapproving lips was a heart of gold – and a lot of love for the Angel sisters.

'Anyway Mrs J, I told you, I've given up on guys. I don't make the same mistakes twice... that's called masochism.'

'Oh... so that's what you do, is it?'

'No, I didn't mean I... I don't indulge in whips and...' I tried, because she was likely to tell anyone who'd listen that Sam from the bakery was 'one of them masochists'.

I ceased trying to explain myself when she disappeared under the table to wipe the floor, I was too tired and it would only get complicated. I opened the oven and let the blast of warmth light my face as I surrendered more rum sultana cakes into the furnace-like heat. I went to the window to see if Tamsin was on her way back with Jacob and, sure enough, there she was in the snow still wearing her 'delivery outfit' and designer heels.

Mrs J joined me at the window. 'She looks like the cat's dinner.'

Together we watched her staggering through the snow in a visor and dark glasses. She and Jacob were throwing snowballs at each other – Tamsin's were small and not very robust, with more of a scattering than a throwing action, but Jacob's were big and heavy and his aim was good, and at one point I feared she'd be knocked out. But after every freezing whack on the head she'd gather herself together, and waving to Tim the butcher in a flirty way, soon regained her flounce through three feet of snow.

'What is she like?' Mrs J sighed, shaking her head.

'She's something else, my sister,' I smiled, my heart filling with love and pride.

Chapter 14

Yummy Mummies in Knock-off Gucci

Tamsin

I think what struck me most about being 'poor' at this time of year was that everyone else seemed to be 'doing Christmas' except me. The bakery was all about the festive season, with glittery toppings and sprigs of holly and snowflake-shaped cookies. The TV was sheer torture, with commercials for glittering liqueurs, breathtaking chocolates and delicious perfume ads where you didn't recall the perfume, just the beautiful woman wandering through it. There was no escape, and for someone who was used to having the money to just buy this stuff, it was a special kind of hell.

I thought about how different this year would be from last, I'd always insisted on the family eating together when we could – and Christmas was the epitome of this. I loved that we spent time together on Christmas Day, but the rest of the year we all seemed to go our separate ways. I wanted to be a 'proper' family and chat about our day over a meal together. But often it would end up with Simon and I at the table alone as the kids gobbled their food and abandoned us. Hugo would be prostrate on the sofa, watching something inappropriate on TV and Hermione would disappear to her bedroom.

Before they broke up for the Christmas holidays the kids were from a wealthy family. They didn't have the usual student worries about paying for rent and food because we covered all that and more. But their new term in January would be quite different... and thinking about it – that might just be the making of them. Only the day before, Hugo had made everyone beans on toast at Sam's – something he'd never have done before. Hugo never cooked and wouldn't have touched baked beans. 'I need to practice,' he'd said. 'No more take-aways and restaurants when I go back to Uni – we can't afford it now.' I felt so proud and hearing that I realised my son would be fine and step up to this new, challenging time ahead.

Being a mum and going through my own kids' growing pains had made me aware of Jacob's problems too. Of course Sam denied he was having problems, but I'd collected him from school and he was always on his own. Sam knew that he didn't make friends easily and some of the kids made fun of him but was so close to it she hadn't really looked at the situation from both sides.

Before I moved in, I'd sometimes walked to school with Sam and Jacob before meeting Phaedra or Anouska for coffee. I'd seen the withering looks from the designer-clad yummy mummies hanging around in the playground in nasty little clusters. Of course they weren't in 'real' designer, it was all rather faux. But I suspected their snobbery and meanness was far more real than their cheap knock-off Gucci handbags.

Sam was attractive, a little younger, but wore huge, baggy jumpers and sometimes even flip flops or sandals in winter. When it was warm she wore vests that showed off her pert figure and you could see the jealousy in their over-made-up eyes. They resented her because she was different – and the fact she didn't even try to join their gang bothered them the most. It was the same at school, I can't count the times I'd had to threaten or hit some bullying madam who didn't understand my sister and saw her as an easy target to mock or threaten. How I longed to do the same for her and Jacob now – wait by the school gates at home time and sort out the bullies.

I loved the fact that Sam was a free spirit and didn't care what people thought – but I worried it was affecting Jacob. One evening, I went into his room and sat on the end of his bed for a chat. I missed bedtime with my own children, who had friends, and probably lovers now, and didn't need Mum.

'Do you like school Jacob?' I asked, tucking him in.

'I don't know.'

'Well... do you have friends who make you happy when you go there? Do you like your teacher?'

'Mrs Robinson's nice, but Josh is a dick.'

'Oh, that's not nice, to call someone that.' I tried not to reveal my shock at such a vulgar word coming from my nephew's rosebud lips.

'No, but that's what he calls me. He says my jumper's too big and my hair's too long.'

'Would you like to get your hair cut?'

'No.'

'Why?'

'Mummy likes it.'

'But do you like it?'

'Daddy likes it.'

My heart broke. I could see he was suffering in his own little six-year-old way but I hadn't yet worked out how I could help my nephew. So after a rather confusing chat about something called 'Minecraft', I kissed him goodnight and left him to go to sleep. Sam was baking downstairs so I joined her and tried to broach the subject of Jacob's hair and being Sam she behaved like I was suggesting he join a cult. She went on and on about him being an individual and accused me of all kinds of evil.

'I just think you could make life easier for him by getting his hair cut,' I reiterated.

'Keep out, Tamsin. Jacob is a good and happy little boy and he is what he wants to be. I will not have him changing for someone else – if some of the kids don't like his hair then hard luck.'

I understood that Jacob's identity and Steve's memory were wrapped up in all this and I knew it was important, but to whom?

'I wasn't suggesting you change his personality,' I said, but a haircut would have been a start. I respected her principles and ideals about being an individual – but at his age, Jacob just wanted to be like his friends, he didn't want to stand out.

'His long "girl's" hair is all the other kids see,' I said.

'Jacob loves his hair like that... it reminds him of his Dad.'

'It reminds *you* of his Dad,' I said, without thinking.

She glared at me, 'Ask him... ask him then if he likes his hair like his Daddy's.'

'No. Because that's a loaded question... you're putting your own loss onto that child. He was twelve months old when Steve died, he doesn't remember what his Dad's hair was like,' I tried to say this gently but she wasn't happy.

'Stop telling me what to do... how to run my life. And keep out of my relationship with Jacob too!' she yelled, running upstairs to the flat like a teenager.

I was only trying to help. I don't know why I bothered, she never took my advice anyway. It wasn't just the way she was with Jacob, she didn't know how to cook pasta, she had sex on the floor and her hands looked like an old man's with bitten nails, but would she get a manicure? I dared to mention it and she bit my head off like I'd told her she had to fly first class to Cannes in her lunch hour.

Then there was the pierced navel and her refusal to marry lovely Richard. I knew it was difficult for her to take another man into her bed (though not the floor apparently) and I understood her reasons. I'd held her hand through it all, but I felt it was time she moved on, cut her son's hair, say 'yes' to Richard – and no to any more piercings.

I hadn't meant to hurt her, but I had to address the hair situation because I believed her own grief might be hurting Jacob. I had to help my nephew – in the same way I'd helped Sam after Steve's death.

After only a week in the hospital she was discharged and I brought her home with me. She'd been a total mess when I collected her, calling for Steve, only wanting Jacob. I'd made sure she had a beautiful private room with apricot walls and matching bed linen, but in spite of all this she was still desperately unhappy.

My friends said I should book her into a really good spa, apparently there's a wonderful one somewhere down south. But I brought her back to the bosom of my family on Chantray Lane and installed Fifi, my life coach on suicide watch. Fifi practically saved my sister's life. Five years later, here she was with her own business, a lovely kid and a nice boyfriend. She'd done so well and I didn't want her to fall at the final hurdle.

Chapter 15

Lusty Firemen and Frosty Macarons

Sam

It was just before closing time and Mrs J was reading Heddon and Hall's tea leaves in a rare quiet moment when I got the phone call from Tamsin. 'I can't get it to go,' she shrieked down the phone, followed by a loud 'OH MY GOD IT'S STOPPED! I assumed she was referring to the van, which Mrs J confirmed with a nod.

I put down the phone. 'If that was in the leaves you might have told me sooner, Mrs J,' I said.

'I've only just seen it. But there's worse to come I can tell you that.'

Great, I thought, and thanks for breaking it to me so gently, and I went to greet my hysterical sister whose screams could now be heard over the van shuddering to a halt outside the bakery. The bonnet was smoking and Tamsin was yelling for help. So there was worse to come... worse than this? Really?

Fortunately Heddon and Hall placated her while I called the garage.

'Call the fire brigade, my love, we need those boys - it could all go up at any time,' cried Heddon, clinging to a tearful Tamsin. But that wasn't necessary – I knew he just fancied a parade of lusty firemen with his frosty macarons and coffee.

Having calmed Heddon, Hall AND Tamsin, I spoke with Fred at the garage, whose opening line was, 'Sounds like your big end's gone, love'; I felt like it had too. I held on to the phone, not understanding a word of his garage-speak, just wanting to know the bottom line – would I have a van for deliveries in the morning? To my despair, the roundabout answer seemed to be 'no', and even worse – no van the following morning or the one after that either. Still clinging to the phone, my mind everywhere else, I tried not to cry as Fred talked worryingly about big ends, back ends and front ends, expensive parts, transmission systems and drive belts, which was just a list of unrelated sounds to me.

'Just... Fred how much? How much and when can it be fixed?' I asked.

Again I was given another list of engine-related words and sounds, but all I heard was 'about a grand'.

'But the van isn't even worth that,' I protested. Then I cried.

I didn't have the money. Everything I'd made in the bakery had been ploughed straight back into the business or used to pay basic living expenses, and what little I'd put aside was for Christmas gifts.

I didn't want Tamsin to see how upset I was because it would only upset her. I could see by her face she was now taking on the guilt and responsibility for the problem.

'I feel terrible, we won't be able to do any Christmas deliveries,' she was sobbing.

'Please don't feel terrible. It's an old van and I'm sure we can find a solution,' I wiped my eyes, tried not to vomit and patted her leg... her other body parts were being comforted by Heddon and Hall. Mrs J was making more tea and Tamsin went on to talk through her 'trauma' like she'd been physically attacked.

'For God's sake, Tamsin, the van broke down, you're fine, get a grip,' I sighed, wondering what the hell I was going to do.

'I'm sorry,' she sighed. 'You're right, I'm being a prima donna, but I've never broken down before, never known the horror of that terrible black smoke coming from the engine.'

'No. Well that's because you've never driven a car older that twelve months old,' I said, trying not to sound bitter.

'Sam. It's not a crime to own a new car, you know – just because you choose to drive some dilapidated old...'

'Well isn't that just typical. The very fact you say that I "choose" to drive an old van says it all. You think I have a choice, Tamsin, but I don't, because I can't afford a newer, more reliable vehicle. Like most people in the real world.'

I was angry, and so was she, we stared at each other, both red-faced with rage and resentment and I wanted to tell her to get out of my life. She talked about suffering as a child, but I'd suffered as an adult, I'd been widowed at thirty-one and I'd been left with scars too.

'Ladies, ladies, now, now,' said Hall, ever the peacemaker. 'Let's not get upset... we need to think about how we can make lemonade from these bloody rancid old lemons we've been handed,' he smiled.

'I just don't know what to do,' I sighed. 'I can't afford to get the van fixed and we have literally hundreds of orders to be delivered before Christmas.'

The boys gasped theatrically.

'We'd help you but our van is packed with Christmas stuff and permanently on the road this time of year,' Heddon said, rubbing Tamsin's back.

'Thank you, but we'll be fine. I just need to think about it,' I sighed, knowing that if I didn't, we couldn't make the deliveries. And if we couldn't make the deliveries we would lose a lot of money, which would be a huge problem for the bakery.

'It's me – I'm the jinx,' Tamsin said, throwing herself onto the table.

'Yes, you are. It's in the leaves... you've brought nothing but bad luck and there's more to come,' Mrs J added. I rolled my eyes, I wasn't in the mood for Mrs J's predictions or my sister's attention-seeking theatrics.

Tamsin lifted her head, she looked crestfallen but said, 'We shall rise to this challenge!'

I tried to 'play nice' but pointed out a thousand pounds was more than 'a challenge' where I came from. Heddon and Hall clearly felt the tension and announced their departure, saying they had to 'decorate some glitzy balls'. I wasn't sure if they were referring to Christmas balls or each other's, but we all hugged goodbye and they skipped off into the snowy night.

Tamsin and I were left alone at the table, glaring at each other. We had loads to do before morning when I would have to phone all the deliveries to cancel, postpone or ask if they could collect. But Tamsin was still in fantasy land, talking colours and themes and how we could stage events and parties and catering and 'transform the bakery's fortunes' with a makeover and a 'Christmas Launch'. As usual I felt like we were speaking in different languages and her loud voice and sweeping gestures were too much for me. My sister and I had always been on different planets but I was worried she was still on 'planet Tamsin,' where money was no object.

'I don't have the money for makeovers,' I sighed. 'As much as I'd love the bakery to look like a white wonderland – I can't do anything without a van.'

'Not in the short term, but sweetie, we need to think beyond tonight. Oh God I'm exhausted, I've been through so much – I could just book myself into a spa... that's what I need, a lovely massage and... a big man's feet. Oh God, Sam, you haven't lived until a big man has walked up and down your back...'

'I feel like he just has,' I sighed.

How could she even talk about a spa at a time like this? 'Look. I don't know how many times I have to tell you, Tamsin. We can't ignore the boring, gritty day-to-day stuff by brushing it under the carpet and talking about bloody spas and launch parties. I have lived in my world for some time,' I explained. 'And like most other people's lives it's messy and sometimes not very pretty to look at. Unfortunately I can't just spend my way to happiness or solve problems by buying myself another designer dress, and as of ten days ago – neither can you.'

She got up from the table and went into the bakery kitchen where she began banging trays around and slamming cupboard doors. I wondered seriously about what we were going to do – not just about the van, but the fact we just couldn't live together.

I am laid-back, but even I was beginning to wonder when it would all end and there would be peace.

It felt like suddenly my life was falling apart, just when I'd thought things were coming together and this Christmas I would be able to celebrate for the first time in years. But Tamsin and her bags of pointless possessions had taken over everything; her presence was affecting my relationship with Richard because we could never be alone; and time I should be spending with Jacob was being sucked up by Tamsin's endless, high-maintenance demands. She was getting involved in Jacob's life and hair, banging on about 'holding events' when we didn't have the time or the money and now the van was just one more thing – and she just didn't get it that no van meant no business.

Then I heard Jacob calling.

After I'd given him his tea, I'd sent him upstairs with his laptop and asked Mrs J to sit with him for a little while until I could close the bakery. She was no doubt now napping on the sofa, so I was a little concerned he may be scared or worried on his own.

'Mum... Mummy...' he called downstairs.

'Yes sweetie?' He didn't answer and as Tamsin appeared in the kitchen doorway wiping her hands, we both looked at each other.

'Sweetie are you okay?' I called again. The look on Tamsin's face mirrored mine. Our previous irritation with each other dissipated as we had both instinctively responded to his call, united in our love for Jacob.

'Yeah. Mum... what's gay nympho?'

Tamsin screamed and covered her face with both hands.

'Get off that laptop NOW,' I shouted, flying up the stairs, Tamsin in hot pursuit.

'Oh my God he's watching gay porn...' she was yelling from behind me. I could have sworn the laptop had a parental lock on, but what did I know? As far as I was concerned he was playing Minecraft, how on earth had he found himself on a porn sight? It wasn't any old porn sight either, I thought, mounting the stairs two by two – it was quite specific... gay nymphos.

'I'm phoning Tana my therapist...' Tamsin was shouting. 'She can sort this... there are retreats we can send him to.'

Ignoring Tamsin, I tore into the room and snatched the laptop from him, unable to imagine what he must have witnessed.

'Mum... what are you doing?' he whined.

I stood with the laptop in my hands. I couldn't see any gay nymphos on the Minecraft site, but it occurred to me I wouldn't know what to do if I did... the joke was I'd have to ask my six-year-old to get rid of them.

I didn't want to scare him, or alert him to something he may not understand, so trying to make it sound like Tellytubbies, I said; 'Can you see any of the little... gay... nymphos... here?' At that old Mrs J's head was up and she was wide awake.

'Oh what are you saying to the lad now?' she hissed, like it was a daily occurrence for me to ask my child to find porn on his computer.

'No, Mrs J – you don't understand, he asked me what gay nymphos are... and I...'

She stood back, shocked, then leaned in to look at him, her nose touching his. 'Jacob,' she shouted in his face, 'what are you doing with gay nymphos on your laptop?'

'I'm not...'

I stepped in, moving Mrs J aside to try a more gentle approach.

'Darling, why did you ask Mummy what gay nympho means?'

'I didn't... I said what does game info mean?'

'Oh...' I didn't know where to put myself as Mrs J put her hands on her hips and shook her head slowly, looking at me with sheer disgust, at which point Tamsin appeared in the doorway with her mobile clamped to her ear.

'Tana? Thank God! This is an emergency... we need your help, we've just discovered my six-year-old nephew is addicted to gay internet porn...'

I finally managed to calm everyone down and convince my sister and Mrs J that Jacob hadn't been downloading anything untoward and his internet activities were innocent. But it was just another exhausting half hour of my life I wouldn't get back. I was beginning to feel like I was in a surreal world where I had no control and no one was listening to me. Tamsin's noise filled my head and what would normally have been me having a quiet conversation with Jacob ended up with me screaming 'gay nymphos' in his face, to the soundtrack of Mrs J's tutting and Tamsin's hysterical call to some therapist. When, I wondered, did my life get so crazy and loud and most of all – when would it stop?

❄ ❄ ❄

The following morning Richard came over. Jacob was at school and Tamsin had gone to argue with someone at the bank and during a few precious minutes alone in the bakery kitchen he asked again about being together at Christmas.

'For God's sake, Richard, I don't know what I'm doing tomorrow, let alone Christmas,' I'd snapped. 'We don't have a van and without it I'm in serious danger of losing my business – I may not even *have* a Christmas at this rate.' I was aware I'd been quite short with him and also aware I was beginning to sound like Tamsin. Her brusque, business-like manner was infectious, as was her stress.

'I think we should talk,' he said. I nodded, I didn't have time for this but Richard looked so serious I asked Mrs J to keep an eye on the shop while we went upstairs and, judging by her face,

I'm sure she assumed we were going to have wild sex. I didn't care what she thought, Richard obviously had something to say and we couldn't talk in full view of customers. My mouth felt dry as I led him into the living room, Tamsin's bin liners had crept further onto the sofa in the past couple of days so we had to sit on the floor.

'I can't go on like this,' he sighed. 'I don't want to push you into something you aren't ready for Sam, but I won't wait forever.'

My heart did a flip. Was he finishing this? It was the last thing I'd expected – Richard was always around, he'd said I was everything to him. I felt my heart begin to thud in my chest.

'Am I just wasting my time? I'm not an idiot, Sam. I won't be strung along.'

'God I never thought you were and I'm not stringing you along... I told you from the beginning. I'm not sure I can do forever, not after Steve,' I said. Richard nodded, but I could see he was hurt by the fact I still couldn't let him in.

'Someone or something wants a piece of me every minute of every day at the moment – and I can't take much more...' I started to cry and he put his arm around me.

'I understand. And I won't be the one more person who makes life hard for you. I'd wanted to be the person that takes away your troubles... if you'd have just let me.'

'I'm sorry Richard. I can't...'

I could see his eyes were sad even in the dimness of the tree lights, but I was so tired and worn out I couldn't take it on. I didn't have the energy for yet another emotional casualty – even if it was my own victim.

'I'm sorry,' he said. 'This is too much for both of us – we seem to want different things Sam, I think we should say goodbye so we can both go and find them.'

I nodded, big tears dropping down my face. He stood up while I watched the dying embers of the fire send up little smoke signals. Mrs J would say it was the spirits telling me to stop him leaving, to kiss him better. But I had to kiss me better first.

He left silently and I watched from the upper window as he trudged home in the snow, shoulders hunched, head down. A wave of sadness overwhelmed me, I didn't want to hurt this man, but in my own mixed up way I suppose I was trying to protect both of us. I may be the woman he wanted, but I couldn't be the woman he needed. I had to protect my life and my heart... Love and loss had devastated me once already.

Perhaps in the long term it was best for me to let Richard go? I couldn't give him what he wanted, a committed relationship, a ready-made family – and yet ultimately wasn't it what I wanted too? I knew I was being stupid – and perhaps if I'd been brave enough to take a chance, I might finally have found what I was looking for... but I just couldn't do it.

Chapter 16

Sauvignon Blanc and a Seafaring Threesome

Tamsin

The following day we ordered a taxi to drive me and all the deliveries around the area. The taxi driver was called Keith and on the journey he told me all about his three baby mothers and his current girlfriend's weakness for crack. It was like a real life Jeremy Kyle and I half hoped I'd see him again to find out what happened next. Things hadn't been great between Sam and I, so I felt, as the big sister, it was up to me to make amends, so that night I joined her to work late in the bakery.

'I've been thinking,' I announced as she slaved wordlessly over cupcake batter. 'I know you're worried about the van situation and I hope you don't think I'm interfering,' I said pointedly, 'but I called Gabe.'

Sam looked up. 'Why?'

'Well. Given that Gabe and I have a little unspoken, unfinished, 'thing' between us, I asked if he might help us out with deliveries until we can get the van fixed. I hadn't heard from him since the bodice-ripping incident but asked if he could do me a favour. He said yes straight away, which I took as a good sign so I asked if he might help us out with deliveries until we can get the van fixed. I said we'd pay him petrol money... worryingly he said we could 'come to some arrangement', and if I have to prostitute myself for this business, so be it,' I giggled.

'You wonderful, wonderful... old tart,' Sam said, reaching her arms out to hug me and it felt good being able to help her again.

'He asked if I'd be joining him on deliveries and I said yes and that seemed to seal the deal for him.'

I blushed, just thinking about our telephone conversation, it was quite delicious, and I flushed again remembering how my eyelashes had batted down the phone line.

Sam seemed so relieved. 'Oh Tam, you've saved my life – and my business!' She'd jumped up and down like a little girl and we'd danced around the bakery together to celebrate. I saw a couple of people pass by and to my horror realised they were yummy mummies from the school. Sometimes I really do think she asks for it, I thought, as Sam swept me across the floor like bloody Fred Astaire and the yummy mummies peered in, nudging each other with smirks on their faces. Sam was oblivious and while fox trotting across the bakery floor I stared hard right back at them through the window. The next time I looked they'd gone.

'So, let's celebrate the solving of the van issue,' I said. I'd found a warm bottle of cheap Sauvignon in one of Sam's cupboards and poured us both a glass to toast before we started work.

'Here's to no talk about men, money, vans or business,' I said as we clinked glasses.

Sam agreed, but within minutes was asking if I'd heard from Simon.

'Mmmm I don't want to talk about Simon either – quite frankly he can toss off.'

'Nice mouth,' Sam said, laughing.

'I am such a potty mouth on Sauvignon Blanc, it makes me say things I wouldn't normally dream of uttering,' I giggled, feeling the welcome warmth of the white wine fill my chest. 'As Rosalind Rice discovered last summer just before her yacht company went tits up,' I went hot, recalling my horrific faux pas on board Sky Dancer.

'They were launching their latest model and I was languishing on deck sipping what I assumed to be a decent wine, but it was in fact a new world Sauvignon,' I curled my lip. 'Anyway, I was three sheets to the wind when Rosalind's husband sauntered up, and in front of everyone gesticulated toward my décolletage and said "Would you like a threesome?"'

Sam had stopped kneading, mouth half open in shock. 'Rosalind's husband? Oh God, what did you say?' she asked, a smile playing on her lips.

'Well, I was outraged. I slapped his face and called him a filthy pervert. Not words I would use normally in polite company,' I explained.

'No, but it's not every day someone's husband propositions you in polite company is it? She'd temporarily stopped kneading the bread to take all this in.

'So what happened?'

'Well, when Rosalind's husband recovered from shock and asked why I'd reacted with such vitriol to his comment, the Sauvignon had really kicked in. I heaped even further abuse on the man, informing him very loudly that I wasn't into his dirty little sex games. I said I was both horrified and surprised that Rosalind was married to such a disgusting scum pig,' I grabbed a chair and sat down, Sam was enthralled.

'You never told me this bit of gossip... Rosalind - a swinger? She's such a stuck up bitch too...'

'Mmmm. Let me finish,' I waved my hand in the air. 'As I shrieked obscenities at her husband, Rosalind wept, and silence descended on Sky Dancer, their 200-foot yacht. Everyone was staring and he was looking at me with such shock and horror it occurred to me that I may have misunderstood and the Sauvignon had caused me to perhaps overreact to what he'd said.'

'Nooooo.'

I nodded. 'Oh yes, it was mortifying. I was wearing a low-cut Versace that evening, it was rather chilly on deck and it transpired that he was looking at my goose bumped chest and asking if I'd "like a fleece on".'

Sam was now doubled up laughing, and though it was a painfully embarrassing story for me to tell, I had to join in. 'Anyway, that's what I'm like on Sauvignon Blanc... it colours my imagination, I tend to think of everything in a sexual way... or is it that more to do with my age?'

Sam was still laughing, now wiping her eyes on her tea towel.

'Thing is, Rosalind still isn't speaking to me,' I sighed, warming to the theme and enjoying Sam's laughter. 'You can laugh, it cost me a fortune in floral tributes to apologise.'

'Nothing says "I'm sorry I called your husband a disgusting scum pig," like a bouquet of spring blooms,' she roared laughing.

'I was never invited to sunset cocktails on Sky Dancer again,' I said, a wave of sadness coming over me. 'Says it all really, doesn't it? One word out of place and suddenly you're out, thrown bodily from the social circle. Forget a 200 foot yacht, I'd be lucky to be invited to one of Mimi's pole dancing classes now.'

'I think you'll find calling someone's husband a filthy little pervert and a disgusting scum pig is actually more than just one word out of place, Tamsin,' she said. 'Anyway, they've had a bumpy ride themselves this past year, haven't they? I would feel sorry for them, but they were so obnoxious, always looking down their noses at everyone...'

'I wonder if people are saying that about me – now I don't have money anymore?' I said, almost to myself.

'Yeah... some will. And they can fuck off,' she snapped. 'Do not work yourself up into a lather about fair-weather friends who turned up to drink your champagne and criticise your lifestyle and wallpaper. People who really care about you will still be there, Tamsin, and not gossiping and spreading rumours about you and your marriage.'

She said this with watery eyes and my heart went quite floppy, my own eyes filling up at the thought of everything that now lay ahead.

'My marriage?'

'Oh, you know... just jealousy... only gossip.'

I thought for a moment about Simon and what we had... what I'd thought we had, together.

'I know people talked, even Mrs J told me she thought he'd got someone else when he left.'

'Who cares? You were always too good for him. I like you better without Simon. And now you're on your own, I reckon you might just start to like yourself a bit more too.'

I wanted to hug Sam, but she was full of flour and sticky buttercream, and as much as I love her there's only so much grease a Prada blouse can take.

'Given how hilarious you are on Sauvignon, might I suggest a second glass?' she asked, smiling. I nodded. It was nice being here with my sister, laughing, drinking. Sam could even make me smile about the bad bits of my life – she got things into perspective for me and made me realise there were other things going on.

'Oh Sam, how did I get into this pretty pickle I'm in?'

'Being evicted from the posh Rotary Club Wives you mean?' she sighed.

'There was no "wives" in the title, we were all fully fledged Rotary members.'

'Yeah... whatever... that's what they told the wives in Stepford too,' she smiled, handing me a second glass.

'I am a lot of things, but I'm certainly not one of those kept women who haven't a clue,' I said.

'Really? Do you know how much your weekly supermarket shop used to be?'

'Not... really because I got Mrs J to...'

'Do you know how much you paid to heat your home in winter? Or how much you owed on your credit cards?'

'Okay, I take your point. I lifted my foot off the pedal of life – as it were. Being married to Simon had turned me into a dependent, pathetic "Real Housewife of Chantray Lane" type, who had everything done for her. But it's not what I wanted, Sam.'

'Don't knock it,' she laughed. 'I'd give anything for someone else to pay my bills and do my shopping while I swan around boutiques before a light lunch with wannabe WAGs in the latest French bistro.'

'It wasn't quite like that,' I said, indignantly, while wondering if she'd been spying on me it was so bloody accurate. 'Anyway, it's all in the past now – gone are the days of French bistros and footballers' wives. And yes, I am ashamed of myself, I should have known what our debts were and how much a loaf of bread costs... but I've spent my whole life worrying and as a child I would cry myself to sleep most nights.'

She looked at me, we were both leaning on the ovens trying to keep warm

'I was so unhappy.'

'I know and I hate that you went through all that, but you mustn't forget there were golden moments too, Tam.'

I didn't answer her... I wished I could shake it off, and perhaps with Sam's help I could. But some days it just came in on me – the past.

❄ ❄ ❄

Mum couldn't afford to buy us much, what money we had went on Dad's whisky and what Santa brought was usually a disappointment. I'd watch Christmas films and ads on TV of perfect families, with a dad carving the turkey, a mum presiding over Christmas pudding and smiley-faced children opening their presents. I'd imagine the wreaths on the door, a fire blazing and gifts around the tree, how I longed for a Christmas like the families on the telly.

I remember going to my friend Karen's house when I was about eleven years old. There was a green and gold wreath on the door and the Christmas tree was the most beautiful I'd ever seen. Her mum was smiling in a beautiful shiny kitchen, and later she brought us warm mince pies on silver doilies. They had a colour TV and a video and her dad put tinsel round the room and poured sherry into strange shaped glasses. 'They're called schooner glasses. Mum and Dad always have sherry in them,' Karen said, like she was letting me into a family secret. How I envied her life, her parents and those very special shaped sherry glasses. I can laugh now at the kitsch glassware and how the child in me saw a perfectly average family and thought they were royalty. But back then I thought Karen was the luckiest, richest girl I'd ever met. I wanted to feel like she must feel, live like she did – and I wanted it so much it had become a stabbing pain in my stomach for the rest of my life.

And despite having had enough money for a hundred turkeys and a million gifts since then – it occurred to me I'd never actually achieved this 'Christmasness'. Living in Sam's world had made me realise that perhaps Christmas wasn't something you *achieved*. Perhaps Christmas could only be planned so far and the rest was down to the messy unpredictable nature of human life? In which case, I thought – who cares what colour your baubles are?

❄ ❄ ❄

'I've been thinking... about the future,' Sam said later that night.

'Whose?'

'Ours actually,' she looked down at her feet. I followed her eyes... bloody flip flops and black painted toes – in this weather. For once I kept my mouth shut – what did I know? 'Look, we've not always been the best of friends... we're totally different people, but turns out we're both in what you would call "a pretty pickle" and I would call "deep shit".

'I'm going to be sick,' I said, lunging into the back of the bakery and arriving at the downstairs bathroom sink just in time. I threw up, vowing never to touch Sauvignon again while wiping my face on a towel that had seen better days. It was rough and scratched my face dry rather than blotting it as my own soft towels did. I saw myself in the mirror and wondered where the years had gone. How many Christmas parties, carol services and theatrical productions had I presided and fretted over? And for what? I had spent the past twenty odd Christmases spending time and money on other people. I had probably ignored my own family's needs to tend to those people who were now not answering my calls (you know who you are).

I tried not to cry and walked back into the bakery where the warmth of cinnamon penetrated my nostrils and my heart. Sam must have seen in my face that I was feeling fragile and she put both her arms around me.

'What I was going to say about our future, was you can stay as long as you need to and if I sometimes get cross it's just because you're one of the most annoying people I know. But I love you and I'm here for you.'

'Oh Sam, you've been so good to me – you're even putting a roof over my head.'

'Hardly Tam... it's a shared bed in a tiny room in a very small flat. It's nothing like the glamour and luxury you've been used to.'

'I know you always thought I was having this amazing life... there was a time when I thought that too. But it was meaningless – and you were right about the people, they were shallow and selfish. They only want you when you're winning.'

'I've been saying it for years. How many festive fucking canapés can a woman serve before she's accepted into a world like that?' Sam huffed, angry on my behalf, which touched me.

We both laughed at her comment, humour relieving the pain temporarily.

'You've had enough wine, I've made you some tea,' she said. 'Mum always said there was nothing like a nice cup of tea when life was shit.' That word again, Mum used words like that – usually when she was 'ill', and though Sam didn't know it, for Mum 'a nice cup of tea' was usually a mug containing a nice splash of whisky.

I watched as Sam gently pasted some cupcakes with syrup. It was quite therapeutic to see those thirsty cakes quenched with warm syrup and I was hoping she'd frost some so I could watch that too – then lick the spoon. I was hurting inside but found this whole process quite comforting.

She looked up from what she was doing. 'Do you remember Nan baking?' she asked.

I nodded. It was only the times spent at Nan's that were truly happy as a child.

'The house was always warm and smelled of food cooking,' I sighed, salivating at the thought. Perhaps it was these times I needed to think about when I considered the past – when we stayed at Nan's and she read us stories and fed us cake. I'd spent a fortune in therapy over the years, but the way to deal with the past was to embrace the Christmases on Hyacinth St when Granddad brought home mistletoe insisting Nan kiss him underneath it. 'You silly old sod,' she'd say, faking reluctance when he tried to claim his kiss. Nan and Granddad's tree was always a real one. I could smell the pine and feel the prickly dark green fronds.

'I always thought it was just luck that we were there on the day the tree was decorated but looking back they must have planned it that way.' I remembered once, before Sam was born, being discovered alone at home by a neighbour. She must have called Nan and Granddad, who came to collect me. They had no car and walked through the wintry streets in the middle of the night, and the following morning when I woke up in their cosy home I ran downstairs and found a Christmas tree leaning against the wall. Granddad must have gone out first thing to get it before I woke.

Once, another Christmas time, we arrived late to my grandparents after my parents had been rowing. A policeman took us in the car and when we got there, Sam, who was about five years old, saw the tree waiting to be dressed. She asked granddad if we could decorate it and I kept telling her we couldn't because it was almost midnight. But Granddad said, 'Oh it's better after midnight – the fairies come out to help.' He brought in the box of decorations, the old paper chains, the cracked old baubles, all breathtakingly beautiful to us. We gasped at the glass owl, the little wooden rocking horse, the favourite and familiar blue Cinderella slipper – while Nan made hot chocolate. Later, she came in with a box of Quality Street sweets she said she'd found in the back of the cupboard. Now I realise she probably had those chocolates there for a reason – for a night like this when we'd be rescued from our parents. Once Granddad had worked out which light was broken in the string of multi-coloured fairy lights, Nan put the plug in the wall and Sam whispered 'fairies'. The lights and the baubles twinkled and we ooed and aahed and Sam said she could hear the bells on Santa's sleigh.

I had spent thousands of pounds and as many hours planning and decorating my own Christmas trees since, from traditional red and green, to post-modern purple. But do you know what? They never captured the essence and beauty of Christmas the way Nan and Granddad's tree did that night.

I was suddenly dragged into the present by Sam, who was now whipping up frosting.

'I'm going for cranberry,' she said. 'The cake's sweet, so the cranberries should be a good balance.'

She split the frosting into two bowls and handed me one with a palette knife.

'What?'

'Frost some cakes,' she smiled. 'If you're going to hang around here you might as well make yourself useful.'

I smiled, took the palette knife and began to work on smoothing the buttercream onto the sponge cakes.

'And no licking the spoon,' she said. Here in the kitchen Sam was the boss, she was 'the big sister' for once and surprisingly I didn't mind her telling me what to do. I didn't have to think or worry or take on any responsibility for anyone else. It was like taking a holiday away from myself – and despite all my worries, I liked the freedom.

'You are clever,' I smiled. 'I wish I had a skill like you do, especially now. I could help more with the business.'

'You say you have no skills but you do. You have an eye for design and you're a great PR person, you can put people at their ease, chat along and make them feel good about themselves. In that way, you can do so much more than me.'

She was being kind. 'I suppose I have a modicum of what you might call "people skills",' I sighed. 'Yes I can design interiors, come up with a table-scape when I have to. In the past few years I've been involved in some quite unique "events" – but it's not about skill, it's all done with a cheque book.'

'It's not just about the money. You've said it yourself, money can't buy taste,' she said pointedly, a reminder of how judgemental I'd been in my designer-clad ivory tower. 'I feel so bad, Tamsin... you've always been there for me, helped me through such bad times – I wish there was a way I could help you.'

'Sweetie, Simon and I owe thousands, not to mention the cost of potential divorce proceedings when we will be funding the lawyer's villa in St Tropez. You couldn't possibly help me... I don't mean to sound ungrateful.'

'Well you do. Ungrateful, pompous, rude and patronising... to be precise,' she sighed.

'But I deliver it all with great style and class,' I smiled.

'Tamsin making fun of herself... that's new and different?' she was shaking her head and smiling and the radio was playing 'Once in Royal David's City', while we sang along, frosting cranberry cupcakes. And it felt just a little bit like Christmas.

Chapter 17

It's Going to be a Cold, Cold Christmas

Sam

A couple of days later I woke at five a.m. to freezing conditions. I had baking to do for the day, so once dressed, rushed straight downstairs to turn the ovens on. Despite a jumper and woolly leggings, I also had a blanket around me to try and keep warm, it was always so cold first thing and I couldn't afford to leave the heating on all night. I boiled the kettle for tea and waited for the ovens to heat up when I heard something at the door. I went to answer it, but by the time I'd unlocked and unbolted everything, all I felt was a blast of cold, snowy silence when I opened the door. I popped my head outside and looked both ways but couldn't see anyone.

Thinking I must have imagined it, I turned round and closed the door quickly, trying to keep the heat in, when I noticed a brown envelope on the floor. Intrigued, I picked it up and when I opened it discovered a gorgeous watercolour of the bakery. It was so pretty and delicate, it almost sparkled, the fairy lights twinkled and each little cupcake was painted in beautiful pastels.

I knew it was a gift from Richard, I had no idea he was so talented… but what touched me most was the love and time that had clearly gone into such a beautiful, detailed picture.

He'd taken so much care in creating this, and tears sprung to my eyes just thinking about the way things had been, and the way I'd dismissed him. It was selfish, I'd been thinking only about me. I held the watercolour to my chest, my eyes stung – what had I done?

❄ ❄ ❄

Tamsin kindly took Jacob to school that day so I didn't have to bump into Richard. It was still raw, I'd been tired and tearful the previous couple of days and I didn't want to see him and make a fool of myself, I needed time to think.

'He asked if you were okay,' she said when she got back. She looked under her mascara lashes at me, pretending to feign indifference.

'Well, I finished it. He's made it quite clear he's not going to hang around – so don't go reading too much significance into his enquiry.'

I changed the subject and asked about Simon, which soon shut her up. I hadn't heard any more rumours about him 'running off' with another woman, so assumed Phaedra's comment in the restaurant was just a repeated rumour, but I did wonder.

'I don't even want to say that arsehole's name,' she snapped.

'Wow – listen to her with her Chantray Lane mouth,' I mocked. 'I don't think Anouska would approve.'

'She can shove it up 'er arse as well,' Tamsin hissed. We both looked at each other and laughed, the working class Mancunian never far from the Yves Saint Lauren surface.

The door jingled and some rather well-heeled customers came in and Tamsin's demeanour changed instantly. From suggesting someone 'shove' something up their arse, she manoeuvred seamlessly into 'Good morning ladies, how "lavely" to see you. Now what can we tempt you with? Do please try a soupcon of our divine gingerbread...' I watched in awe at her amazing ability to put negative thoughts away in boxes and forget about them, almost instantly. I could see the 'ladies who lunch' were completely transfixed, and she talked their language. It reminded me of the way Richard had enticed the yummy mummies that day he'd served coffee. At the thought of Richard my stomach turned over, I felt guilty about the way I'd treated him... and I was missing him. I was missing him so much I had a deep, permanent ache in my stomach that intensified when I thought about him. I had never expected to feel like that again and seeing the beautiful watercolour he'd painted so lovingly had made it even worse. But I was soon dragged away from thoughts of Richard with Tamsin's news.

'I finally got a text from Anouska last night, she seems fine and made me feel so much better about everything,' Tamsin announced after selling a huge amount of gingerbread and cupcakes to the ladies and taking several big Christmas orders from them. She was smiling, and leaning against the counter.

My stomach lurched. I'd never trusted Anouska and the fact she only texted and never called kind of confirmed that for me. I was convinced she'd simply been pumping Tamsin for information about her money and her marriage to take back to the other 'Real Housewives of Chantray Lane.'

I didn't want to spoil Tamsin's happiness. Anouska might be a good friend, but I'd seen the way she looked at Simon when we were last at one of Tamsin's candlelit suppers – and it had irritated me. So I kept quiet and just agreed that it was great they were back in touch.

The following morning Tamsin appeared in the bakery at seven a.m. in top to toe glowing in midnight blue Gucci. This was her first day delivering with Gabe and she had that old spring in her step.

'Looking good. You're back girlfriend,' I said, offering up my hand in a high five.

She waggled her arm a bit, not sure quite what to do and giggled like a schoolgirl.

'Don't leave her hanging,' Gabe laughed. He and I had filled the van and he was waiting, arms folded, by the door, like her driver (it might have been quicker if Tamsin had helped us load, but – baby steps). I noticed a look pass between them and wondered if my sister's new-found glow had something to do with Gabe's presence.

Tamsin disappeared to put her lipstick on and I followed Gabe outside into the early morning white-out.

'I'm so grateful for this, Gabe,' I said, leaning on the back of his truck. 'I'll pay you once we get... sorted.' He was rolling another fag and waiting for Tamsin.

'I don't mind at all, Sam, I don't want the petrol money, I'm doin it for Tammy... about time someone treated her right.'

I saw the look in his eyes as he pulled on his cigarette; there was something almost mystical about Gabe. Tamsin said he'd arrived in the snow like an angel (which was a bit of theatrical licence because he'd been hanging around since late Autumn) and she was right – he had that faraway look and I wondered if he actually had genuine feelings for Tamsin and wasn't quite the player we all thought he was.

❄ ❄ ❄

With deliveries now back on thanks to Tamsin and Gabe, I was feeling much more positive about the The White Angel Bakery's future. Tamsin was so on board with everything and despite being irritating and in my face at times, I really appreciated all her help and decided to show her my appreciation the only way I could.

'So I have been thinking about... the bakery, and your situation – and Christmas and I just wonder if the answer is in front of us,' I said, when she returned from deliveries later that day.

She gave a puzzled look. 'The mere mention of Christmas sends a jolt of spiky tinsel through my veins Sam,' she sighed. 'I had planned so much, booked caterers, venues, guests. Now it's all cancelled, and most of the time I can cope, but there are moments when I am overwhelmed by it all and just can't face what has happened to me.'

'I know – and I just think that you deserve more, you deserve a purpose and a future and we should embrace the fact we've been thrown together in adversity. Why don't you come into the business with me... we can be partners. What do you think?'

I thought Tamsin was going to cry. Her eyes filled up and she hugged me so tight it almost hurt.

'Sam I would love that.'

'Okay, let's shake on it. But I think we need to talk about parameters,' I said, giving her a look.

She nodded eagerly, like a little girl who'd just been told if she was good Santa would come.

'I am the boss in the kitchen... but I just think your talents for organising and PR will be invaluable – oh but you still have to do deliveries indefinitely,' I added, before she got carried away and started employing staff.

'Yes of course,' her eyes were twinkling. 'I adore being here and helping out and I'd love to think that I could keep doing that. The bakery is a sanctuary to me... but Sam, how can I be a partner? I have no money.'

'You don't need money to join me in the family business - you're family,' I said. Now get the kettle on – you're also the tea girl.

Chapter 18

Desperate Housewives and Cheshire's Chattering Classes

Tamsin

The deliveries went well with Gabe, he drove safely, (only touched my knee once, and sadly I think that was unintentional) and we were back at the bakery by eleven. I have to admit I was a tad disappointed when he pulled up outside and just said he'd see me same time tomorrow. As I climbed out of the truck and waved coquettishly, he set off into the whiteness and my heart flopped a little into the snow.

The last time we'd been alone together he'd pushed me face down into designer cushions and given me a questionable but skilled and delicious massage. Now it was like we were back to the beginning, he being polite almost monosyllabic and me being vaguely in charge and keeping my silk pants on throughout.

'Did he try anything on?' Sam asked as soon as I walked in. We knew what a tart he was and I was almost embarrassed to admit he didn't.

'What's wrong with me, Sam? He's had every desperate housewife in Cheshire – rumour has it he even had Mrs Robinson who teaches Jacob – and let's face it, she's no porn star.'

Sam just laughed. 'I think you should give it time. Perhaps he thinks you're better than a quick one up against the trellis?'

'Oh I do hope not,' I laughed. 'I was looking forward to that trellis.' I surprised myself these days, I was becoming quite vulgar, but Sam thought I was hilarious.

❄ ❄ ❄

Later that day I asked Mrs J if she fancied a last hurrah at the house. 'There's still some stuff to take and we can dust all the furniture while we're there and Heddon and Hall said they'd come and collect it later,' I explained.

Mrs J was up for it. She said she'd had enough cupcakes to last a lifetime and longed to clean something that wasn't covered in jam or lubricants. I think she was referring to cooking oil, but I didn't ask just in case – who knew what Mrs J had seen on her cleaning journey through the bedrooms of the chattering classes of Cheshire?

Sam gave me the afternoon off and we grabbed a lift off 'our Lawrence', who didn't say one word as he drove us the ten minutes to my old place. He didn't even say hello or goodbye, he didn't need to, his wife spoke for both of them, and ended every sentence with 'didn't you, Lawrence?' I sat in the back and wondered if he was dead and she'd just propped him up against the steering wheel, his foot resting on the accelerator. Mrs J would never have noticed his lack of response and just continued to talk until we got there.

Once inside my old home, I stood in the hall, waiting for homesickness to fall over me like a veil. I'd felt so unmoved last time I visited, but I was numb then from everything that had happened - surely this time I would feel something? I gazed at my lovely film star stairs, ran my hands along the perfect Farrow and Ball-painted walls and waited. Nothing. I still felt nothing. It was a very beautiful house but it didn't fill me with longing as I imagined it would. The pale grey 'Elephant's Breath' walls weren't as stunning as I'd remembered. They whispered to me of a time in my life when I was very unhappy and very alone.

I turned to the Christmas tree, still here, dressed in white, waiting like Miss Havisham for her groom to arrive. I breathed in the scent of pine forests, hoping for that Christmas hit. I waited, I looked – I breathed in only sadness for what might have been.

Wandering through the empty rooms, I tried to dig deep and find some good times... they were in here somewhere, weren't they? I wasn't unhappy all the time. I thought of the parties in the big room, family birthdays at the kitchen table, cosy, suppers straight from the Aga. Then I remembered one of the parties – it was Christmas and Simon had come home late, I was stressed, the caterers had let me down and so had my hair. I looked and felt dreadful with a cold and while everyone laughed and drank and glittered around me I just sneezed and wanted to go to bed. Simon had been vile to me and I had no idea why – I don't remember much about that party except the fact that no one could find Simon when I fainted.

But yes there were some great times in this family kitchen, I thought, walking through my bespoke clotted cream nirvana. The children were small when we'd moved here so there had been lots of birthdays, some parties on the lawn with balloons and a children's entertainer. Then Mrs J would make pizzas and we'd have amazing birthday cakes shaped like castles, tanks and fairy tale princesses. But as hard as I tried to recollect, I couldn't remember one of the kids' parties where Simon had been present.

And those cosy kitchen suppers I'd seen in middle class homes on TV that I'd try to recreate? Simon would turn up late from work, say he'd already eaten and there'd be a row about it. He'd end up storming off to bed and I'd sit on my own, playing with a seafood linguine and finishing off the wine.

I realised then – Simon had left me long before that night. Our marriage had broken up years before and I had just been too busy worrying about interior colour schemes and the latest handbag to notice... or perhaps that was why I obsessed about those things? Because there was nothing else.

I made a cup of tea for me and Mrs J. I saw Mimi's picture glow on my phone for the third time that afternoon. When would she get the message that however low I was in the Real Housewife hierarchy, I could never be friends with a lucky lap dancer. I turned my phone off, but as I poured boiling water on the tea bags, I thought about how awful it must have been for Mimi never to be accepted into Chantray Lane. I was getting a taste of that now and it was so horrible I wondered how I could continue to do the same to Mimi... yet at the back of my mind I wondered if I could trust her. Had Anouska and Phaedra finally accepted Mimi and asked her to find out what was happening with me? I couldn't believe that my old friends didn't want to know what I was doing, how I was feeling, even if only to discuss with everyone else.

That day at the house, I'd felt nothing – but I went back to the bakery and I felt arms around me.

From the moment I walked into the little shop, it felt like a cosy sanctuary from the big cold world. It made me realise I had to stop haunting my old house like a ghost returning to the empty rooms, re-living the past. It was time to let it go.

'This is our future now,' Sam had said. 'We can make all our dreams come true in this place of bricks and mortar... and love and cake.'

I was touched, this had been my sister's dream and now she was sharing it all with me, and for the first time in my life I felt like I belonged.

By asking me to be her partner in the bakery Sam had given me a future and I was determined to embrace it and forget about the past. My kids had flown the nest (along with my husband) and though I had very little, I was actually happy in the present, and I wasn't sure I ever had been before. I wasn't lusting after the latest season's clothes, the newest kitchen gadget, the most fabulous holiday. I just enjoyed helping Sam, I loved the warm scent of cinnamon, vanilla and contentment that permeated the air around me - and for the first time in a long time I felt useful. Spending time with Gabe was good for my soul too and in his own way he made me feel desired. The awkwardness of the first few deliveries had settled into something more flirty and each morning I'd climb in his cab and he'd tell me I was hot and I'd say it was my age and we'd laugh. I loved to watch him lifting the huge trays of cakes with ease and waltzing to the door or entrance and imagine what it would be like to sleep with him. Sam said I should be more upfront, but I didn't consider it ladylike to proposition him to a quick one in a truck full of festive patisserie. So we just continued to tease each other and flirt and I would glance discreetly at his denim thighs as he drove, but despite us having great fun and a frisson fizzling between us, he never once leaped on me or suggested we do anything inappropriate in his truck. To my deep disappointment.

Chapter 19
Fairy Lights and Frosty Windows

Sam

We worked incredibly hard over the next few days – Christmas orders were coming in and we virtually lived by the big oven, making tea, chatting, looking at recipes, laughing at silly things that only sisters can share.

Since Tamsin had been pulling her weight and helping out our relationship had definitely improved. She now had a purpose, a future and it was good for her. Spending time with Gabe seemed to suit her too. According to Tamsin nothing had happened between them, but he was a good influence on her. Gabe kept her grounded and stopped her from taking herself too seriously, which had been one of her worst flaws.

We had a routine of putting on the kettle at midnight, making a pot of tea and sitting by the fairy lights to have a break together while baking for the next day. It felt so Christmassy just sitting by the window, looking out onto the snowy white square framed by white fairy lights and frosty windows.

'I've never known it snow for so long,' I sighed, sipping my tea.

'It started when the bailiffs came,' she said.

It had all seemed so unreal since then, so many changes. It was like the snow had brought with it an ending but also a new beginning.

'God, it feels like months ago, but it's only two weeks. What do you miss?' I asked.

'Nothing,' She said, without hesitation.

'Really? But what about Simon and your friends?'

'I don't miss any of them. Simon's called the kids, he's been trying to call me too. He left messages saying he wants me back, we were meant to be together.'

I was surprised. 'You wouldn't go back with him would you?' I asked.

'No... he doesn't want me and I don't want him. He's just panicking I'll take him for everything he's got in a divorce – but he doesn't have anything,' she laughed. I don't miss him, but I miss the early days together when we'd first met and we were both so vital and enthusiastic, our whole future laid out before us.'

'Yeah... I remember that with Steve. But I've had to remind myself that's all it is – a memory, a lovely memory to add to the photo album in your head. Take it out, look at it – but don't let it hold you back.'

I heard myself and smiled. I should start practising what I preached – it made perfect sense for both of us to leave our pasts behind, not to forget, but to face them and move forward.

I was just thinking about this when my phone rang, it was a number I didn't know and when I answered a voice said, 'Hi this is Tamsin's friend, Mimi.'

'Oh, hi Mimi,' I looked at Tamsin, who had a puzzled expression on her face. 'Tamsin's not with me right now – but I'll get her to call you,' I said. 'She'd love to hear from you I'm sure.'

I came off the phone and Tamsin looked cross.

'Look, she just wants to find out if you can make it to her party. She's worried about you – she hasn't seen or heard from you and she says she misses you.'

'Really? She didn't want to gossip about my situation? Didn't ask how much we owed? Or the phone number of my favourite caterer?'

'No Tam, she's what normal people call a friend... and I think she genuinely cares about your welfare.'

Tamsin seemed surprised and even a little flattered.

'She was a lap dancer, you know,' she said, almost to herself.

'So what? I did a bit of dancing when I worked in Spain.'

Tamsin clutched the worktops like she'd been stabbed – the diva was never far away.

'I didn't take my clothes off, but I danced with men, lured them to the bar and got them to buy drinks.'

'Why?'

'I was paid by the club to do it. I stood outside the club with leaflets and flirted and guys spent their money – it's not quite the same, but it wasn't any better than lap dancing.'

'Oh my God, Sam.' She looked at me warily. 'Is there anything else you want to share.'

'Apart from my time as a prostitute in Berlin and a drug addict in Amsterdam?'

'I take it that's a joke?'

I nodded.

'So all this time, I've been blackballing Mimi from every social event while welcoming my sister, the bar room dancer?'

I nodded.

We looked at each other for a few seconds, then she started laughing and I joined in and before long we were holding on to each other, tears of laughter rolling down our cheeks.

'I told you, Tam, you should never judge a book by its cover... you don't know everyone's story – even mine. Have some humility... Mimi was a lap dancer, not a murderer.'

She was still laughing. 'Give me her number – I'd better give her a call. I'll tell her my sister's looking for a lap dancing partner – you two could start your own act.'

❄ ❄ ❄

Things were going well and mine and Tamsin's working relationship seemed to be good for business. We'd increased a couple of big orders as Tamsin had used her charm on the manager of a local hotel and convinced a tea rooms and a grocers to use our bread and cakes.

'We've had another big order,' I said to her one morning as she teetered down the stairs in Jimmy Choos and a Vivienne Westwood suit with black and yellow stripes. I read the email order form – 'The lovely lady in the designer dress' apparently seduced someone into ordering all their Christmas cakes from us. Go Tamsin. I reckon you've really got a talent for selling.'

'Fabulous! I just feel so alive. It's amazing to discover in your forties that you are good at something.'

Gabe came in at that point, shaking snow off his boots and beaming at her.

'Do I look okay?' she asked, giving us a twirl.

'Yeah... you look hot, but do you have to wear those stupid shoes?' Gabe sighed. 'Yesterday she got her heel stuck in the bloody snow and nearly broke her ankle,' he said to me, rolling his eyes. She giggled and I caught a look between them. I loved the way he teased her making her go all girlish.

'These "stupid shoes" cost a fortune, poor little Jimmy Choo slaved in his cobbler's studio stitching these by hand,' she said in mock reprimand to Gabe.

'Well, if you change your mind there's some of my wellies behind the door,' I smiled and continued to work as Gabe loaded the van and Tamsin teetered around him like a high-heeled wasp.

Eventually Gabe started up the van and Tamsin was just getting in her side, which was a high climb for someone in heels and a tight skirt, when we heard the rip.

'Christ it's torn,' she shouted, and I gather Gabe was laughing because she was now admonishing him and telling him how much it cost while half in and half out of the van.

'Calm down, Tam,' I said, helping her out.

'Look, go back upstairs take the beautiful suit off and in my second drawer down you'll find my jeans and jumpers. They aren't designer, but they are far more suitable for deliveries and it doesn't matter if they get ruined in the snow.' She wasn't happy and stomped off in quite a tizzy.

'She's a bit pissed off,' I called to Gabe, who just laughed and lit up a fag.

'She'll get over it,' he smiled.

I went back into the shop and thought about how the two of them were together; he didn't pander to her and even when she tried to boss him around, he let her think she was in charge, but really he just let it go and she forgot. He had her back and she knew it. Minutes later Tamsin appeared on the stairs in my jeans, looking ten years younger without the fuss of designer clothes and grown-up heels.

'You look great – so different,' I said.

'Yeah... this little jumper's not bad is it? Whose is it?'

'Mine.'

'No... I mean which designer?'

I rolled my eyes; 'You know I don't wear designer clothes.'

'I know, I just hoped against hope I'd come across a gem in your pile of chain store cast-offs,' she smiled.

'Cheeky bugger – now get those stupid shoes off and put these wellies on and get to work,' I said.

She struggled with the wellies. I could tell she was biting her tongue, but then abandoned them on the floor.

'I'm sorry – I can't they are awful – so unflattering, they do nothing for my leg length.' With that, she teetered out into the snow in my old jeans, cheap jumper and Jimmy Choos. One step at a time I reminded myself as I stood on the doorstep holding the wellies like her mother and when Gabe worked out what was happening he got out of the truck and walked round to the passenger side. He calmly took the boots off me, and opening the truck passenger door, grabbed one of Tamsin's legs and while she wriggled and giggled he slowly but firmly took off one Jimmy Choo. For a split second my heart was in my mouth as he held the shoe in his hand and then threw it over his shoulder into the deep snow. Tamsin screamed like she was in pain and tried to struggle as he pinned her down and took the other shoe. By now he was laughing as she lashed out at him, and by the time the second Jimmy Choo flew through the air I was waiting for the Tamsin explosion. I held my breath in horror as Gabe picked up a wellington and despite her struggling and screaming he put the first one gently onto her foot, then took the other one and did the same. Then I realised, she was only pretending to fight him off – and to my relief and amazement – she was giggling.

They eventually set off and as I watched them go I thought about how much my sister had changed and how she was literally shedding her old life – and stepping into a new one.

Chapter 20
William, Kate and a Right Royal Christmas
Tamsin

I had been so busy with deliveries and fending off Gabe all morning I was exhausted. It seemed Sam's cheap old jumper and jeans were far more alluring to him than my gorgeous designer suits. I always knew the man had no taste – and after wrestling me to put awful supermarket wellingtons on my feet, he couldn't keep away. I have to say it was fun fighting Gabe off – little did he know I enjoyed it as much as he did, and whilst I definitely wanted it to go all the way – there was a time and a place.

Returning to the bakery, I waved Gabe off and went inside. I was instantly soothed by warm gingerbread hovering in the air, infusing the place in rich, treacly fragrance. It was also very calm and lovely - a couple of women were enjoying coffee and mince pies at a table and Sam was behind the counter putting out freshly baked rum truffles in Christmassy boxes. The perfect Christmas scene, I thought as I picked up one of the boxes.

'They need a red ribbon,' I said, playing around with a box, a little Christmas wrapping and some ribbon lying on the side.

'Wow, that looks lovely,' Sam said, and asked me to do some more. I enjoyed doing this, and as we put them on the counter, the two ladies at the table made approving noises. I saw this as my chance to leap in and prove to myself I could make something of being a saleswoman.

'Good morning ladies... soo Christmassy with the snow and everything, isn't it? I just wanted to show you these new boxes of truffles we are presenting for Christmas.'

'Lovely,' they both said in unison. They licked their lips, they were so damn desperate to have them.

'Maracaibo, or Porcelana cocoa is grown on small plantations in Venezuela. I'm sure you're familiar with the Amedei chocolatier in Tuscany?'

They both nodded. They weren't.

'Well, the same bean used in these truffles is used to make their Amedei Porcelana – said to be the most expensive in the world.'

In my former life I'd attended a gourmet pudding weekend – of course we didn't eat a thing it was all too fattening – but fascinating nonetheless. At the end we'd had a fun chocolate quiz, but I'd revised hard and won (I always like to win) and still remembered random chocolate facts – who knew they'd be so useful?

'My sister is not just a pâtissier, she is also a master chocolatier, the chocolate is full-flavoured, takes on the rounded marble of truffle, yet is yielding in texture. She adds the finest French cognac flown directly from Paris and the result, ladies, as you can see, is sublime... exquisite.'

They were looking at me like two children being read a story – they were hooked, they wanted more.

'Kate and William have ordered several boxes to gift the family this Christmas,' I added, watching their eyes widen. Then, finally, when I had their full attention, I gave them the price. 'They are £5 a box for six truffles... a snip, I think you'll agree.'

Manicured nails clawed at the beautiful boxes, smoky eyes darted everywhere, while Chanel-glossed lips panted with the wanting. I knew the Kate and William line would get them agitated.

'My husband asked me to buy small gifts for his business associates – I've left it late this year – I could get them all a box of these truffles?' the blonde said, breathlessly, imagining how fabulous these truffles would make her look to her husband.

'What a great idea,' I smiled. 'So how many can we make for you?' I asked.

'Can I order one hundred please?'

I was a little taken aback. 'Boxes?'

'Please... I'll need them the day after tomorrow, is that possible?'

I nodded, but didn't meet her eyes, knowing Sam would go mad. That was six-hundred truffles in two days. I was better at this selling business than I'd thought – and Sam couldn't grumble we needed the money.

'Oh you know what?' The redhead started, not wanting to be outdone. 'They are so gorgeous I'm going to give them to our clients – and friends too. Make my order one hundred and fifty,' she gave a sidelong look at the blonde that said 'gotcha girlfriend.' I knew how these women ticked and they were in the palm of my hand.

At this point Sam appeared at my shoulder like a rather negative little monkey.

'I'm sorry but...' she began.

'Sam, please. Let me handle this,' I said, gently putting my hand on her arm.

'But Tamsin, there's no way I can make that many...'

'It's fine,' I said over her, smiling reassuringly at the ladies who lunched. 'My sister is a little concerned, she's been told by a certain "family who will be spending Christmas in Sandringham" that on no account must she recreate the same chocolates for anyone else. It's all about exclusivity in those circles, but I won't tell if you don't.'

The women were now virtually fighting each other to be the first to get their credit cards swiped while I smiled benignly and took their cards in turn.

Once they'd left, their orders safely made, I looked at Sam. 'So... I have just taken a total of £1,250.' I held my hand up for what Hugo always called a five high or something, but Sam just looked at me stony faced.

'If I remember rightly... the phrase is "please don't leave me hanging around here",' I said, my hand still in the air.

She ignored this. 'Tamsin – I know you want this business to succeed as much as I do, but you have just taken money under false pretences. That chocolate isn't used in Tuscany, nor is it from Venezuela, it's from the bloody cash and carry. And Prince William and Kate? Hello, they haven't been anywhere near the shop, let alone ordered truffles.'

'Who said anything about *Prince* William? I just said William and Kate had called, and I'm sure, in the year that you've been open, people by those names have bought cakes.'

'That would hardly stand up in a court of law,' she sighed.

'Look Sam, those women were label queens. They would buy my used tissues if I told them they were designed by Alexander McQueen and Lady Gaga had wiped her armpits with them. Remember I once paid 200 quid for a sweaty T-shirt signed by Madonna... I had the bloody thing framed until we found out it was a money-making scam from the boys at Hugo's school. God only knows whose teenage sweat I'd had expertly mounted in that gilt-edged box frame.' I shuddered at the thought. 'What you have to remember is, those women don't care about the chocolate... they'll never eat it, nor will their friends. They just want it in their lives to make them look good.'

'It's dishonest, Tamsin, I'm not comfortable with it.'

'Oh Sam, lighten up,' I said, hearing myself and never imagining in my life it would be me saying this to her. 'It's called selling. I seem to have a knack for it... I just put a few of my old designer dresses on eBay to make a few pennies and sold them within the hour for six hundred quid – all because I said they were, "believed to have been owned by Monégasque Royalty".'

Sam frowned.

'Oh I didn't say who, but of course everyone is thinking Stephanie of Monaco.'

'But it's a lie.'

'Prove it.'

'I don't have fucking time – I have to go to Venezuela via Tuscany to get the chocolate for the 5 million bloody truffles you just agreed to make,' she yelled.

'Well get on with it then,' I shouted back.' And stop bloody swearing.'

She was genuinely cross, but it was all quite good-natured. I quite enjoyed the yelling and the arguing with Sam, it reminded me of when we were younger and she'd borrowed my best top or used my mascara. It wasn't serious but it helped us get stuff off our chests. I hadn't been able to get anything off my chest for a long time. I poked my tongue out at her, made an online order for 400 truffle boxes and felt a frisson of excitement for the first time in years.

Chapter 21
Christmas Cupcakes and Sumatra Wahana

Sam

So Tamsin had taken the biggest single order ever and I was quite frankly panicking. I really had no idea how we were going to meet it, but I knew we had to. We decided to work late into the evening and make a good start, but by midnight I was exhausted. We'd barely made a dent and I also had an oven full of cakes to take out for the morning. Tamsin seemed to have found her second wind and had gone from very low to very high, and urged on by her selling success that day was now making future plans.

'Anyway Sam… now all our van worries are over, I've been thinking.'

'Oh,' I said, leaning on the oven for support. I had never been so tired – I wondered if I was coming down with something. I'd only just got over a bad dose of flu and all the stress was probably bringing it on again… Mrs J had said bad things would come to us in threes. First it was Tamsin, then the van, next it would be me, ill in bed and unable to bake.

'Next weekend is the last weekend before Christmas,' Tamsin was saying from behind a huge bag of flour. 'Why don't we stage a Christmas cupcake event?'

I wished she'd be quiet. I was glad she was taking an interest but as always she was ambitious and getting ahead of herself. 'I don't... know. It would be such a lot of work and I...' my head was throbbing. My shoulders and neck ached with exhaustion and I felt like I might fall over if I stayed up another minute. The very idea of taking on even more work horrified me.

'We will make it irresistible...' She went on and on and I couldn't actually hear words any more. She was clutching at her forehead channelling Martha Stewart and I'd really had enough for one day.

Only my sister could use the word 'stage' as a verb when talking about a little bakery selling cakes. 'Tamsin, we can't...'

'Stop with the negativity, Sam... I don't want to hear the word "can't". We *can* get the bakery looking fabulous and Christmassy. We'll do a big community event...' She gave me a 'don't interrupt me' glare, so I didn't, I just carried on mixing sugar icing and pretended she wasn't there.

'And don't go on about having no money – I get it. Christ, do I get it, darling! I'm quite aware of how desperate things are – I've been drinking bloody Nescafé for two days, my freshly ground Sumatra Wahana is but a distant memory floating on a Sumatran coffee breeze.'

'Yes, and at that price it will have to stay a distant memory.'

'Oh stop being so bloody boring about money,' she snapped. I had to smile wearily at that because Tamsin had always gone on about money... How things had changed in such a short time.

'Are you okay, love,' I heard her say when she'd eventually stopped yapping.

'Yes... no actually, I don't feel great.'

'Why don't you go to bed?' she said, putting on her apron. 'I can wait for the final batch to come out of the oven.'

I was grateful and desperate to lie in a darkened room, but made mild protesting noises.

'Go on... I'll watch the cakes. And I'll make some notes about our Christmas Cupcake Event too,' she added, as if it was something we'd just agreed on. She wasn't letting it drop, she was like a dog with a bone our Tamsin, but I was relieved to see the old sparkle coming back into her eyes as she donned her apron and picked up her notebook. I couldn't believe the change in our Tamsin, If you told me a month ago my sister would be living in my 2-bed flat and working as a delivery driver cum sales rep cum baking assistant in my little bakery - I would have said you were mad. But now it seemed completely natural.

I wandered upstairs and as soon as my head hit the pillow I was out until much later when I was woken by a smell... I lay there for a few seconds trying to work out what it was. Then I realised with a start. My heart lurched, and I sat up, trying to gather my faculties – it was smoke. I leaped out of bed and ran into Jacob's room where he was sleeping soundly. I took a deep breath, gathered him in my arms, checked his breathing and carried him into the living room. I realised now the smoke was coming from downstairs and though it may have been stupid to walk towards a fire, I had no choice, we couldn't stay upstairs there was no way out up there we had to go down. So with Jacob sleepy in my arms, I ran through the smoke now billowing through the bakery, curling and growing by the second. I ran out into the square relieved to taste the chilled air, breathing in deep lungfuls and hugging Jacob.

Then I realised. 'Tamsin... where's Tamsin?' I said out loud. I had to go back in, so threw my mobile to Jacob, told him to stay exactly where he was and not follow me inside, but to press 999 on the phone.

'Tell the person at the other end the White Angel Bakery in Cheshire Square is on fire,' I yelled and forced my way back in to find my sister.

I pushed through the smoke, now much thicker than it had been only seconds before, and felt something soft at my feet. 'Oh no... Tamsin?' I fell to the ground, desperately scrabbling along the floor, unable to see anything... then I felt it, Tamsin's cashmere shawl lying on the floor. I was tearful now, fearing the worst, she could have inhaled smoke and might be unconscious. She could be anywhere in there, my eyes were stinging with the smoke. I could barely see but thought there was something red under the counter, was it one of Tamsin's shoes? I lunged towards it, hoping to pull her out, but when I finally grabbed at it, she wasn't attached. I tore around quickly, desperately trying to make out what was in front of me while calling her name. Was that her lying on the floor in a heap? I staggered towards the shape I could just make out through the smoke, but it was just a pile of boxes. Then I saw her leaning against the wall, but that was the fridge, my mind was playing tricks and all I could shout was 'Tamsin... Tamsin.'

Suddenly I heard her, a faint groan from somewhere near the oven, and I shot over to the sound, the acrid smoke now burning the back of my throat.

As I got nearer to the oven I could see she was half slumped over it. 'Oh Sam, I left them too long... they're burned... they're burned...'

I grabbed her around the waist and she yelped a little and probably suffered severe whiplash as I hurled her over my shoulder in a fireman's lift. I don't know where I got the strength from, my legs were buckling beneath me, but I had to get her out of there and I pushed hard against the smoke and the dead weight and the burning pain in my eyes and throat. Finally reaching the door, Jacob ran to open it but I screamed at him to get back and we all landed outside in the snow, the smoke chasing us like a dragon through the door.

We lay on the ground, both gasping. I was telling Jacob we were fine, but tears were running down my face as I looked at Tamsin.

Then the fire brigade and an ambulance arrived and the fire was soon put out. It was all very dramatic and emotional and I wept as I watched with relief and worry. Tamsin was shaken, but seemed okay and I insisted I was fine; the paramedics wanted to take Tamsin to the local hospital, but she refused, telling them she'd been through much worse and just needed a decent cup of coffee. She kept asking if anyone had any Sumatra Wahana on them. They probably thought she was feeling the after effects of the smoke and speaking in tongues – or asking for something illegal. I didn't even try to explain, just assured the paramedics and firemen that I would look after her.

They eventually departed, leaving us sitting on the floor in the bakery. I looked at my sister, her beautiful clothes were ruined and her hair was singed and smoky. I noticed a graze on the side of her face where she'd fallen into the oven. 'Oh Tam, your hair, your face...' I was expecting her to start thrashing about, her appearance was always so important to her, this could be the last straw.

'Oh it doesn't matter about my bloody hair,' she said. 'Sam, the bakery... I've destroyed it... it's all my fault.'

'It's not your fault,' I said. 'The main thing is we are all okay, it could have been so much worse.'

'I must have fallen asleep... the cakes are burned... the truffles you'd started... our biggest order. What are we going to do now?'

'I don't know, but I think it might be time to cut our losses and admit defeat, love,' I sighed. In the madness of making sure Jacob and Tamsin were alright I hadn't considered what the fire meant for the business and it was slowly beginning to dawn on me.

We sat among the carnage of the fire, two women who'd both been to hell were back in the middle of it again. The kitchen was blackened, the oven was ruined and the coffee shop area was smoke damaged. The White Angel bakery was finished and I sat in the middle of the room just taking in all the damage. Then I thought about Mrs J's prediction that three bad things were going to happen to us - perhaps she was psychic after all?

Chapter 22
Random Acts of Christmas Madness

Tamsin

It felt like a death, another loss. Poor Sam – her lifelong dream was in ruins. The bakery couldn't bake and so would now be closed. What else could we do? There was no money for a new oven, and the insurance would take a lifetime to come through. Sam was calm and kind and kept telling me it wasn't my fault, but I knew she was devastated, and I could barely look at her. I felt so guilty and I hated myself... however many times Sam said it was her fault for using old faulty ovens, I still felt responsible.

'Will you call our customers who have orders for Christmas and tell them we'll have to cancel?' Sam asked me.

I nodded, she obviously found the prospect of making those calls too painful. I couldn't bring myself to do it straight away, but I did think on my feet and discreetly phoned the women about the huge truffle order, telling them we'd had a call from the wife of a footballer in LA. I hinted she was a fashion designer and once belonged to a famous girl band and we had to do her order first as it needed to get to her in Beverly Hills. I said she'd asked me to ask them if they minded receiving their truffle orders a little later as a favour to her? Of course they were falling over themselves to oblige - a late order of truffles was no problem, a privilege in fact. I put the phone down with a smile – until it dawned on me I may have to call a week later and cancel completely – which celebrity or member of the royal family could I blame that on?

I was worried about Sam, both emotionally and physically. I would have expected her to rail against this, go skip-hunting for ovens and bake those cakes against all the odds, but for once she didn't.

She'd lost her dream, her future, the one thing she'd clung to since Steve's death and it broke my heart to see her like this. She said she'd already paid the rent on the bakery until January so we all had somewhere to stay until then, but we'd have to find work and somewhere to live after Christmas.

Sam said she could go back to teaching, and I decided the only thing for me to do was to sell my stuff. Mrs J offered to come with me so I asked Gabe if he could drop us off at The Rectory and we could go through what was left and what was sellable. And so it was with a heavy heart I headed back to The Rectory again and while waving Gabe off I tried to explain to Mrs J why we were there.

'We need to do an inventory,' I said.

'An in what?' she asked.

'We need to go through everything in the house we can sell, and catalogue, box, and label it all. Then we write each item down on a spreadsheet under different classifications and…'

'I thought I was here to do some light dusting?'

'You are,' I said, abandoning my plan to have Mrs J as assistant, it would be far quicker to work alone. If she wants to dust, let her dust, I thought.

I had spent most of the afternoon listing and boxing stuff that we could sell and was just about to start on the dining room when the doorbell went and my heart almost stopped.

I wasn't quite sure what the exact arrangements had been with our creditors and our solicitor. I wasn't even sure if I should still have the keys and be allowed access and was worried I'd be caught. Those bailiffs were very passionate about their work and if I was trespassing, then God help me, I'd be all over The Advertiser the following week being hauled from my home with a coat over my head like some has-been z-lister. Those men could enter from anywhere – like a scene from the Embassy siege. Big, bald-headed men landing on roofs and windowsills, crashing through windows shouting 'We know you're in there,' so at the sound of the doorbell I hurled myself onto the floor, keeping well down. Fortunately, the floor was polished oak so I was able to slide seamlessly along on my back, using my legs to propel me forward. My aim was to avoid the big window in the door, should anyone decide to press his bald head against it for a nosey.

I was shimmying along the hall floor between rooms when I heard a rustle at the front door, and an envelope dropping onto the mat. Looking up, I came face to face with Mimi staring in the glass, mouth open, just watching me slide along the floor like an insane person. I didn't know what to do, so put my nose in the air and continued to slide forward into the piano room like it was the most natural thing in the world.

For a while I lay face down under the piano, not quite sure what had just happened but wondering if I'd had a breakdown. Unfortunately Mrs J was in there dusting the piano and the look of surprise on her face matched Mimi's as she got down on all fours to inspect me.

'What the bloody hell are you doing now?' she asked, screwing her eyes up like she couldn't believe what she'd just found while dusting.

'For God's sake Mrs J – a woman can't even slide on her own oak floor and lie under her own baby grand without everyone wanting her story,' I huffed indignantly. From under the piano.

'You make me die laughing you do,' she said, almost to herself while carrying on with the dusting.

I ignored her and stayed under the piano until I was sure Mimi had gone, then I leaped into the hall and grabbed the thick silver envelope Mimi had posted. As I opened it, I found a stunning purple invitation adorned in silvery Christmas glitz inviting 'Tamsin plus one' to celebrate Christmas at Mimi's Musical Evening: 'A celebration of Christmas in song.'

'The bitch!' I hissed to no one, or so I thought.

'Who are you complaining about now?' Mrs J called from the other room.

I screwed the invitation up and threw it in the bin. Christmas had always been mine. 'I owned Christmas,' I said out loud. I was the one who held the musical evenings and the festive soirees – this was just rubbing salt in the wound. And how fickle they all were! We'd always gasped in amusement at Mimi's exploits, I'd laughed behind my hand along with the others at her pole dancing, her penchant for purple and fruit flavoured lubricants. But I wasn't laughing now – Mimi was queen of Christmas and I was nothing.

Hurt and rage were filling my head and giving me such a migraine I had to get out – so I grabbed my keys, but just as I was leaving, Sam turned up with Hermione, Hugo and Jacob.

'We thought we'd come and get you,' she said, walking into the hall. 'You weren't answering your phone. I was worried... after the fire and everything that you might...'

I nodded and tried to be bright for the kids. 'Sorry, Mimi's stalking me,' I said. 'I turned off my phone.' I suggested Hugo take Jacob into the spare room upstairs where some of Hugo's old toys were and Jacob could choose what he wanted. Sam wandered up with them, probably to supervise – it was a wise move, who knew what Hugo would produce from behind his wardrobe?

I went into the kitchen where my lone kettle stood and decided to make a final cup of tea before packing it away for the last time. Hermione wandered in and nodded at me before going straight to the fridge. Of course there was nothing in there and despite it all we giggled.

'Automatic response,' she smiled. 'No wonder I'm such a porker.'

'You're not, your beautiful...'

'You okay, Ma? Shouldn't you go and see a doc or something?'

'No – just a little smoke inhalation, a few smoke-singed hairs. I'm fine – it's the bakery that's died.'

'Shame... it was so cute, like a fairytale shop, you loved that bakery.'

'Yes I did, I do - but I feel for poor Auntie Sam, she's put so much into it.'

Hermione nodded earnestly.

'But what about you? Are you okay, darling?' I asked, aware that so much had been happening I hadn't spent enough time with my kids since they came home for the Christmas holidays. Some Christmas!

'Yeah I'm okay... well no, I'm a bit pissed off to be honest, Ma.'

My heart sank. I thought the kids had been coping a little too well considering their world had come crashing down and their father had abandoned them.

'I'm sorry, darling. It's bloody awful isn't it... how everything's just turned to... well, shit.'

'I know, Ma... pure, evil shit... I am so done with it all...'

I put my arm around her.

'Talk to me, Hermione, tell me how you're feeling.'

'So I am just about ready to come off "snapchat", as for Twitter... jeez. Note to people with genitalia as their profile picture – I DON'T follow back. I mean, Billy no mates... saddos. Seriously?' With that, she slammed the huge fridge door and slumped on a stool at the island.

'Darling... when I said tell me how you're feeling... I was talking about the house and Dad and everything.'

'Yeah... Oh God... yeah... totally. Shame about the place in France... and as for Dad, WTF?'

'Yes quite. What does that mean?'

'What the fuck, Ma... I mean seriously?'

'Mmmm. Don't swear, Hermione.'

'Ma, I'm eighteen, you can't tell me what to do.'

'I know I fucking can't,' I said, suddenly overwhelmed by it all. 'I can't tell anyone what to fucking do anymore.'

She looked shocked; 'Hey enough with the mouth, Ma. Are you feeling okay?'

'Yes,' I smiled and reached for her hand. 'Whatever happens in your life, Hermione – promise me you'll do what *you* want to do. Don't do anything just to please a man – be yourself... or you'll lose yourself.'

'Preach it, Ma... no guy tells me what to do...'

'Yeah and keep it that way,' I squeezed her hand. 'So, are you staying at Sam's tonight, love?'

'Nah, going over to Kate's.'

'Oh Kate with the lovely red hair? How is she?'

'Good. She's heteroflexible now.'

'Oh. Really?' I picked up my phone feigning calm indifference. Heteroflexible sounded complicated and rather messy – whatever it was – and given my problems with the internet I wasn't Googling *that*. After a financial meltdown, the breakdown of the van and now the fire, I assumed we were done waiting for 'event number 3' (after Mrs J's premonition that 3 bad things were going to happen to us). I hoped number 3 was the fire and not my daughter screaming out of the closet and running off to some lesbian love nest with Kate. I watched as my daughter gazed into her phone – and despite my new laid-back approach to life, I had to ask, the mother in me needed more details. 'So... heteroflexible? What does that... entail? Exactly?'

'You're straight, but shit happens.'

'Indeed,' I held my breath and counted to ten, just hoping that letting my lovely daughter spend the night at Kate's wasn't inviting that 'shit' to 'happen'.

I looked up from my phone, but she'd gone. The little girl who used to sit on my knee and demand my attention, my bedtime stories and my love was now big enough to find it all somewhere else. My heart ached for the children I once had.

Mrs J wandered in and I handed her a mug of Darjeeling.

'So... it's all gone tits up again?' she said with her usual hallmark of tact and good taste.

'I suppose you could say that.'

'Meant to tell you. The two gay lads came over before and moved a load of fancy Christmas stuff into the other room – don't suppose you'll have much use for it now.'

'Mrs J, I'm not dead – I still intend to celebrate Christmas.'

'With a bloody big reindeer? What you gonna do? Ride 'im to Lapland? You make me laugh you do.'

'So glad I can entertain you,' I smiled politely, concerned that Heddon and Hall had completely lost it.

'I hope they haven't bought some ghastly giant inflatable reindeer – that's just what I need right now.'

Mrs J laughed loudly at the prospect, and told me it was my own fault for wanting everything and then forgetting I'd ordered it. She had a point which was annoying - in fact she was often annoying but I didn't know what we'd do without her. I'd told her I couldn't pay her, but she was good enough to be there for me, dusting, vacuuming and providing a running commentary on my life. I think she was on autopilot and programmed never to stop dusting and talking.

She insisted I go and have a look at the decorations, and wandering into the den I was overwhelmed at the sight before me.

Mrs J was right – a beautiful white reindeer big enough to ride on was standing proudly in the middle of the room, surrounded by glitter curtains, huge white snowflakes, baubles of every size and several small trees. In the dim light of the room everything sparkled, and despite knowing we wouldn't be able to use any of this now – the little child in me gasped!

Heddon and Hall had planned further festive decoration after the 'Christmas lights switch on'. Unfortunately, as I'd paid for it all in advance and not cancelled, the stuff had been delivered regardless of the fact I didn't live here anymore. The good news was it meant more stuff to sell, but the thought of selling off this perfect white Christmas broke my heart.

'Oh it's just... exquisite,' I whispered, walking around the white sparkle. Running my hands along softly folded piles of shimmering gossamer, twinkling glass, I stroked the reindeer as though it were alive. Despite everything – here, after all, was Christmas.

'Bugger me it's a big un in't it?' Mrs J was suddenly at my side.

'Yep, a huge beast... I don't suppose your Lawrence would like it for his shed?' I laughed.

'He'd think I was as mad as you if I went home with that,' she was nudging me and laughing along.

'Yes I am a bit bonkers, aren't I?'

'Well, you've always been over the top – but you're a good lass really.' I glanced over at her and in that instant I saw such tenderness in her eyes. I'd never seen that even from my own mother.

'Ha ha... I don't know what we're gonna do with you. You break the van, jump on Gabe, set fire to your sister's business and...'

'Thank you Mrs J I don't need the list – and I didn't "set fire" to anyone's business... as for Gabe...' I started.

'And you're still talkin all posh... you're all fur coat and no knickers, our Tamsin,' she laughed as she left the room, 'our' Tamsin hanging in the air. And despite the fact she was criticising me as usual, the 'our' made me feel all warm inside.

I walked towards the small window and watching the falling snow spiralling from the whitest heavens, I made a wish. Sam and I used to make wishes on snowflakes when we were little. Funny what you wish for when you're a kid – mine was always that Dad would allow me to pour his drink. I loved how important it made me feel and how close I felt to my dad. As an adult I could see how heartbreaking it was that this was the only way a little girl could feel close to her father. Why was I allowing his ghost to haunt me still?

Slipping off my shoes, I wandered over to the white deer, I had this sudden child-like urge to sit on it. With some effort I mounted it and was soon looking down at all the white Christmas splendour. I felt small, like a little girl again. I stroked the deer's neck, whispering gently that everything would be fine, but when I looked up the door had opened and Hugo was watching me. My son seemed to have a knack for catching me in strange situations and just when I'd managed to convince him of my sanity, he'd witness me doing something inappropriate or weird again.

'I was just... I was just riding the deer,' I said, unable to think of anything else. I suppose it made a change from internet sex and romping with the gardener.

'Ma,' he said, incredulously. 'What is wrong with you?'

'I don't know, Hugo... everything I suppose,' I sighed, big tears dropping onto the deer's white fur. I expected Hugo to leave, he was a young man now and his mother's actions embarrassed him at the best of times, but this was the worst of times. For a few seconds we looked at each other – what a tableau we made, a crazy middle-aged homeless woman on a life-size deer and her poor student son at a total loss as to what he should do. But then he came over to me, as I sat atop the deer, and he put his arm around my waist and hugged me close.

'I don't know what to do, Hugo,' I said, stroking his hair like I had when he was little. I'd vowed never to let my kids see me vulnerable, my mother had been vulnerable all her life and I'd watched her succumb to my father. He'd turned her into a weak wretch who couldn't even protect her own child. I grew to hate her as much as I'd hated him. I had no respect for the woman who cowered in corners preserving herself while her own daughter was beaten... but who knew what drove her? Who knew what her demons were and her mother's before her? My Dad wasn't the only one I had to learn to forgive.

'You were always the one who knew what to do,' Hugo said, rubbing my back.

I nodded and tried to smile. 'And I will again, Hugo, don't worry... '

'I'll never forgive Dad for doing this to us,' he sighed.

'Your dad couldn't cope, but I have to take some responsibility, Hugo, I never asked him about the business, never shared his worries or picked up on anything. Dad probably hates himself far more than you hate him - don't carry it around with you all your life, it'll only destroy you - forgive him, let it go.' I didn't want my kids to miss out on a relationship with their father – he may not have been a good husband, but with time he could still be a good dad.

'It will take a while – he's phoned me and Hermione, but we won't pick up.'

'Do me a favour, next time, pick up – for me.'

We hugged and within seconds Hermione had walked into the room.

'I thought you'd gone to Kate's?'

'Nah, she's straightening her hair – I mean how can she control her life if she can't control her hair? Doh.'

I nodded, bemused and confused... perhaps hair straightening was all part of the heteroflexible lifestyle? I didn't ask.

'Anyway, what crazy shit is going down in here?' she said.

'Are you referring to the three million quid's worth of Christmas stuff lying around? Or do you mean crazy shit, like Ma sitting on a stationary Rudolph?' Hugo recovered himself quickly, wiping his eyes and moving away from me lest his little sister see his vulnerability.

I climbed down from the deer – with the help of both my kids – and asked them if they'd both step outside with me. As we walked into the hallway, Sam and Jacob appeared at the bottom of the stairs with a big box of Hugo's old Lego.

'We're going outside, come with us?' I said.

They looked at each other – no doubt concerned at what this mad old smoke-singed woman was going to do next, but they followed me anyway.

As they all put on their wellingtons and coats in the porch, I slipped into my Louboutins and held both my children's hands as I had done when they were little. The three of us stood in the middle of our huge lawn and waited for Sam and Jacob to join us.

'Snow angels?' Sam said, with a twinkle in her eye.

'Snow angels,' I confirmed with a smile and Sam and I both lay down in the snow as the others watched in barely concealed horror (my kids) and unbridled joy (Jacob).

Sam and I both giggling made star shapes in the crunchy whiteness and were immediately joined by Jacob.

'Dudes, this is some crazy shit,' Hermione said, lying down next to Jacob, who repeated exactly what she said. Hugo and Hermione roared laughing at Jacob's 'crazy shit,' comment and I wanted to laugh too but couldn't let Jacob think this was funny.

'You do realise he'll say that at school now and I will be hauled before the headmistress?' Sam said.

I caught her eye, she was about to tell Jacob off, but she ended up laughing along with the kids and I joined in.

When we'd eventually stopped laughing, I made everyone form a circle, lying down in the snow, our legs banging into one another and our noses almost dropping off with the cold. We lay for ages in the deep, white silence, snowflakes hurtling down and melting on our faces, our lips and eyelashes. We talked about the fire and how lucky we'd been to have survived, and we talked about the future.

'I'm selling everything and giving the money to Auntie Sam,' I said.

'No you're not, I was stupid pinning all my dreams onto the bakery in the first place. What kind of businesswoman am I? One old van, a faulty oven... I was asking for trouble. I have no savings left, and one gust of wind and I was down. No, I need to be realistic and stop dreaming,' Sam sighed.

'No, you must never stop dreaming.' I said, half-sitting up. 'That's what I did – I stopped dreaming years ago and look what happened. Sam, I won't let you give this up - I'm going to sell everything and get your dream back,' I announced.

'Oh Ma, you are such a drama queen,' Hermione said.

We all laughed at that and lying in the snow, looking up at a dense, white sky we talked about what we would do at Christmas and then we moved on to past Christmases.

'One Christmas Eve I remember Auntie Sam and I creeping out into the night and lying in the snow for ages.'

'I remember,' said Sam. 'We were waiting for Father Christmas.'

'Did your mummy and daddy tell you off?' Jacob asked.

'No,' Sam giggled. 'No one even noticed we'd gone – and Father Christmas never came.'

'Ma... Sam... I hate to break it to you, but Father Christmas doesn't exist,' Hugo monotoned.

'Don't be stupid, Hugo, of course he does,' Jacob piped up.

We all added our own jeering 'yeah Hugo, don't be so stupid.'

'You've got to believe. And it's not just Father Christmas - snow angels exist too,' I smiled to myself, 'if you believe in angels then anything's possible.'

My worldly teenagers sniggered, but Sam and Jacob, like me, were more open to possibilities – we had been through so much we wanted to believe – and for us something magical *was* in the air.

I turned my head in the snow to look at Sam, her cheeks ruddy in the cold, and my baby sister smiled back. 'I've always believed in angels,' she said.

Chapter 23
Sex in the Kitchen and Love on the Rocks

Sam

There was nothing else for it, the fire was the end of The White Angel Bakery and we had to make different plans now. I was devastated, but tried not to let Tamsin see because it only made her feel worse and she'd been through enough. It had broken my heart the following morning to turn customers away but what could I do? The bakery was blackened inside and there was no oven. Tamsin was constantly trying to come up with ideas and plans like 'a cupcake truck' and 'a pop-up shop', but it was too late and I asked her to cancel all the orders. I was depressed, felt very lost and still had the beginning of the flu and no energy to do anything.

Meanwhile, Christmas was still heading towards us like a juggernaut and despite the bakery coming to a standstill, everything else was carrying on. Jacob had finally learned his important two lines and on the evening of the Nativity play we made our way carefully through the snow in a taxi. There had been some stage nerves and a bit of stroppiness regarding Jacob's costume, but I managed to calm Tamsin down in time. She wasn't happy that I'd made his donkey head with papier mâché and grey paint and demanded I call her seamstress and ask her to create 'a life-like donkey head' within the hour. I reminded Tamsin, not for the first time that it wasn't the RSC and we couldn't afford it anyway.

So, after much drama at home, the three of us arrived for more drama at St Stephen's Primary School for the Nativity Play.

'I can't believe how grown up Jacob seems,' Tamsin said as we sat in the audience waiting for everyone to come in.

'Do you... think about Steven? I mean, of course you do... but on nights like tonight?'

'Yes,' I said. I didn't want to talk about it. I didn't want to have to tell her that a day didn't go by when I didn't wonder and wish and imagine how it might have been with him by my side. Recently I'd been so busy and so involved in the bakery I'd thought less about Steve, but then the fire had taken all the distractions away again. Why couldn't I ever hold on to the stuff I loved? Even Richard, the most perfect, kind, lovely man in the world had walked away because I wasn't prepared to commit to him.

'I'll be rather relieved when this play's over,' I whispered to Tamsin as the lights went down. 'He's been in character so long I'm worried he'll have an identity crisis and think he's a donkey.'

'Oh the cost of therapy for that one,' she sighed theatrically. We both smiled – my sister could be very funny when she wanted to be. Still smiling, I turned away from her to see Richard sitting down in the empty seat next to me and I took a sharp intake of breath. I could feel the blood run to my face. I felt guilty about the way I'd been – and rude because I hadn't acknowledged the lovely painting he'd pushed under the door. I meant to, but hadn't had time to do anything other than clearing up debris and cinders for the past few days. Richard nodded and smiled as he sat down and I smiled awkwardly back.

'You okay?' he whispered. 'I just heard – about the fire.'

'Yeah. No one was hurt, except the business,' I shrugged, in an attempt to appear braver than I felt.

I really hadn't wanted to bump into Richard, let alone sit with him. It wasn't because I didn't want to see him, it was just that being near him reminded me of what we had, what might have been if things had been different, if I'd been different. And my heart ached. As I watched Mary and Joseph begin their endless search for a room, I smelled the cold night air on him. I tipped my head slightly in his direction, breathing in his scent, then realised this might look weird if anyone saw me. I shouldn't be sniffing ex-boyfriends at school plays and if Tamsin realised what I was doing she'd have something to say – loudly.

Then Jacob came on stage and my heart spilt onto the floor. When he neighed, he sounded more like a siren than a donkey, but he was so earnest, his performance brought tears to my eyes. And by the time they'd found the stable, I was very much aware of Richard's thigh warm against mine. I didn't move, just let it happen, getting a sick kick out of the imagined intimacy.

Then the three kings arrived with their gifts and Richard's hand reached out to mine and held it gently, caressing it with one thumb and reminding me of what I was missing. Richard's brand of sex was gentle, caressing, caring – but I tried not to think too much about that and concentrated on the three kings and their ludicrous gifts. But I wanted him so badly I thought I might explode there and then in the middle of St Stephen's school hall with the choir singing 'O Little Town of Bethlehem'.

How inappropriate, I thought, as the gold frankincense and myrrh were dished out. This is my son's school play and all I can think about is sex. I'd slept with a few men, but rarely had it been so tender, so gentle, so good. It was this caring side I'd told myself was controlling – but Richard wasn't like that, I'd just been looking for excuses not to love him. And sitting so close, just breathing him in like a weirdo and remembering how good it was made me realise I did love him – and I wanted him back.

When the lights went up, I breathed a heavy sigh and turned to Tamsin first, who was wiping a tear. 'My gorgeous little nephew,' she said, almost laughing at herself. 'I'm being so silly at the moment.'

My eyes were damp too as I turned to Richard. We didn't need to say anything – we'd said enough throughout the performance. 'Thank you for the painting,' I smiled, 'fortunately it wasn't destroyed in the fire – I had kept it by my bed.' I wanted to kiss him but that might lead to me wanting to take all his, and my, clothes off. 'The Bakery's a mess, though,' I sighed.

'Can I do anything to help?'

He looked at me with such softness and warmth I felt my knees go weak and I seriously doubt anyone has ever felt such powerful sexual urges after or during a primary school nativity play. Tamsin would have labelled it 'indecent' and I couldn't meet her eyes.

Much later that night when Tamsin and Jacob were asleep I heard a gentle knock on the bakery door. 'I came to see how you are after everything,' Richard said, looking around at the carnage caused by the fire.

'I'm okay. I'm moving out in January, I'll probably have to go back to teaching for a while.'

'Oh that's a shame, you've worked so hard,' his eyes were greyer and more twinkly than I'd remembered. The open door brought a freezing blast to my naked body underneath my dressing gown, so I invited him in.

He closed the door behind him and walked into the bakery kitchen, I followed, commenting on the smoke-damaged walls.

'The landlord will have to have it all repainted, but there's no structural damage,' I said, leaning on the remaining countertop, facing him, aware my dressing gown had slipped slightly to reveal some cleavage.

'Good,' he looked right back at me and stood against the wall. He wasn't going to make any moves, the message was clear, it was up to me, the ball was in my court.

I slowly walked towards him and, close up, could feel the heat pulsating from him. He was as excited as I was, and within seconds I had reached up and kissed him full on the lips. He kissed me back, as my hand slid down to his groin and I slowly undid the zip on his jeans. I looked up at him, the excitement in his eyes was tangible but he gave little away, he was playing hard to get, and I loved a challenge.

I pushed my hand inside his jeans, feeling the hardness, the building tension, and opening my dressing gown I turned us round so I was against the wall. Then I brought him towards me, and holding onto his neck, I wrapped my legs around him and pushed him inside as his strong arms slid under me, supporting me against the wall. We couldn't help ourselves, we were both consumed with such passion it was a matter of minutes before it was all over.

The climb down was slightly awkward and we both laughed, embarrassed at what had just happened. 'I'm sorry, I just had to...' I smiled.

'Don't ever apologise for something like that,' he laughed.

We went upstairs and lay together in the dark (both covered in case my sister decided to pop in or Mrs J felt like wandering through to give a running commentary) and we just talked. Richard spoke about how his father had walked out on them when he was only ten years old, leaving his mum with four children. I knew about this, but he'd never really talked in detail to me before and that he was willing to share this made me feel even closer to him.

'I went from being a carefree little boy playing on his bike and stealing the neighbour's apples to looking after two little sisters. Mum had three jobs just to keep food on the table,' he said, explaining how he'd grown up 'looking after girls.'

'I think that's why I've always been a sucker for a lost lady in distress,' he smiled. I wondered if I had been one of his lost ladies, it went some way to explaining the caring nature I'd sometimes railed against. I saw his desire to spend Christmas together as him trying to take over my life, in the same way I felt Tamsin did, which is why I fought it so hard. But Richard didn't want to control me, he just cared about me and Jacob, wanted to look after us and be part of a family again.

The following morning I woke and there he was, lying next to me on the floor and I felt brighter, happier more alive than I had for some time – it just felt so right him being there. I walked over to the window, it was still dark outside and the snow was falling faster and faster, frenzied snowflakes whirled to the ground and disappeared in orangey whiteness. I went back and snuggled next to him, watching him sleep, and when he woke he smiled and kissed me. I kissed him back and as the snow fell silently outside we lost ourselves all over again.

❄ ❄ ❄

I was bundling Richard out of the door at 6.30 when Tamsin appeared at the top of the stairs, almost banging into us. She was in full make-up, hair tied up and wearing a little Prada number in Winter White, 'I'm breakfasting with friends,' she said, mysteriously. I was intrigued, but she wasn't offering any more information. She then greeted Richard like a long lost friend, she'd only seen him the previous evening at the play – and didn't know about the evening's development but she was keen to make him welcome. I didn't want her butting in and ruining things at this delicate stage so bundled him out before she could ask if he liked it enough to put a ring on it.

I stood at the bakery door, watching him walk off into the snow and I had the cheek to feel a little hurt because he hadn't asked to see me again. But he wasn't going to put himself on the line again, and I didn't blame him - I still had some chasing to do. And this time I wasn't going to let him go.

'You need to decide what you really want, madam,' was all Tamsin said, from behind me.

I knew exactly what I wanted – at last. I'd stupidly rejected the only man I could finally trust with my bruised and battered heart and it was now up to me to win him back.

I suddenly ran for the door, whipping it open and sprinting into the early morning blanket of snow. 'Richard,' I heard myself calling after him. 'Perhaps we could get together again?'

'Yes I'd like that,' he called back, turning around and stamping his feet on the ground to keep them warm.

I had run outside without a coat and was shivering with cold. 'Okay, great. When?' I wasn't playing games any more, I was going to hand him my heart as he had his.

'I... I'm sorry, I'm working late this week then it's Carole's Christmas party at work... she's asked me to be her plus one.'

I was shocked. 'Carole?' His ex? Ella's mom? Who he was still technically married to!

'Yeah... her boyfriend dumped her... she needs an escort and muggins here offered,' he laughed nervously.

Ah, it was all beginning to make horrible sense now. He wasn't playing hard to get – he was going back to his wife. I felt such a fool.

'Oh great. It's good that you two are... it's good for Ella.'

He walked back towards me, his voice lowering as he came nearer. 'Yeah it's been difficult for all of us and…'

'Yes... yes, of course,' I bumbled. Like a moron. I didn't want to hear all about their love-in and turned to go back inside feeling like an idiot.

'Yeah... but you and I should get together soon,' he was walking away, raising his finger on the 'soon', like he was talking to a mate about a casual drink in the pub.

'Yep,' was all I could manage before running into the shop to sob on Tamsin's shoulder just like I did when I was a little girl.

'Talk about bad timing,' I sobbed. 'Stupid Sam spends almost a year with someone, dumps him and then finally falls hard the day after he decides to give his marriage another go.'

'Oh love, it's one thing after the other at the moment, isn't it?' she sighed.

'I wouldn't mind, but I slept with him last night... he might have mentioned his plans before we ripped each other's clothes off. I didn't think he was like that – I thought Richard was special, I thought he cared about me.

Tamsin wiped my tears and brushed my hair back from my face. 'If it's meant to be – it will happen,' she said wisely. 'I blame this snow – it's turning everyone's heads... it's like we've all gone mad.'

Chapter 24

A Breakfast Meeting and a Red Hot Date

Tamsin

I felt terrible - like I'd destroyed everything Sam had worked for and it was now up to me to give my sister back her dream. But with no ovens and no money there was little I could do – yet I couldn't bring myself to call our customers and cancel their orders. Something inside was telling me not to close the door on The White Angel Bakery' yet and I was damned if I was going to throw it all away without at least trying to resurrect something. Sam seemed to lack the energy and drive to even engage in a conversation about starting again and I was worried the depression she'd had after Steve was returning. She was permanently pale and tired and I was worried about her, but being Sam she just carried on saying she was fine.

I had a plan - made some calls and arranged to meet Heddon, Hall and Gabe at a nearby cafe for breakfast, and once I had my team assembled I made my announcement.

'I want to re-open the bakery before Christmas. I intend to honour the orders, re-open the bakery and restore my sister's faith in me – and herself,' I added.

'Absolutely, mon chérie,' Hall said. 'But aren't we being a soupcon ambitious, after all, my love... you don't have long and the bakery is a blackened shell.'

'No we don't have long,' I sighed. 'We need to act immediately, which is where you guys, "Tamsin's Angels" come in.'

Heddon giggled and they all looked at me, Gabe even put his knife and fork down for a second. He took a long drink of orange juice and his lips were wet. I had to avert my eyes.

'I want to clean up and transform the bakery – using all the Christmas stuff at my house we can recreate the winter wonderland I was planning for The Rectory – in the bakery,' I said.

'Do you mean a makeover like on the telly? Covering Sam's eyes and saying "you can open them now",' Gabe asked.

'No,' I said. 'The last thing my sister needs is some MDF-constructed nightmare and bloody Alan Titchmarsh appearing from behind the hedge, shouting "I bet you didn't expect me to pop up from your petunias did you?"'

'No class, darling,' Heddon and Hall nodded in agreement.

The boys were only too willing to help and Heddon and Hall wrote me a cheque there and then for a loan to buy a new oven. I wept with gratitude and we arranged for them all to turn up the following morning and start work.

Gabe dropped me home in his truck and I mentioned that I had been invited to Mimi's party that evening.

'Are you going? You know Mimi, don't you?' I asked, provocatively.

'Yeah I know Mimi – I did her trellis.'

'Mmm, so I heard. I wonder if you'd care to be my plus one?' I heard myself ask.

'Yeah... I'll come along,' he said. 'Pick you up about 8?'

So, not only was I going to Mimi's party, I was taking a 'plus one'. I felt nervous and excited and happy all at the same time. If I was going to move forward and move on from my life with Simon, an evening with Gabe would certainly be a push in the right direction. I was beginning to feel like the old Tamsin, but this time I was stronger and more independent, not relying on my husband for money or feelings of self-worth.

'I'll see you later,' I said, kissing him on the cheek. I couldn't wait.

Chapter 25

Life-size Reindeer and Christmas Carnage

Sam

Tamsin had decided to take up Mimi's party invite. And being Tamsin she couldn't just get dressed and go – there would be hours of 'hair and make-up' and parades of various gowns plundered from the bin bags lying around the flat.

'My hairdresser Debbie is coming over – she says since I've spent thousands with her over the years she'll do it gratis until I get myself together,' she said, pouting into a hand mirror.

I was pleased for Tamsin. She was finally getting her life back, albeit quite a different one. It was little things like getting her hair done for a party that mattered to her and a good looking guy as her escort was just the boost she needed.

'Oh by the way,' she called from the bathroom. 'Debbie said she'll do yours... and Jacob's hair too, if you would both like a trim?'

Mmmm. She'd said this when she was out of the room, because Jacob's hair was a touchy subject. I wish she'd leave things alone and stop bloody interfering, I thought. Debbie the hairdresser wasn't just about Mimi's party hair – she was about Tamsin trying to get her own way – again. 'No, thank you,' I called, but she'd gone, or was pretending she hadn't heard me. I knew my sister, and if I didn't address this she'd carry on and have us both with a short back and sides by this time tomorrow night, so I went to the bathroom. I could hear the taps running – she was washing her hair in preparation for Debbie – and I just went straight in.

'Oh you shouldn't just walk in on someone's bathroom...' she started.

'No and you shouldn't just walk in on someone's life,' I replied. 'I know what you're up to – you think you can turn Jacob into Little Lord Fauntleroy while nobody's looking. You think you can convince him to have his hair cut while I'm busy downstairs and before we know it he's looking like something from the bloody 1940s. Why don't you take him to church while you're at it? That's something else I don't want him to do – religion – but obviously I'm only his mother – as his auntie you have the final say.'

'No I don't.'

'No. You don't, Tamsin... so why are you trying to get your own way? We have had this conversation – he DOESN'T WANT his hair cutting. He loves it long, like his dad used to wear it.'

She was shaking her head in a very annoying 'know-it-all' way I thought she'd dropped.

'He wants his hair short like the other boys. He's fed up of being called a girl and gay and...'

'There's nothing wrong with being gay...'

'I'm not saying there is, and there's nothing wrong with being different... but I told you before, at his age he doesn't *want* to be different.'

'Are you trying to tell me you know my son better than I do?' I was so angry now. 'Let's ask him shall we, Tamsin? You aren't listening to me, so perhaps you'll listen to Jacob when he tells you he is happy with his hair long,' I shouted, going into the living room to find my son.

'Jacob, Jacob, auntie Tam and I want to ask you something,' I called, trying to fade the volume and aggression from my voice, but not succeeding. I found him watching TV, apparently oblivious to the drama unfolding around him. 'Jacob – would you like a lady to come here and cut all your hair off,' I asked, trying to make it sound as bad as possible. I waited for the complete and total rejection of this ridiculous idea, followed by my absolute final warning to Tamsin about keeping out of our lives. But to my deep disappointment, his little face lit up.

'Can the lady give me hair like Toby?'

'What's Toby's like?' I asked, knowing he had never heard of them but willing him to say 'Bon Jovi circa 1973'. But of course the answer he gave me was 'short'.

He must have seen my face drop and looked at me like he was trying to figure things out.

'Mum... if Daddy sees, will he be upset if I have my hair cut?'

His question ripped at my heart.

'Oh sweetie no – of course he won't. He'll be happy if you're happy, darling.'

He smiled, satisfied with that, then looked at me again this time with worry in his eyes. 'Mummy, will *you* cry?'

I reassured him again. I felt like a terrible mother – Tamsin had been right and I hadn't even seen it. I'd been letting Jacob struggle and get picked on – I'd been projecting my own feelings of loss onto Jacob without even realising. Jacob was so young when Steve died he'd only seen him in photos and wouldn't remember his Dad's hair.

'Okay sweetie – let's get the lady to cut your hair then?'

'Yay,' he said and clapped his pudgy little hands together.

I walked onto the landing and banged on the door. 'I guess you know my son better than I do,' I said loudly and stomped downstairs, wondering if, at 36, it was perhaps time to get my own long hair cut when Debbie arrived.

A little later Tamsin came down with her hair in a towel turban, full lipstick on tight lips and an obstinate swish in her walk. Joan Crawford couldn't have done a better entrance.

'I won't ask Debbie to cut his hair if you don't want it doing,' she said, tentatively. I was surprised at this, she usually railroaded over me – perhaps this life change had taught her some tact?

'It's fine. You're right, it's what he wants. It was me who wanted him to keep it long – like his dad. He can be "different" when he's older... if that's what he wants.'

'And if he doesn't you can make him be "different",' she giggled. 'That's a joke,' she added.

'I get it – you controlling bitch... that's a joke too,' I grimaced.

I'd always been keen to point out how bossy and controlling Tamsin was – and there was me trying to keep my son's hair long, because I wanted it like that. Perhaps the Angel sisters weren't that different after all?

❄ ❄ ❄

Once Debbie had given us all a trim – yes I succumbed to Debbie's scissors too – Jacob seemed to light up. He loved his new hair and couldn't wait to go to school on Monday and show his friends.

I watched Jacob admiring his new cut in the mirror; 'Please don't say 'I told you so,' I murmured to Tamsin.

'I wouldn't dream of it,' she sighed, studying her fake, wine-coloured nails studded with 'an occasional diamond', as she put it. She couldn't afford a manicurist and had spent all afternoon doing them herself.

'It's as well we don't have a business, because I'd have been serving on my own all day today, while you breakfasted with friends and did your nails,' I said. 'And you certainly couldn't bake with those on... do they come off?' I asked.

'For God's sake, Sam, that's like asking "does your leg come off?" Of course they don't, they might be fake but they're glued fast. Have you never worn fake nails?'

'No... why would I? That's like asking me if I've ever worn a fake leg, I have my own.'

She rolled her eyes and flounced off to get dressed. I could tell she was excited – but she was nervous too. Tonight she'd be stepping back into her old life for a guest appearance and I wondered if she was ready.

'I'm taking Gabe,' she said, her eyes shining. 'I want us to be the stylish and surprise couple at the party. Fasten your seatbelts it's going to be a bumpy night,' she hissed, in her best Bette Davis. I just hoped Mimi had the stairs to justify her entrance.

Earlier, Heddon and Hall had arrived in a flurry of white sparkle and cashmere and deposited the whole of Tamsin's lost Christmas in the back of the shop. I was climbing over bin bags in my bedroom and a life-size reindeer on the landing (I told her we didn't have the room but she'd conveniently forgotten).

'There's nowhere else to put everything,' she'd said as Debbie tugged hard at her shiny black bob. I'd reminded her that in January we had to leave. 'If you bring any more stuff into this tiny flat I will invite Channel 4 to make a documentary about it, "My sister the hoarder".'

'Yes, my love,' she said, 'after Channel 5 have made "My sister the bar room dancer",' she smiled sweetly. I wasn't going to live that one down.

Leaving me to live with her Christmas carnage was so typical of Tamsin. She was used to having people to tidy up and finish off, and after I waved her off I sat amid the white snowflakes and reindeers piled up in the corner feeling alone.

Seeing Gabe collect Tamsin and tell her she looked gorgeous then watching them go off arm in arm had been a painful reminder of Richard's absence. I imagined him at home with Carole, mistletoe hanging, eyes meeting, rediscovering each other after and falling in love all over again after their time apart. It was my own fault – I left it too late and he wasn't hanging around for Miss No Commitment. I made a cup of tea, watched X Factor, had a little cry and felt slightly better.

❄ ❄ ❄

Later I wandered down to the ruins of my business and looked out of the window onto the square. It was dark, just a few fairy lights in the trees and the scattering of confetti-like snow coming down again, it was relentless this year. I gazed for a long time at the white landscape outside, the snow getting deeper, another layer of the white blanket of silence descending over everything. So much had happened recently I could barely take it in and having lost my business and the man I loved my heart felt almost too heavy to carry. I hoped Tamsin would enjoy herself at the party – perhaps if my sister got her life back on track it would be good for both of us. I'd realised since she came to live with me that our lives were entwined and if she wasn't happy, then neither was I – and I knew it was the same for her. I went back upstairs to check on Jacob, hoping the Angel sisters would one day be able to find happiness at the same time.

Chapter 26
Low Flying Louboutins and Sex in the Snow

Tamsin

Mimi's party was amazing. Gabe drove us there and we arrived to the kind of sparkly Christmas event I would have been proud to stage. Of course, I wouldn't have gone with the colour scheme, which was a dodgy purple, but apart from that I had to give it to Mimi – she could host a party.

I climbed from the truck and walked with Gabe down the winter pathway which led to the main front steps. As we walked together in silence, hearing only the sound of Herald Angels, I turned and looked at him.

'I'm a bit nervous, Gabe,' I confessed.

He stopped in the darkness, a halo of fairy lights all around him and he took my breath away. He looked like an angel with his mid-length hair and piercing blue eyes and his smile was beatific – I reached out and touched him to see if he was real and for a moment our eyes locked. Then he took my hand, kissed it gently, and led me up the garden path to Mimi's Musical Extravaganza.

Once inside, my heart leapt at the sight of the magnificent tree. Forest green pine dressed in vibrant, shiny purple stood proud in the centre of the room (though I would probably have put it in the hallway – a little brash to have the tree in the living quarters). The staircase swept forever, a huge swirling mass of every shade of purple from deepest violet to the lightest lavender swirled around the banisters and swept into the room with the stairs. Magical!

Mimi greeted us excitedly – dressed in a figure-hugging glitzy purple number many would have avoided with her ginger hair and skin tone, but she rocked it.

'Oh Tamsin, how good of you to come – you have no idea how much I've missed you,' she beamed. She seemed genuinely delighted to have me there, and when I peered round to see if Anouska or Phaedra had arrived, she seemed to know what I was thinking.

'They aren't coming,' she said. 'They never do. None of the ladies from Chantray Lane ever come to my parties or coffee mornings. That's why I'm so touched you did.' Her effervescence seemed to disappear momentarily and she grabbed a glass of champagne from a passing waiter.

'Mimi... I'm touched you invited me,' I said giving her a warm hug. Mimi and Gabe nodded hello, but neither seemed interested in the other and I felt a wave of relief wash over me.

Funny how I'd become so territorial about Gabe, it wasn't like we were in a relationship, but I didn't want any other women getting their claws into him.

Gabe went off to get us some drinks and I asked Mimi if she'd heard anything about Phaedra or Anouska. 'What have those girls been up to?' I asked, 'I've been so busy I haven't had a chance to call either of them... has Anouska had her kitchen done yet?'

She seemed immediately uncomfortable; 'Let's not talk about her – she's really not worth it.'

I was surprised at this reaction – perhaps Anouska's kitchen was amazing and Mimi was jealous? Oh, the relief at not living in their world any more, I thought, as Mimi showed me round her beautiful home. I waited for that stabbing pain of envy and loss to hit me in the stomach as she took me from one exquisite room to another and then paraded her Chanel handbags and her stunning shoes on the pure silk bedspread. But I felt nothing but pleased for her, I wasn't judging Mimi – if that's what got her through the day then good for her. But it wasn't for me – not anymore.

Why hadn't I seen this before? Mimi was, a genuine, loyal friend who just wanted to be one of the gang. I'm ashamed to say I was one of the gang who'd excluded her from everything and been so blinded by my pre-judgment of Mimi I hadn't seen the lovely woman she was. Ten years younger, a few pounds lighter and a hell of a lot prettier than me and the other Wives, I realised it wasn't just the lap dancing we disapproved of. Without Phaedra's bitchy whispers and Anouska's back-handed compliments about her were based on nothing but pure jealousy.

The champagne flowed, the canapés were stunning and the music... the choir, the singing was just amazing. I sat with Gabe on a huge chunky sofa and we drank champagne and talked like it was the first time we'd met. It felt like I'd never even seen this handsome, well-dressed man at my side. He was so attentive, so interested in me and made me feel like the most important person in the room – something my husband had never done. After the choir, things kicked back a little, and a floor appeared from nowhere, with little lights around it. A DJ had seamlessly appeared behind two decks and was providing the kind of sounds you just had to dance to; 'Do They Know it's Christmas?' Wham's 'Last Christmas' and all the mad, bad and sad seasonal songs in between.

As the music played I sat close to Gabe, which caused my pulse to quicken, I hadn't felt like this for many years – if ever.

'Shall we?' he whispered in my ear. I wasn't quite sure what he was asking, but I nodded and walked on to the dance floor (in what I hoped was a sensual way) where he joined me. He was so sexy, so laid-back, nothing and no-one seemed to bother him... and so very easy on the eye. He took my hand and electricity sparked so brightly I was sure everyone felt the sparks fizzing. We danced opposite each other, our bodies close but not touching. Our eyes were locked and I had this uncontrollable urge to touch him, to run my hands through his hair and hold his beautiful face in my hands. I'd never seen him in this way before – it was like he'd been touched by magic, his rough edges smoothed down, his smile sexier, his eyes bluer. The music slowed and we moved closer, his arms now round my waist, mine on his shoulders and my face in his neck. I breathed in his smell – no Monster Munch or musk tonight – he smelled of burnt candles, cedar wood and cinnamon, so delicious I wanted to lick his neck like a cat. I stopped myself, but after a few more minutes of close dancing I couldn't take any more – I wanted him and I knew he wanted me.

'Do you want to leave?' his voice was husky in my ear, his lips warm on my flesh and I melted on the dance floor.

I couldn't speak, but my body language must have said it all, and within minutes we'd left the warmth and noise of the house and were running through the snow still holding hands.

'Where are we going?' I panted as we tripped through the whiteness, my heart was in my mouth. 'I can't run in these shoes...'

'You know what happens when you wear silly shoes,' he said, grappling me to the ground, making a grab for my shoes to try and take them off while I squealed like a girl.

'It's okay I can walk, I can walk,' I shouted through laughter. 'Not the shoes... not the shoes...' I screamed as the first scarlet-soled Louboutin flew through the air, quickly followed by the second. I screamed in mock horror, but I didn't care – the shoes were beautiful but they didn't work in my new life.

'What do I do now? I can't walk in bare feet,' I protested through giggles. And he swept me up. Just like that, he lifted me into his arms and strode through Mimi's landscaped acreage like Hercules. I clung to him, my red silk dress damp with snow, my arms bare, my feet shoeless... but I didn't feel the cold. And when we finally arrived at a shed, he carefully put me down, fiddled with the lock and used his shoulder to push the door open. He pulled me into the pitch black interior, pushing me gently against the wooden wall and lifting up the scarlet silk. I was naked underneath – I wanted a smooth silhouette, but no underwear had other advantages that night, and as the damp wood held my back, he lifted my legs around his waist. His lips were on my mouth, my neck, his hands were everywhere and we just kept going on and on and on. I was in a trance, I'd never felt such overpowering feelings of lust before and when he finally released himself gently, I was weak, exhausted and happy.

We half sat, half lay against the wall of the shed. My eyes had become accustomed to the lack of light and I could make out garden forks, plant pots and huge bags of compost leaning against the wall. The smell of soil and damp wood filled my nostrils and I suddenly felt cold and felt for him with my hands, running my fingers through his hair. Instinctively, he took off his jacket and put it around me, just like they did in the films, and I felt beautiful, loved. Neither of us spoke – words would have seemed clumsy and inarticulate after what we'd just experienced and despite the most wonderful Christmas party going on in the £3m house, I just wanted to stay there forever in that damp old shed with him. How things had changed.

After a while we had to move, it was very cold, so he carried me back through the snow to his truck. He was tender and gentle and sat me on the front seat like I was a piece of porcelain. Turning on the heater in the cab, he asked if I was warm enough, I nodded and smiled.

Gabe drove slowly through the whiteness, more snow was coming down and we could only see a few feet in front of us. The heater was blasting, the windscreen wipers were squeaking and John Lennon was singing 'and so this is Christmas and what have you done?' on the radio. I couldn't believe what had just happened. I had never, ever, had sex in a shed before, it just wasn't like me to lose control like that... this man had such an effect on me.

I felt so young and beautiful that night. The blood was coursing through my veins and I was filled with an energy and excitement I'd never known before. Gabe was amazing, and being with him just made me sparkle, but I had to keep reminding myself I mustn't get too carried away. I was just another bored wife to Gabe and I told myself I mustn't lose sight of that and believe it was anything more than wonderful sex. It had disoriented me, making me realise I'd never had real passion in my life – not like I had tonight, with him.

Who was I? Had I lost myself? Or found myself? It was as though the map of my life had been mislaid, my journey suspended, my compass buried in the snow. Along with my Louboutins.

Chapter 27
Fake Breasts and Drizzled Nipples
Sam

Tamsin had staggered in about 4 a.m. the night – or rather the morning – of Mimi's party. She was pissed and giggling and almost fell into bed.

'Tam, you've woken me up, you noisy sod... so how was it?' I turned the lamp on and sat up in bed. 'Your dress is wet… and where are your shoes?'

'Oh Gabe hurled them into the snow again. Louboutins this time,' she giggled.

I watched her staggering around the room barefoot, wet through but without a care in the world, and it struck me again how much things had changed. Even as a teenager she'd never come home late after a party, always too worried about what was happening at home. Then with Simon she'd never drink more than a glass or too – worried what he'd think, what he'd say. For the first time in her life she seemed free, and it was wonderful to see her finally having fun.

'Oh Sam, it was great... Gabe was gorgeous,' she sighed. 'I don't know what it is about him, but he makes me do terrible things,' she giggled.

'What sort of things did he make you do?' I'd asked, the look on her face suggested it was either illegal or involved more than two people.

'We had sex… outdoors... in Mimi's shed,' she blurted, looking at me like she was unsure of my reaction.

'Fantastic! Good for you, there's nothing wrong with sex in a shed, on a park bench, a beach, the back of a car... I've done them all.'

'Oh my god,' her hands flew to her mouth. 'Sam, you are such a hussy... was it good... in the car?'

'I don't kiss and tell, you'll have to find that out for yourself, Tamsin.'

She giggled again.

'You really like him, don't you?' I said.

She nodded. The sparkle was back in my sister's eyes for the first time in forever.

'He's really kind, he makes me feel special.' She had that far-away look in her eyes. 'Sam, I've never been happier than this past couple of weeks, with you and Jacob and the bakery itself. I feel like I belong.'

'I think it's because it's what *you* want to do,' I offered. 'You're living your life – not Simon's. You never really bought into that corporate world of yachts and golf and posh dinners, did you?' I asked.

She shook her head. 'No. I saw all that tonight again at Mimi's, the fake smiles, the fake friendships... and, goodness me, the fake breasts and teeth! You should have seen them, Sam. No, I didn't belong there tonight. I like Mimi but I don't want to be her, I don't want her life or her handbags. I had such a wonderful time though, in the past I wouldn't have enjoyed the party, I'd be obsessing about who her caterer was, what produce they used and how I could secure them for next year. Tonight I didn't give a toss what Mimi had drizzled on her nipples... I meant nibbles.'

'From what you say about her, you were probably right first time,' I laughed.

In her slightly inebriated state Tamsin found this hilarious and we laughed loudly about Mimi's nipples for some time.

She clambered into bed. 'You know, my therapist told me I was always seeking acceptance because my father rejected me. Ha, I didn't need to pay £120 an hour to be told that,' she laughed, without bitterness.

'I've been thinking about what you told me about Dad and the way he treated you – I've been trying to work it all out,' I started gently. 'And I think because you saw him at his worst, drunk, and aggressive, he was forced to remember that when he looked at you. When he was sober, all the guilt and self-loathing were reflected in his child's eyes. I know it's hard to understand, but he hated himself – not you, Tam.'

'That makes a kind of sense,' she said, 'even after a night of shed sex and cocktails.' She looked over at me and we smiled. 'I just wish he'd realised the damage he was doing then he might have changed,' she added, more serious now.

'He stopped drinking, didn't he?' I stroked her hair.

'But it was too late by then. I never forgave him, so how could he forgive himself? And to think I believed Simon was my salvation. My perfect marriage – as unlived in as my beautiful home.'

'Oh Tamsin, you mustn't see your life with Simon in the same way you see your childhood. Don't dismiss it all as painful and dark... there were good times and good people in that life too. And you have the kids.'

'I just find it hard to see anything but ghosts in my life. Apart from you and Richard I've only known transparent, insubstantial people who faded away when I needed them most.'

'But you haven't faded away. You may have felt weakness throughout your marriage but you never showed it and your kids are strong and forthright and…'

'Yes. A little too forthright at times,' she laughed.

'Yes but Tamsin you stopped the cycle. Hugo and Hermione are their own people, however you felt inside and however small and insignificant Dad or Simon made you feel, you taught your kids to believe in themselves. *You* gave them self-belief, something you never had.'

'Thanks Sam... you might be my little sister, but sometimes I feel like the little one.' She lay still for a while, thinking then pulled the covers over us both; 'I'm tired... let's get some sleep, we've got a big day tomorrow,' she sighed, dropping off.

'No we haven't. It's Sunday, we're not doing anything.'

She didn't answer, so I nudged her in the darkness, but she was gone, no doubt dreaming of sex in the snow and a pair of lost Louboutins.

We were like detectives, my sister and I. We were working on cold case files long buried, feelings hidden, pasts covered up. We'd never know why our father drank or why our mother's self-esteem was so low she stayed with a man who hurt her. Simon's abuse was subtle, but it was just as cruel, and it would have continued until Tamsin either fought back or shrank to nothing. Sometimes things happen for the best – and it was beginning to look like their devastating financial loss might be Tamsin's gain.

Now we just had to put the pieces of our past together and create a picture we could both accept and live with. Then perhaps my sister would find some peace.

Chapter 28

Makeover Madness and a Winter Wonderland

Tamsin

The following morning I was up with the lark. I'd run out of my Sumatra Wahana so forced myself to drink three cups of disgusting instant coffee, but on only four hours sleep even that wasn't going to be enough. It was cold, every muscle ached from my 'outdoor activities' with Gabe the night before (Oh God, did I really do that?) and I had a hangover. But when the bakery doorbell jangled and the boys came pouring in I was so ready for it and leaped to greet them.

'Darling, we have come to save Christmas,' Heddon announced. They were both dressed in white and carrying bags and boxes of all kinds of what they described as 'festive frou frou gorgeousness'. I squealed with joy and clapped as they swept around the bakery, talking me through their design plans while I added my own thoughts and ideas.

Gabe was making a start on cleaning the walls and was going to paint them and I found every excuse I could to brush past him – it was like electricity between us whenever we touched and I could tell he felt it too. After some flirtation and lingering looks I forced myself to focus on the job in hand. 'Tamsin's Angels' were about to turn The White Angel Bakery into the Winter Wonderland I would have had at home... but it was going to be so much better. I was so excited I could barely contain myself and popped back upstairs to see if Sam was awake. She was in the kitchen, hair on end, looking like death.

'Are you okay, sweetie?' I asked.

'I'm not actually, Tam, I've got a headache, I've been sick and I think I'll go back to bed... would you mind keeping an eye on Jacob?'

This was perfect. I was sorry she felt ill but it meant she'd be out of the way for a few hours so we could get a good start and we could surprise her. That way, what she saw as impossible (to re-open the bakery before Christmas) would hopefully seem very possible by the time she saw it.

I woke Jacob, gave him some toast and told him we were doing a top secret surprise for mummy and Gabe needed his help. He couldn't have been more excited if I'd told him Father Christmas was here and within minutes, he was downstairs, and under Gabe's fatherly tutelage, Jacob worked alongside him scrubbing soot off the walls like it was a dream job.

I made hot drinks, put on a little Michael Bublé and did what I always do best – supervised – or as Sam would say, 'bossed everyone around,' but someone had to keep the boys in order – especially Gabe. The bakery had been cleaned after the fire, thanks to Sam and Mrs J, and was spotless, just needing a light dust and lots of paint. We dragged the reindeer and all the glass ornaments and baubles into the shop and once Gabe had finished painting the walls we didn't wait for them to dry but just got on with styling.

By mid-afternoon it was starting to look like a bakery again. The walls were painted perfectly, the tables had the most exquisite cloths, and fairy lights were dotted everywhere. We hung glass snowflakes from the ceiling in a spectacular 'ice-scape' as Hall referred to it; the flakes were all glass, different sizes and shades of white, and the boys had found a glass top with lace effect for the counter, which was so pretty I almost cried.

Then I almost cried again because stupidly I'd been so obsessed with reindeers and glass baubles I hadn't considered the tree. But would you believe, Heddon and Hall had – and within minutes Hall came back from their little van carrying a beautiful, pure white Christmas tree, which brought tears to my eyes.

We all dressed it and I even allowed Jacob to put a few pieces of Lego on there – as long as they were white. After a gruelling day, we were ready for 'the reveal'. The glass and crystal baubles were glittering through the tree fairy lights, the snowflakes sparkled from the ceiling and the whole place twinkled.

I told everyone to be quiet, and I went upstairs to get Sam.

Chapter 29

The Beating Heart of The White Angel Bakery

Sam

I'd known something was going on downstairs that morning, but I assumed it was just the boys visiting for coffee and that Tamsin had kept them downstairs so they could chat and squeal (which they did – a lot!) without disturbing me. A quick coffee with Heddon and Hall could easily turn into an improvised opera or a joint rendition of West End show tunes. And despite them being downstairs, I had enjoyed a Christmas musical extravaganza from my bed courtesy of Heddon, Hall and Tamsin – accompanied by Michael Bublé.

After a particularly gutsy rendition of Ave Maria, Tamsin appeared in my bedroom doorway and suggested I get up.

'Come and have a cup of tea downstairs with me and the boys,' she said. 'It will make you feel better.'

Then Jacob appeared at the bottom of the stairs and told me to close my eyes. I looked to Tamsin for confirmation and she beamed at me and nodded before taking my hand to guide me. I hadn't a clue what was going on as she walked me down the stairs then apparently through from the kitchen into the shop front. She positioned me in the shop, touched my hand and Jacob shouted; 'You can open your eyes now Mum.'

I couldn't believe what I saw – the bakery had been completely transformed. Before the fire it had been a cosy, if somewhat shabby, little place, then a burnt out shell and now... it was still cosy and welcoming, but white and sparkly and very, very beautiful.

The walls had been painted a pale sheen of icy white, gossamer angel wings were scattered everywhere, and fairy lights glinted like diamonds all around the room. By the window was the white reindeer, huge and proud and glistening under several amazing snowflake chandeliers all coming from the ceiling at different heights, in varying shapes. I just walked around in a daze as everyone looked on smiling. They'd cleaned up my tables, covered them in sparkly cloths and tied the mismatched chairs with huge white satin and palest blue bows. The counter glittered under all of the twinkling lights and in the coffee shop stood a beautiful white Christmas tree. I didn't know where to turn my eyes and they rested for a second on the tree, adorned in white and silver baubles, glass, diamanté, pearl – and was that Lego? – with one, heart-shaped scarlet glass bauble half way up.

I walked over to the tree and, trance-like, I gently touched the scarlet glass, searing in the white glitter.

'The Bakery's new beating heart,' Orlando announced, bowing theatrically. I would normally have rolled my eyes at this, but his sincerity and all their goodness just filled my own heart with sparkles.

'It's the most beautiful bakery in the world,' I started to cry and looked over at Tamsin, who was glowing. 'I love it, I just love it – thank you,' I said, wiping my eyes.

'Oh and before you start going on about money and ovens... the boys have given us a small loan to put a deposit down on a brand new oven. It arrives first thing tomorrow – which is probably as well, because we still have a hell of a lot of orders,' Tamsin said.

'No we don't... you cancelled.'

She looked at me.

'You didn't cancel them, did you?' I said, my heart doing a little jog.

She shook her head and I felt my face drain of blood at the thought of the work and the speed we had to get everything done.

'Are you up for a few all-nighters, Tam?' I asked.

'You bet,' she beamed.

❄ ❄ ❄

Later, when everyone had gone home and Jacob had gone to bed, Tam and I sat alone together in our white wonderland and I just gazed around me, taking it in.

'I know Heddon and Hall are great interior designers,' I said. 'But there's so much of you in here, you gave yourself to this, to the business and I just feel so grateful.'

'It was driven by self-interest,' she said, modestly. 'Being here, building a new business reminds me of the past – the good bits, when Simon and I were starting out. It was all so exciting – everything mattered because we had nothing,' her eyes grew fiery at the memory. 'Whatever happens with the bakery, even if it's a great success, which I hope it will be – I don't want to lose me again.'

'You won't... I won't let you. I don't think I realised how much you'd bought into this... the bakery,' I said, gazing around at the gorgeous decorations, still taking them in. 'I assumed after the fire, you'd just find something else.'

'It's our dream, you said so yourself. I came to you with nothing Sam and in a short time I feel like you gave me my life back – but a better version.'

'Yeah but these last couple of days, I've taken my foot off the gas, I've been tired and achy – and I'm ashamed to admit it but I'd given up. You carried on for both of us.'

'That's what being part of a team is all about,' she said.

'Yes but it's also what being sisters is all about.'

❄ ❄ ❄

I hadn't failed to notice Gabe's presence at the bakery and the glances that passed between him and my sister. And whilst I couldn't be more pleased for her, it was a stark reminder of the fact my own relationship with Richard was well and truly over. He hadn't called since our night together and Tamsin said it served me right if he was just using me – he obviously felt like I'd used him for the past twelve months.

On the Monday morning after Mimi's party weekend Tamsin had kindly offered to take Jacob to school. I was grateful – I was busy baking, but equally I didn't want to bump into Richard and Carole playing happy families at the school gate.

Tamsin was happy wading to school through the snow in her Gucci snow suit (obviously) and since having his hair cut there'd been no more reports of name calling and Jacob was making more friends each day. On the second day of Tamsin taking him in she'd asked Heddon and Hall to help out and Orlando turned up in his white Aston Martin – much to my horror and Jacob's delight.

I was very grateful for the help taking Jacob to school but after a few days of Tamsin, Orlando and a very posh car - I decided my son needed a splash of reality and I needed a sniff of Richard (not literally... oh, okay, perhaps). Jacob had been disappointed not to be driven in style and almost had a tantrum when he found out he'd be with me.

'But I want Auntie Tamsin and Uncle Orlando to take me in their lovely car,' he'd stropped. According to my son, all his friends had thought Tam was on the telly and had her own show, which of course she did – in her head.

Arriving at the school gates felt very strange that morning. Kids were coming up to Jacob and giving him high fives and yummy mummies were ruffling his short hair and saying 'what a cutie he is' in my earshot. It made a change from the way they backed off like he had nits when his hair was longer. Had a mere haircut created these superfans?

It wasn't long before I spotted Richard across the playground. He was chatting to a group of mums and dads and I felt a stab in my heart. I was relieved to see he was on his own and not with Carole but tried not to make it too obvious I was looking. I had just said goodbye to Jacob when a couple of 'mummies' wandered over rather self-consciously. I recognised the blonde one, she'd laughed at my homemade rucksack once and her friend had made a very audible remark about my shorts on Sports Day.

But for some reason these two glamour queens seemed very eager to be my friends. They were all over me asking how the bakery was doing and asking where my sister was.

'Are your sister and Orlando... together?' one of them asked.

'No, he's in a relationship,' I said. I didn't 'out' him there and then, I thought the blonde highlights and 'man bag' he carried might have revealed where his preferences lay – but apparently not. They ooed and aahed and made ridiculous small talk, but I couldn't join in like Tamsin clearly had. I was relieved when Richard turned up at the side of me.

'You walking my way?' he asked. I nodded, gratefully and eagerly, and said my goodbyes to my fawning audience as we walked off.

'My sis and Orlando have certainly made an impression on the yummy mummies,' I said as we walked in synch.

'Yeah, she is so funny. I had to laugh at her yesterday getting out of that car in her fancy clothes and dark glasses, Orlando rushing round to the passenger door to open it for her. Hey, and

Jacob – he's a rock star at the school since your sis started doing his PR.'

'Yeah, well after his hair cut he says everyone treats him like a boy now... so she was right on one thing.'

We walked in silence for a while and I was just about to ask him how things were with Carole, when we were caught up by another group of women.

'We've been looking for you, Sam,' said one of them, like we were old friends. She was blonde and pretty, wore bright pink boots – I'd noticed her before – but she'd never noticed me.

'Why?' I asked, alarmed. 'Is Jacob okay?'

They laughed self-consciously.

'Yes, he's fine – we just wanted to ask if you fancied meeting up for lunch at the pub on the day the kids break up? We go every Friday lunchtime and we thought you might like to join us?'

I was amazed. After all this time why did they suddenly want my company? I didn't want to be rude, but it was the last thing I wanted. If they couldn't accept me before, why now?

'I'm sorry, I'm working at the bakery,' I tried a smile.

'Is it going well? We heard about the fire,' one of them said, looking stricken, the others all nodded.

'It's great now thanks – it's been tough, but we're getting there.'

I was so unused to this attention it freaked me out. Then they all asked individually if we could swap mobile numbers so they could 'keep me in the loop, socially'. I was mid-swap when Richard leaned in. 'I'll get off, Sam, I have to speak to a client at 9.30, so see you around,' he said in a low voice. Richard worked with computers, he rarely spoke to clients, if anything he used email and I wondered if this was just an excuse to go. I watched him walk away through acres of white and disappear as my new 'fans' milled around me, admiring my hair, my clothes, my 'lovely eyes'.

What the hell was going on? I was very confused and because of these stupid women Richard had now gone. I didn't want this; I'd never wanted these people to befriend me. For the past eighteen months I had felt their stares, their unspoken ridicule, and like when I was a kid at school, I'd just kept my head down. Funny how people didn't really change, the template we make as a child stays with us, a few modifications here and there – but the women hanging around the school gate were exactly the same as the girls they'd once been.

I couldn't put my finger on it, but as I walked home, alone, I wondered if this new-found adoration had less to do with me and more to do with my meddling sister. And later, when I told her what had happened, she fobbed it off too easily... no inquisition, no details required, she just laughed and said, 'People.'

'No it's more than just a random decision to include me,' I said, making eye contact. 'Have you told them you'll hit them if they don't make friends with me – like you did at school? Because if you have I'll be furious.'

'How ridiculous. I haven't said anything, but I think it would make life easier for Jacob if you're part of the mummy brigade.'

'Really? Oh God, I'd end up thumping them, the way they dance around each other, twirling and gossiping and moving from camp to camp. Who's in favour this week? Who's out of favour now? I don't care.'

'Well, perhaps you should.'

'No. Today those women were like zombies, staggering through the snow to paw at me and touch my hair –what the hell is going on?'

'I told you Sam, it's the snow – it's sent everyone mad.'

I shrugged, perhaps Tamsin was right and this white-out had created a dislocated reality for all of us. I couldn't explain it any other way.

I wasn't going to let annoying women stop me collecting Jacob, so later that day I wandered back to the school delighted to see my son surrounded by lots of friends.

I stood near the school entrance, waiting for him, and was soon joined by Richard. I was pleased to see he was alone and despite him now being 'taken,' I still wanted to be around him. I just hoped I could get over him one day.

We chatted about the kids for a while then he looked and me and said; 'You seem preoccupied, a bit pale, are you okay... with everything that's going on?'

I nodded. 'Yeah, I've not been too good - I'm fighting flu I think.'

'I just thought you seemed a bit overwhelmed with it all.'

'Oh it's been quite a few weeks what with Tamsin, then the van, then the fire, but things are getting back to normal now.

Mind you this morning was a bit much with the desperate housewives.'

'Yeah it looked like it, they all want a bit of your limelight, don't they?'

'What do you mean?'

'The reality show... everyone's talking about it.'

'I still don't know what you mean...'

'It's okay, the cat's out of the bag, Tamsin's already told everyone. I'm not surprised, I always knew you were a bit of a star, Sam... and now you're getting your own TV show.'

Chapter 30

Melting Snow and a Sudden Goodbye

Tamsin

You'd think I'd killed someone the way Sam went on – accusing me of telling outrageous lies in the school playground.

I mean I didn't actually say that Sam was starring in the UK version of *Real Housewives...* I may have suggested that a TV company had approached her about a TV reality show about housewives set in Cheshire. The rest was just Chinese whispers set off by that blonde in the nasty pink boots. And as I said to Sam, 'When one of those women in their faux designer snow jackets asked me if Orlando was a TV director, I may have been vague in my response.'

I told Sam it was a psychological experiment, but she said it was just an outrageous lie. I knew I was on dodgy ground, but when I saw how well Jacob's hair cut had been received by his contemporaries I'd wanted to do the equivalent for Sam. And seeing those awful women hanging round the school gates looking for someone or something to gossip about I gave it to them.

'It wasn't malicious,' I said. 'It's given them a purpose, something to get up for in the morning, a reason to put their stupid lipstick on.' I'd known it wouldn't take much to appeal to their fame-hungry hearts.

Sam needed some credibility in the playground, but her degree in education and talent for baking wouldn't cut it with those women. They wanted the shallow glamour of TV, a wad of cash and their own fifteen minutes of fame. I knew this because I'd been just like that myself once, and when I climbed out of Orlando's Aston Martin that first morning and heard one of them say 'she looks like a woman off the TV,' it inspired me.

'It hasn't done you any harm, I bet those women are hanging off your every word at the school gate,' I pointed out to Sam.

'Yes they are – and I hate it. I don't want or need people around me like you do Tamsin. You're the star of the show, you always have been – I'm happy to be in the wings watching. I hate the attention – and it's all so fake anyway, they don't like me they just think I can get them a part on "The Real Housewives of bloody Cheshire".'

'I'm sorry. I didn't set out to tell lies and get you into all this, it just sort of happened and before I knew it was all around the playground and little kids were asking for my autograph,' I said.

'Oh I can imagine – I bet you put on quite a show, Tamsin.'

'Well, I have been admired for my theatrical bent. I'm even thinking of joining the local Am Dram, though after last year's Mikado it would be hard to top Orlando's Yum-Yum.'

But she wasn't interested in my thespian plans, she just kept banging on about how she was being harassed at the school gate by zombies.

'Oh it'll die down, you're a seven-day wonder, love,' I added and changed the subject to something about cakes. She was soon distracted.

I was secretly pleased. Sam wasn't as cross as she would normally be about me 'manipulating' her life, as she always put it. Perhaps she was beginning to see that if she'd allowed me a little manipulation now and then she would benefit from it. I think she was also beginning to realise that my 'interfering' was because I only wanted the best for her. I didn't always go about it the right way, but implying that she was about to star in her own reality show to stop her being bullied was definitely a step-up from threatening to beat up the girls at the school gate as I had when she was twelve.

She asked me to make it quite clear to the other women when I next saw them that it had all been a big lie.

'Okay, I'll say it was a misunderstanding,' I said. 'Lie is such a big word, Sam.'

She'd rolled her eyes. 'They will see for themselves when the TV show doesn't actually happen. You can call it what you like – either way I will look like a dick.'

'Oh and I suppose turning up for school dressed like a hippy, doing wheelies on Jacob's bike and starting snowball fights in the playground didn't make you look "like a dick"?'

'I'm me. I will always be me and whatever you do or say, you can't change me,' she snapped.

I suppose she was right. I had to begin to build my own life now and Sam needed her space. So I decided it was time to start my house-hunting with much more seriousness. I thought it might be worth taking a look at a few little cottages and an old schoolhouse that was up for rent, so called Gabe. I told him my plans and he offered to drive me round to the viewings in his truck, which was exactly what I was hoping he'd do.

I finished early in the bakery that afternoon; Sam and I had pretty much pulled an all-nighter to get those truffle orders ready and it almost killed us. It was nice to be out driving with Gabe, arriving at various houses, him linking arms with me as we strolled up pathways, opening doors and at one point putting his arm round me as we knocked on a door. People assumed we were a couple and neither of us bothered to say we weren't – I think we both quite enjoyed it.

'I think that woman thought we were runaway lovers,' I said as we pulled away from a thatched cottage. It was beautiful inside and out but I knew I'd never be able to afford the monthly rent.

Gabe laughed. 'Yeah, I reckon she thought you were the lady of the manor and you'd run off with one of the servants,' he looked at me.

I felt a fizzing in my chest as I gazed back into his blue eyes.

'How romantic, it's like a film isn't it? You and me, driving through the snow a few days before Christmas – looking for a home.' I could imagine him in the bedroom of that cottage, stretched out on antique lace, holding onto the metal bedstead with one hand and me with the other.

He smiled and pulled up in the car park of a pub. 'Come on, I'll buy you supper,' he said.

I was delighted. This was the end to a perfect day, being with Gabe made me feel happier than I had for a long time. He was attentive and kind and I felt like he really listened to me and didn't view everything I said as an opportunity to mock me or make me feel small. Being with Gabe had made me realise how desperately unhappy and unloved I'd been with Simon. Gabe had no money and didn't care about the future, he didn't drink the best wine or eat in the finest restaurants – and that was all good with me. As we walked through the car park the snow seemed to be finally losing its grip on our world and in the silence you could hear it melting, trickling through the trees. It felt like a new beginning.

The pub had a welcoming glow about it and walking inside I tasted hops, laughter and warmth. I'd never been there before, I didn't even know it existed, but I loved its old-fashioned red velvet seating and swirly red carpet – something I would have hated before. But here, with Gabe, everything just seemed to have more intensity, and when he came back to our table with drinks, I pulled him to me, kissing him passionately. I felt like my veins held fire, my whole being was alive and I finally had something to live for – a future on my terms. My past had been tough, but it had made me the woman I was – I could do anything, I was strong and independent. And I liked me so much more now.

"So which house shall we have?' I joked when our food arrived, a steak and kidney pudding for him, fish and chips for me. That afternoon I'd enjoyed playing at being a couple with him. It was a pipe dream, but I liked the idea of one day sharing my life with someone like Gabe.

I crunched on the beer-battered haddock, it was delicious – the chips were piping hot and salty, with lashings of tangy vinegar. A little grease trickled down my chin and Gabe wiped it off with his finger.

'I never ate fish and chips in my other life,' I said between mouthfuls, 'too fattening… I didn't know what I was missing.' I didn't want miniscule bits of foam or drizzles or smears of ridiculous food costing an arm and a leg any more. Now I was enjoying real food, real life – and I loved how it tasted.

'So, what are you doing for Christmas?' I asked. I wanted him to join us, in fact it wouldn't be the same without him – for me. There would be lots of us at Sam's on Christmas day, and one more wouldn't make any difference – we had very little, but we would share it.

'I won't be here for Christmas,' he said, finishing his food.

I was surprised, and disappointed.

'Oh are you going to stay with family?'

'No. I'm just going away for a while.'

'A while? You mean days? Weeks?'

'Who knows?' he shrugged.

'But where are you going?' I swallowed the batter, suddenly it didn't taste quite so good.

'I'm going to find that beach…'

I smiled, remembering that when I'd asked him in another life where he hoped to be in five years' time his answer had been, 'on a beach.' My eyes stung a little and for a moment I thought I might cry, but this was what he wanted and where he was going, I was going in my own direction now.

After we'd eaten we left, and walking through the now dark car park, the snow was melting so rapidly, huge drops of water, like tears were dripping onto the ground.

'The world's crying,' I sighed.

He glanced over at me. 'There's a lot for the world to cry about.'

'You've made me happy,' I suddenly said, stopping to kiss him on the cheek. 'I don't know how I would have got through all this without you. I didn't think it was possible, because no man has ever treated me as they should – until you, the last man on Earth I would have expected it from. Thank you.'

'My pleasure,' he smiled, opening my door to help me up into the truck.

'When do you leave?' I asked.

'Tomorrow. An old mate of mine's got a van – he'll help with deliveries until Sam's sorted the repairs.'

I was bereft, but grateful. I'd been so shocked at his leaving I hadn't even thought about the practicalities. But how like him not to leave us in the lurch – Gabe was a reliable man you could depend on. And he'd changed me. When he'd thrown my designer shoes away he'd hurled all my pretentions and prejudices away too. He'd shown me what really mattered and I was heartbroken to see him go.

As we drove back I glanced at Gabe, thinking how I could have loved him. I could have moved into that little thatched cottage and lived happily ever after with him in that big double bed, but he wanted something different. And I'd learned that you can't make people do stuff they don't want to do – however much you want it yourself. Perhaps Gabe and I were just about the here and the now and the comfort of strangers? He had no plans for tomorrow or next week – he just lived in my life for a while and I'd loved him being there with me. Gabe was my Christmas angel and though I would be sad to say goodbye I knew, somewhere deep in my heart, that he'd always be around if I needed him.

Chapter 31
Sex, Secrets and a Sister's Lies

Sam

While Tamsin spent a pleasant evening with Gabe, I was baking... and baking... and baking. My back ached, my legs ached, and I felt awful, but I kept on whisking and stirring and frosting – desperate to get us back to speed before Christmas and honour all those orders. Thank God Tamsin had refused to cancel them – and with the makeover and bakery re-opening, hopefully we'd soon be back on track. I was just grabbing a tray from the front of the shop when I spotted a figure walking down the hill. It was unusual to see anyone around at this time of night, especially during the week. I leaned against the door and gently put the bolt on, suddenly feeling very vulnerable alone at night in the shop. The figure drew nearer and in the dark it was hard to make out, but as he got closer I could see it was Richard. Just seeing him made my heart feel like it had stopped and I wanted to press my face against the bakery glass window to get a closer look at him. Fortunately, I realised just in time that from the outside my face pressed against the glass as he walked by would make me look like a crazed stalker and wasn't going to make him love me again. So I just watched from the kitchen, out of view. I expected him to stop, glance in, look for me even – but he was just walking, his head down, past the bakery. My heart did a little unexpected skip and I couldn't help it, I quickly unbolted the door and rushed out into the night calling his name. He turned, surprised to see me. I wanted to run and hug him, but his body language was definitely saying no.

'Where are you off to in the snow at midnight?' I asked in a light-hearted, jokey way.

'Home,' he said, with a faint smile.

'Oh... have you been anywhere nice?' I tried not to sound like an obsessed bunny boiler, but failed.

'I... I've been out with Carole, it was her works do.'

'Oh yes, I forgot it was this weekend (I hadn't, I'd tortured myself for days imagining him swirling her round the damned office party). Was it good? Did you... have a good time? 'I pulled an inquisitive face, expecting more, desperately pretending to be okay with it but he offered me nothing.

'Come inside, if you like?' I said. Judging by his face perhaps the reconciliation with his ex wasn't going too well.

'Thanks,' he came through the door, stamping his feet on the floor to get the snow off.

'This looks good,' he said, gazing round the 'new' bakery.

I explained about the makeover, showing him various little highlights – the glittering snowflakes hanging from the ceiling and the scarlet heart on the tree.

'You okay?' he suddenly said, with an intimacy I remembered.

'Yeah, I'm okay.'

There was an awkward silence, I couldn't ask about him and Carole, it was none of my business, but it was all I could think about.

'Is Tam's still here?'

'Yes... she was the one who got Jacob to cut his hair.'

'Good... about his haircut, I mean. It looks better short.'

'Really? I wanted him to keep it long, I thought he did, too.'

'He was teased mercilessly at school, Sam.'

I shrugged, feeling a little guilty I'd allowed it to go on so long. There was silence for a moment as we both looked at each other, unsure suddenly what to say. Then Richard spoke into the quiet. 'What we had was good Sam, I loved you... still do.'

'What about Carole?'

'Oh we danced and we had a laugh and we'd both had a drink...'

'You don't have to tell me, it's okay, it's not my business...' I couldn't take the details it was too painful.

'No, I want to tell you.'

I didn't look up, I couldn't let him see how much what he was saying was affecting me.

'She wants to get back together...'

My heart was pumping wildly and my eyes were burning, I couldn't cry in front of him, but the thought of losing him, the reality of Richard loving someone else completely floored me. I realised how much I needed him and how much I'd taken him for granted. I'd been an idiot, I should have seen what was in front of me, instead of putting obstacles in the way and being afraid of being happy. Steve wouldn't have wanted me to live my life in the past, scared of the present and dreading the future.

'I thought of Ella and being a family again and wondered if it might be worth giving it another try,' he continued.

I nodded, unable to speak.

He was looking at me, searching my face for a response, but what could I say? Then he put his hand on my shoulder.

'When she'd left me for that guy, all I wanted was for her to come back, to have everything as it was. But it's too late – time apart has changed us both... and I've now got a Sam-sized gap in the middle of my heart.'

I was stunned. So all this had been leading up to him telling me that he wanted me back?

'So you're not with Carole?' I asked.

'No... I went to her works party, that's all.'

'But I thought you two were back together...'

'No. Not while you're here.'

Relief washed over me.

'There's a Richard-sized gap in my heart too,' I said, wanting to cry.

I looked at his long eyelashes, the way he swept his fringe back off his face when he spoke and the way he laughed at my daft remarks. I remembered how he'd thought I was hilarious having snowball fights with the kids, doing 100 miles an hour on a sledge and wearing flip flops in the middle of winter. And I thought about the times he'd asked to be with me, for life, for Christmas – and every time I'd turned him down. But the time apart had been a revelation to me. It was only when I had faced life without him that I'd realised how much he gave me, how much he brought into my life and how I couldn't live without him.

I locked the door, clicked the surviving fairy lights on and I suddenly had that Christmas tingle, the one you get when you're a kid when you hear a carol or Santa's bells. As an adult it's more rare, more fleeting, and since growing up I only ever got my Christmas moment on the first hearing of 'Once in Royal David's City', after that it usually disappeared until next year.

'Come upstairs,' I said, leading him through the shop to the flat.

I smiled, and put my finger to my lips to indicate people were asleep. I showed him into the tiny living room where we both sat on the sofa and watched him gazing around the living room.

'I always loved this room... it's so cosy,' he said. 'I see Jacob has been heavily involved in a new design and execution of the Christmas tree?'

Along with our original decorations, Jacob had added Lego characters and cars. 'We were discussing which baubles we liked on the tree and he wasn't sure about the ones I'd rescued from my own childhood Christmases. So I asked him what he thought he would remember about Christmas when he was older, he said Lego,' I nodded.

'Christmas is different things to different people,' Richard said, looking sad. I wondered if, for a moment when he had his evening with Carole he'd hoped to have a family Christmas with her and Ella again.

I reached my hand to touch his face. 'I've been stupid, too obsessed with what I'd lost and couldn't see what I had.'

He put both his arms around me and I decided now was the time to be completely honest with him. I owed it to him to explain why I'd been unable to commit – and if I wanted to keep him in my life and have a future with him and Jacob, he deserved to know the truth...

'The night Steve died, my last words to him were "don't come back",' I began. 'I've never told anyone that before... not even Tamsin. I'm too ashamed.'

He brushed my cheek with his hand; 'Tell me.'

'It had been a stupid row,' I continued. 'We were both working, had a new baby, we were tired and our lives had been turned upside down by this little thing that demanded every moment of our attention. We were both adjusting to our new roles – but sometimes I felt like Steve forgot he was a dad. It was Jacob's first Christmas and Steve had invited some friends over, but I wanted to relax and sleep and just spend time together, our first family Christmas. He didn't get that – he didn't see the problem in inviting people over to celebrate with us and I became angry. I shouted, said cruel things to him and he stormed off. The snow was coming down hard, the roads were icy, and when a car skidded onto the pavement he was killed instantly.'

'Sam, you can't blame yourself for what happened to Steve.'

'But he died, alone on the side of the road thinking I didn't love him...' I started to cry. For five years I'd carried the guilt of my husband's death around with me. Like a terrible Christmas gift, kept in the back of the wardrobe to be taken out and unwrapped each December. Then every Christmas Eve, the anniversary of his death, I would open up that parcel and wallow in the pain and the guilt all over again.

'You've never talked about that night before,' he said.

'I know, I never felt able to until now – with you. If I'd just said yes to his friends, agreed with what he wanted, then he wouldn't have stormed out – he would still be alive.'

'You can't live the rest of your life saying "what if" and blaming yourself for something that may or may not have happened in the past. It's time to let it go, Sam...'

We lay together in front of the fire, both lost in our own thoughts. After a while, I reached up to his face, the tips of my fingers exploring the stubble of his chin. It felt good – prickly and male. I moved closer to him feeling the warmth from his body, he smelt of Richard – outdoors, wet bracken and winter walks. I breathed him in and my heart quickened. We held each other's eyes and in that instant we both knew what would happen next.

As we kissed and quickly began to take each other's clothes off he stopped and stared at me like I was something very special, precious even. He kissed and caressed me and his gentleness surprised me as it had the very first time. Sex with him was slow and loving and different to anything I had ever experienced before. He looked into my eyes and told me I was beautiful as we lay together naked on the floor.

'Before we go any further, can I just ask, this isn't just a show-mance for your Housewives of Cheshire audition, is it?' he smiled.

I nodded. 'You guessed it – come here, let's make great telly.'

We giggled and cuddled and I've never felt so close to anyone as we lay by the crackling fire, the lights from the Christmas tree twinkling, the snow finally melting along with my heart.

❄ ❄ ❄

The following morning I spoke to Tamsin about her lies at the school gate. We needed to get this sorted, I didn't want to relive a scene from 'The Night of the Living Dead,' every time I took Jacob to school. 'They were pawing at me...' I said.

'I'm sorry, Sam, I couldn't bear to see the way those bitches ignored you. I'm just very protective of those I love.'

'So are pit bulls.'

'You're worth ten of those women – who are they to look down on you?'

'Exactly. They are nothing – it means nothing. And their opinion of me is nothing – so don't sweat it, Tam. I don't.'

'You're right of course,' she said in a small voice. The new Tamsin was the gift that kept on giving, I couldn't believe how tolerant she'd become.

'I cared too much about what other people thought didn't I? And in the end what did it matter?'

I agreed. 'So what exactly did you tell the Yummy Mummies?'

She looked away, unable to meet my eyes. 'I told them that as the star, you'd been asked to choose several women from the school playground to star alongside you and be your reality TV 'friends.'

I gasped, but couldn't help smiling at her sheer front. 'You are so bad, Tamsin.'

'I know, I'm so naughty. But allow me one last glorious moment? Let Orlando have his grand finale,' she said, smiling. 'Let me to take Jacob to school tomorrow. I'll tell them the TV company said none of them were interesting enough.'

I couldn't be too cross with her because I was happy. I excitedly told her about getting back with Richard and then at the same time felt awful when she told me Gabe had gone away.

'Oh sweetie, I'm so sorry,' I sighed, putting my arm around her. She was dressed in one of her ridiculous Doris Day pinafores but looked like a lost little girl.

'I'm okay, Sam, really. I had become quite used to him being around – but I'll be fine,' she smiled a wistful smile. 'He says he's looking for a beach. I hope he finds it.'

'Will you be okay?' I asked.

'Of course. It will be a relief to be single. I spent last Christmas imagining Simon in flagrante with the woman from the wine warehouse. How random was that? Mrs J never saw that in my tea leaves.'

I laughed, a little uneasily. Now I was privy to some of the school conversations, I'd heard that Simon had been quite the ladies' man.

'And this year was going to be the same,' she sighed. 'Simon's strange behaviour was worrying me even more than the white fur and crystal table-scape. I couldn't put my finger on it, but there were the hushed phone calls, even more late nights at the office. Phaedra said it was an affair, 'text book,' she'd said. Anouska insisted it wasn't, but what would she know? She'd been in denial for months about her own husband, until she found him face down in Angela Huntington-Whitely. But Simon's behaviour hadn't been about another woman - it had been all about money,' she said, sipping her tea.

I hoped she was right.

'I don't miss Simon, but I do miss hosting parties, especially this time of year. I loved planning the table, the decor, feeding people, making them happy, choosing the music – it's just so much fun... it's Christmas to me. Do you know what I mean?'

'Yeah it's your thing, and you do it so well, it's a shame you can't do it this year, perhaps by next year?' I said.

She shook her head. 'I doubt it, love, I don't even have my own place to live!'

'Mi casa es su casa,' I said, squeezing her arm. We were working side by side in the kitchen and I was high on the scent of cinnamon and vanilla.

Tamsin was missing the limelight, she loved being the centre of attention, the 'go-to' girl for everyone's needs, and everyone's good time.

'Tonight would have been my Christmas soiree,' she sighed. 'I so loved that – dressing the house, choosing the canapés, the people...'

'Only you could use phrases like "dressing the house, and choosing the people",' I giggled.

'Yeah... she never put out knives and forks like everyone else, she always had to have a "table landscape",' came Mrs J's voice from the stairs.

Tamsin and I looked at each other. 'Mrs J... I didn't even know you were here,' Tamsin laughed.

'I think she lives under the stairs and just pops out every now and then,' I whispered. 'She's been here for days, just waiting for something to comment on.' We both giggled.

'We'll make the best of it this year – together.' I put my arm around her and she rested her head on my shoulder.

'What? You're not doing that sworry thing you do every year?' Mrs J appeared, hands on hips.

'Hardly – we can't afford to do it, Mrs J. Besides, you may have noticed, I lost my venue two weeks ago to bailiffs.'

'What about the 500 canapés and bottles of champagne you told me to order in October?'

'You didn't, did you?'

'Yes I always do what I'm told. "Oooh Mrs J, I will die without my Christmas Moet... it's a matter of life and death that you order well in advance, I can't have lady Titterton-Arse, or whatever her name is, getting in first".' This was all said in an over-the-top (but scarily accurate) impersonation of Tamsin.

'So you ordered...?'

'Yes.'

'And we can't...?'

'Cancel. No. But it's paid for, so you might as well have it... 150 bottles of champers and 500 canapés. You'll be able to take a bath in all that drink and you'll still be eating smoked salmon in April,' she laughed, and shaking her head at the sheer madness, continued to dust vigorously, adding as a caveat. 'You lot? You make me die laffin.'

'Shit, shit, shit.'

'You hate that word and you just said it three times,' I pointed out.

'Well, needs must. I have 500 canapés, 150 bottles of the finest champagne, no guests and no venue. And nobody else is laughing, Mrs J,' she called into the dusting, chortling abyss. 'Oh shit again, I just remembered Jesus is coming tomorrow. He's flying in from New York. Do you mind if he sleeps on your living room floor, Sam?'

I smiled, there were already about five people sleeping on the floor – what difference would one more make? Jacob and I could always go to Richard's now things were more concrete between us. He was living in a flat too – but it was Tamsin-free and as it had two bedrooms Jacob and I had spent a couple of nights there already.

'If Jesus is coming, he'll drink all that champagne and scoff the canapés, there will be no waste,' I laughed.'

"You must want to kick yerself,' Mrs J said, wandering back in with a bucket. I was never quite sure what she did, but she seemed to have lots of cleaning accessories about her person at all times, day or night, and as I'd inherited her from Tamsin, I never questioned it.

People had always been surprised at Mrs J speaking to Tamsin like she was a teenager, but now I knew more about Tamsin's childhood, our family dynamic, I wondered if perhaps my sister liked having her around. It was clear that in their own way they had an affection for each other. Despite the personal comments and spiky retorts from Mrs J, Tamsin often hugged her or spontaneously kissed her cheek. Mrs J always pretended to brush her off, but you could tell she liked it.

'Yes, I could kick myself, but I'm already a little bruised, Mrs J. I'm about to take delivery of a champagne lake and a canapé mountain – and I have no guests. So, if you don't mind, I won't kick myself until next week,' Tamsin snapped.

'Well, I don't know what you've got to moan about – you've got ovens and fridges... you might as well have your Christmas "do" here.'

With that, she filled her bucket with water from the tap and headed back upstairs. Tamsin and I looked at each other.

'You know, Mrs J might just have something. Who says a soiree has to be in one's home? We have a ready-made "white Christmas" here and all it would take is a little tweaking, an hour of Heddon and Hall and...' Tamsin started. I could see she already had it planned out on the whiteboard in her head.

'You mean we could have your party here... in the shop?'

'Why not?'

'I'm sorry Tamsin... this isn't a "why not?" moment. It's more of a "why?" moment. We're only just being resurrected from the fire, we have no money, no guests and we are so busy we may have to bring people in off the street to help us make up orders. Oh, and it's less than a week before Christmas. Do I need to go on?'

She shook her head slowly. She wasn't listening and I knew why – she was going to host her Christmas soiree in The Angel Bakery regardless.

'This is the answer we've been looking for, the icing on the Christmas cake if you will. We'll invite everyone, the whole community and their kids and the local press and make it a very special Re-opening for Christmas party.'

I didn't burst her balloon. She was so excited, Tamsin was back doing what she loved best, planning parties and interiors and almost delirious with happiness and purpose.

'A party would be great for the bakery! I reckon we can make enough money from that one day to pay several months' rent AND the van,' she said. Think of it as PR for the business, a showcase of our fabulous baked goods and a message to the world that The White Angel Bakery is back in business.

Now I felt more like listening.

'And it won't just be about that day, that week – or this Christmas. We are a small business, we can offer the friendliness and one-to-one service the supermarkets and bigger shops can't.'

Tamsin's idea was that our customers would fall in love with the bakery as much as we had. It looked magical and now all we had to do was make sure the customers wanted to come back again and again. She said we had to make friends with our customers and what better way of doing that than throwing them (and their kids) a Christmas party?

I couldn't argue with that, even though I did feel like dropping with exhaustion at the thought of the mountain of work we had ahead of us.

'I can see it all now – we won't make this some stuffy, adult only soirée,' she was saying. 'It will be a family Christmas party, a community event, everyone welcome.'

I didn't want to be a wet blanket, but I did point out that thanks to her 'fabulous' sales we had lots of orders to fulfil too.

But she told me in her Hermione voice to 'chill, sister.'

I never thought I'd see the day when she was telling me, the laid-back, easy-going sister, to 'chill'.

Chapter 32

Swiss Peaks, Edible Pearls and Ravishing Queens

Tamsin

On the day before the party, Heddon and Hall arrived just as we were closing the bakery after a long day. 'We are here – your very own ravishing queens – we're going to do you up, darling, and add some extra Christmas style and sparkle for the tomorrow's re-opening,' Hall declared.

It was going to be a huge event and Sam had a million cupcakes to bake so we pushed everyone available into the kitchen to work on the edible stuff. Sam was kneading dough, Hugo beating eggs and Hermione it seemed had inherited my talent for colour and style and was creating some amazing designs with icing. Even Jacob joined in, building his own gingerbread house from the leftover gingerbread.

Sam seemed to get some of her energy back but I was concerned because she still seemed pale and had to keep sitting down. Despite feeling poorly she made several hundred cakes including my personal favourite - red velvet cupcakes with a dash of coconut liqueur and a topping of glittering Swiss peaks. We put all the large Christmas cakes in the window; they were all iced in white, some with Christmas roses, some with edible pearls, but all with sparkles.

Jacob and I went outside to see how they looked as Sam re-positioned them under our direction. When we finally gave her the thumbs up through the window she ran outside to see the finished effect.

Standing on the pavement together, we all gazed at the pyramids of glittery cupcakes, the big frosty Christmas cakes, and the sparkly snowflake cookies. The lights were on inside and though the window was glacial there was a warm glow emanating from the bakery.

'It looks like Richard's painting,' Sam said. I nodded in agreement, she was right, it was just as he'd imagined it – polished and sparkly, all ready for Christmas.

It was late afternoon and quite dark, the glow from the bakery shone on Sam and Jacob's faces and as we stood together gazing in, I could see the red glass heart hanging from the tree. 'We brought the White Angel back to life,' I sighed, and the window glittered with light and hope and cakes – and in the middle of the winter white landscape the little heart glistened like a scarlet secret.

Chapter 33

Snowy Cupcakes and Shimmering Cookies

Sam

The final Saturday before Christmas was our party day, and Tamsin turned up in white angel wings, as did Heddon and Hall, who always jumped at the chance to wear fairy wings. There was great excitement and anticipation – this was our last chance to make enough money to keep the bakery open beyond Christmas. We needed rent, money for raw ingredients and still we had to pay for the van repairs, and now Gabe had gone it was even more vital.

The day was also about giving the bakery and us a secure future beyond next month's bill. It needed planning and strategy, something I didn't do; I concentrated on cake flavours and designs, the colours I'd use, the scones I'd serve in the tiny cafe. I'd never really considered a business or marketing plan. And this is where my sister came in, with her great talent for planning, selling and PR.

Tamsin had called up some 'contacts' from her charity events, which resulted in a front page picture in the Wilmslow Advertiser and a slot on local radio and TV. Of course she loved the media attention, posing in what was left of her designer dresses, draping herself across the bakery counter and talking 'celebrity customers,' of which we had none – but I didn't let on to the press. As she said, we needed to 'ramp up the PR'. My sister knew about these things – and I knew about cake.

The day of the party was not like Tamsin's usual project-managed soirees. It was more happy cake chaos. The reindeer was moved to a special, central spot under the glistening chandeliers and was a real pull. People were out in the square and children were dragging their mums in to see 'the white Rudolph', who then bought cakes from the bakery and were invited by Tamsin to make those last minute Christmas orders. 'Why struggle round the supermarket on Christmas Eve?' she was saying. 'We can have your freshly made bread packed up in bags with your Christmas cupcakes and cookies – a one-stop shop.'

Just walking into the bakery was like wandering into a winter wonderland of glitter and sugar – everyone gasped and smiled and was seduced by the sparkle. The counter was stacked with glittery sugar icicles, pyramids of snowy cupcakes, sparkly macarons and shimmering cookies. White chocolate and meringue frosting whirled around in peaks, creating the perfect snowy mountain topping, and something inside me sparkled to life.

Hugo and I served customers while Tamsin and Hermione offered champagne and canapés, all to the Christmassy soundtrack of 'Jingle Bells', 'Frosty the Snowman' and all the others in between.

Around midday I caught sight of Richard and Ella arriving into the madness and mayhem. I was desperate to see him and I left the counter rushing to him, my arms open. He seemed surprised at my show of affection, and so was I – but I couldn't help myself.

I ran back behind the counter, and within minutes, Tamsin had put Richard to work. Hugo and I were serving customers and Richard was asked to take over from Hermione, who started on a fresh batch of bread in the kitchen with Jacob and Ella's 'help'.

Looking out from behind the counter, Michael Bublé's Christmas album bubbling away in the background, my heart felt like it was stuffed with tinsel. 'Isn't it just gorgeous?' I said to Mrs J, who was serving with me and doing her usual running commentary.

'Lovely! About time you two sorted yourselves out… I thought last week her ladyship was headin to the funny farm!'

I smiled. Mrs J wasn't known for her sensitivity, but as a former member of 'the funny farm' myself I had to smile.

'She's been the talk of the place with Gabe. I told her he only wanted her for one thing… and she gave it to him by all accounts…'

'I did, and I bloody loved it, Mrs J,' Tamsin said. Mrs J was deaf and always louder than she needed to be.

I smiled to myself thinking about how Tamsin had changed, and how her husband, the bakery and Gabe had all played their parts.

And though Gabe had gone to find his beach, he'd left quite an impression on her, throwing her designer shoes in the snow and bringing passion and caring back into her life at a time when she was lost.

Along with the everyday struggles we had with money, van repairs, kids, hormones and lovers, Tamsin and I were finally enjoying being sisters again and sharing our stories. Some days I'll admit that closeness made me feel like I was drowning. Living and working with my sister was claustrophobic and irritating to the point where I felt I couldn't breathe. I loved her so much, but there were moments I could cheerfully have pushed her face in a gallon of cake batter. Then, other days – most days – we'd laugh *with* each other, *at* each other and the rest of the world. We'd talk about our husbands, our lovers, the past, the present and what we both hoped our futures would be.

'I always thought the future would be Simon and I in one of our homes abroad,' Tamsin said. 'But life had other plans for me.'

I agreed. I'd always thought I'd be a teacher, but losing Steve made me re-evaluate my life and when this bakery came up for rent I just knew I had to take the risk. It took me a little longer to take a risk with a guy again though,' I smiled. I'd always thought I'd be married to Steve, have baby Jacob, one day followed by another baby... but that particular scenario wasn't meant to be. There was a new scenario being nurtured now – a new future for all of us just waiting to be grasped.

Both Tam and I had gone to hell and back to be where we were and it may not have been the paths we'd chosen – fate chose them for us – but we were making the most of the journey.

'Losing my home and my husband has definitely had a silver lining,' Tamsin had said. 'I feel wanted, needed again – I used to fill the holes in my life with shopping and Chardonnay – and I haven't been shopping for almost three weeks now. And I haven't had a glass of Chardonnay since, well okay – yesterday – but it is Christmas.

Baby steps, I thought.

Chapter 34

The Delicious Sound of Reindeer Hooves

Tamsin

This is what I loved, the challenge of creating something from nothing, and the fact this would be great publicity for the business added an extra frisson for me. Heddon and Hall set up an awning and tables at the front of the shop and made it look like a cross between a fairy tale and a Victorian bazaar. They'd dismissed all talk of payment, asking only to be allowed to wear various fancy dress (fairy wings and full make-up) and permission to ride the reindeer. How could I refuse?

The party was planned meticulously down to the very date – there'd be time for guests to order for Christmas and the local press and TV could get the story out in time. I used all my friends shamelessly. I recruited Jesus to be the official photographer and momentarily forgetting his Portuguese accent, promised to 'shoot the arse off it', so we could send out press releases after the event too and put the photos on our new website. Mimi's husband, the football manager, donated two tickets for the following Saturday's game and a signed ball by a footballer with strong thighs and a Latin name. Jacob also had a signed ball waiting for him on Christmas Day and even I was excited about him opening that gift – even though I hadn't a clue who the delicious, and apparently very famous footballer was.

Whilst the people I'd thought were my friends never got in touch, plenty of others did, offering their help, attendance – and in the case of the rather handsome butcher in the square, a free turkey.

Sam said it was because I was so friendly and despite Phaedra and Anouska being shallow, selfish bitches (her words), other people had remembered the kindnesses I'd given over the years. But it was more about my parties – I always gave the best parties in the area and this one was no exception, I was high-kicking my way into Christmas after all.

The White Angel Bakery Party started at 10.30 in the morning and the champagne flowed. Sam had made the most exquisite pastries and dainty, snowy little cupcakes and we laid them out on large white tables inside and out. Dusted with sparkle and lit from above (I always light from above, darling), they looked stunning. I'd told Jesus it was a family affair so no coke, no dildos and no swearing – he accepted these conditions but said the swearing may be an issue. 'Well then darling, so as not to offend you're going to have to swear in your "native" language, and I don't mean Mancunian.' So Jesus snapped away, grimaced at the kids and stayed relatively sober while swearing in Portuguese and taking bookings for family photos and future Christmas cards.

Children all took turns on the reindeer, when Heddon and Hall weren't completely monopolising it. I had to have a quiet word with Heddon when a queue of ten crying children had formed and he was refusing to budge because he was waiting for Jesus to 'capture me in reindeer flight'.

In between reindeer rides, Hall had set up Santa's impromptu grotto, which consisted of a gossamer curtain behind which sat a rather corpulent Heddon dressed as Father Christmas. He made lots of ho ho ho noises, while Hall as Santa's little helper danced around in a pink sequinned elf outfit with glittery wings – he looked delicious and the children loved it.

By the time the carol singers turned up at 5 p.m. we'd taken more orders than we could have dreamed of. Sam and I were ecstatic, but just a little concerned about how we were going to get it all done with only four days to Christmas.

'We'll do it,' I said, squeezing Sam's hand, back to the old Tamsin, making everything right again. Sam seemed relieved at my blind faith and I had to smile because I wasn't 100% sure we had the time either – but we were so determined the bakery was going to be a success we'd do anything.

I'd always paid someone to select the music for my own parties, but as Hugo had kindly offered I allowed him to take over the deck. I had been slightly nervous about his choice of music and had a word before proceedings started. 'Now Hugo we need something Christmassy, I don't want any of that rapping stuff you were playing where black people call each other terrible names.'

'So what were you thinking... Nicky Menaj's "Stupid Hoe"?'

'I'm *thinking* "Wombling Merry Christmas",' I said. Sometimes he could be as sarcastic as his auntie.

It was hot inside with the ovens on and all the customers milling, so I wandered outside into the cold evening to listen to the carol singers. It had stopped snowing sometime around dawn and the crisp white ground had turned to slush. 'Silent Night' was filling the clear frosty air, as the black roads and grey pavements emerged slowly from their white burial ground.

Hearing the singing I was transported straight back to my grandparents' house – carols on the radio, a real fire and paper chains hanging from the ceiling. That was a perfect Christmas, no colour scheme, no expensive crackers, festive flower arrangements or organic geese on the table – just us, our family.

Sam wandered out into the night, her face pink with warmth and happiness, she was holding Jacob and Ella's hands. Richard was behind them, his hand on the small of her back, loving her, taking care of her, and it warmed my heart.

I turned from my sister to see Hugo and Hermione walk towards me with polystyrene cups of champagne. 'Happy Christmas, Mum,' they said.

'We are going to be okay, we won't have much but...' I started.

'Mum, really it's all good,' Hermione sighed, putting her arm around me. 'Well, I say all good – I'm having a love-hate relationship with this glitter nail varnish right now.'

She was looking earnestly at her nails and I smiled with relief – glad she had her priorities right. One day she'd realise that nail varnish didn't matter – but for now I would leave her to find that out for herself. Enjoy it while you can, I thought – the real concerns in the world are too big and scary for you just yet.

I hugged them both, my arms around their waists because they were both bigger than me.

'Are you guys okay?' I asked.

'Yeah, we're fine, Ma,' Hugo said and hugged me back.

I looked around at everyone else also having a genuinely good time with their kids – but without co-ordinated outfits or baubles – and for the first time in years I felt that Christmas tingle, I could almost hear the sleigh bells and the sound of reindeer hooves. But when I looked to see where the sound was coming from, it was only Jesus pulling Heddon and Hall through the snow on the white reindeer.

Chapter 35

Psychic Talents and Fallen Angels

Sam

Tamsin's Christmas soiree was a roaring success. The orders poured in and with all we'd taken it looked like the bakery would survive well into the next year. We had done so well I was even wondering if one day we might open another Angel bakery, and that night, after the party, when everyone was cleaning up I put it to Tamsin as we washed up together.

'I love that idea,' she smiled. 'After all there are two Angel sisters, so there should be two Angel Bakeries... but only two, let's not get greedy. We could call the other one "The Fallen Angel" after me,' she giggled, before suddenly becoming quite serious. 'Sam, if things do work out for us, let's promise ourselves we'll never get so rich or ambitious we forget what's important and lose ourselves.'

'Absolutely,' I said. 'It's taken quite a journey to get here – let's not cock it all up.'

'Oh Sam do you have to be so vulgar? Talking of cocks - I have news on Simon.'

'Really?' I was salivating, what was the tosser up to now?

'Mmm I got a call from Anouska earlier,' she said, plunging her hands back into hot soapy dish water.

'Anouska? Is she calling you with gossip because she wants to be friends again?'

'No. Nothing like that – she asked if Simon was with me.'

I was puzzled. 'Why would she call you to ask that?'

'Apparently he told her he was working late at the office... she had no idea he has no office any more.'

'What? I don't understand.' Then it dawned on me. 'You mean Anouska... and Simon?'

'For almost a year apparently,' she sighed handing me a wet dish. 'It explains why he abandoned me in Spain last summer to rush back "to the office". It also explains the absent weekends and the late night phone calls and why Mimi didn't want to talk about Anouska when I asked about her at the party – apparently everyone knows but me. So much for the girl at the gym, Davina from work and the woman in the wine warehouse; it was Anouska all the time... right under my nose.'

'The bitch, she was your friend.'

'Yes.'

'But you're not raging and threatening to shut her down and...'

'Doing my usual Bette Davis? No. Because they deserve each other, they make the perfect couple, both obsessed with money and themselves. And when she finds out he has no money and he's "late at the office" once too often, they will be over and he'll be on to the next one.

'I'm proud of you, Tamsin.'

'Thanks. I'm proud of me too. And there's something else... I wasn't completely surprised about Anouska, I knew because I'm psychic.'

'Okay... how many fingers am I holding up,' I said, putting my tea towel down and my hands behind my back. It was a game we played as kids to see if we could read each other's minds – we couldn't.

'Oh that's child's play for an expert like me. Don't you remember? In my Darjeeling leaves when Mrs J saw a clown I saw Anouska's face! She was the vulture circling around the dead corpse of my marriage. I have a rare talent, who knows where this could lead.'

'Hermione's right, you are such a drama queen,' I said. We carried on washing and drying and laughed about the possibility of her future as a psychic in a double act with Mrs J.

'I will only use it for good,' she said. 'My talent scares me too much.'

She wasn't joking, and as much as she'd changed, I loved the fact she was still her over the top self, still able to provide high drama on any occasion. Our lives had changed so much in such a short time and though some of it was going to be tough, there were silver linings. Even Christmas Day would be different this year and we talked excitedly of the big family Christmas in our tiny flat.

'It will be great fun,' Tamsin smiled. 'I am just so grateful for us all to be together, it could be in an old garage... as long as we are all together, as a family.'

It wouldn't be anything like the Christmas she'd planned. 'There will be a table and there will be knives and forks,' I warned, 'but nothing will match, there won't be a theme, a colour scheme or a 'table-scape.' Hugo and Hermione had said they were just glad the dinner would be edible – which would make a change from when Tamsin cooked.

Everyone else had either gone home or gone to bed and it felt good just to chat with my sister. I'd wanted the bakery to be the one thing I achieved on my own. After Steve I'd been too scared to fall in love again because I couldn't bear to lose that love, as I had with him. And through Richard I'd learned that it's okay to ask for help, it's okay to let people into your life, you can't keep them out because there's a chance they might leave or die.

As for Tamsin, she said she would have liked there to be something more with Gabe – but it wasn't to be and for now she was just happy to be with family, working in the bakery and waking up every morning with a sense of purpose and a future. The two of us working together was organic, we were sisters after all, and though we were different, we were good together. She'd changed so much – what happened to her had made her far calmer, less demanding, less controlling and there were times when she was actually fun.

'I thought I didn't have a future that night, when the bailiffs came,' she said. 'I didn't know which way to turn, but you were there for me. I know it will take time but the success of today's party has given me such a lift – I'm starting to believe in myself again. I hope it's done the same for you.'

'It has and you've been amazing.' I'd wondered all along if she would crumble, that one day her surface brittleness would crack and she'd fall apart – but she'd been so strong.

'You too, sweetie,' she put her arm around me. 'It's ironic isn't it that Steve was taken from you by a man who'd had a drink... and my childhood was taken from me by a man who'd had a drink too.'

'Perhaps it's time to forgive those guys who had a drink and start to take back what's ours. Steve's gone, but I am still very much alive! I'll always love him, but I can't live in the past any more, and neither can you.'

She blew her nose and smiled through her tears. 'I'm sorry. I am being very selfish... I can't begin to understand how awful that must have been for you, a young wife and mum losing her husband so... pointlessly.'

'I used to think like that, but this is the first Christmas I feel able to move forward. I've changed and I'm coming to terms with life and what it throws at us. I'd put mine and Jacob's life on hold, clinging to our old life and old ways, keeping Jacob's hair long because that's how his dad wore it, refusing to let Richard in and really do Christmas because Steve died on Christmas Eve. But it's time for us to live a new life. I don't want to be defined as "that poor young widow" anymore. And Tamsin you have to do the same or the past will destroy you. You can't anaesthetise the pain with a new handbag anymore. You've had to face everything that's happened to you, both as a child and in the recent past, but I'm proud of you, big sis.'

She seemed surprised, shocked at how much I'd guessed about her. We sat for a while at the little window table. The snow had started again and already a thick white blanket had covered the square, burying sound and covering our thoughts. It was late and quiet and we were both exhausted from the day, but the hope blossoming in my tummy was like a crocus pushing through the snow.

'I've always been the know-all, the big sister who has to give the advice, be there to wipe the tears and clean the wounds of life... but all the time I should have been listening to you,' she said.

'No. We have to listen to each other.'

Then she put down her cup and went over to her handbag on the counter.

'I almost forgot... an early Christmas present – well, the only one,' she laughed. 'Happy Christmas, Sam.'

She handed me a beautifully wrapped, small oblong-shaped gift. I looked at her while taking it from her outstretched hand. I slowly opened it and inside was the most beautiful picture, a watercolour of our Grandparents' home.

'It's Hyacinth Road,' I gasped. The picture was so detailed, so pretty, a golden glow coming from inside, a wreath on the door and the wonky old Christmas tree in the window. I felt huge tears run down my cheeks.

'Where did you get this?'

'From my memory. You told me to let go of the past... but to remember the good times and move forward. Richard painted it from an old photo I had, but it wasn't taken at Christmas, so I remembered the happy details at Christmas for him to paint.'

I looked into the picture and my heart fizzed with love – for Tamsin for being so thoughtful and Richard for painting it so carefully, with love. I was so lucky to have him in my life. There would always be a corner in my heart for Steve, but someone else loved me now, and I was finally ready to let go. I studied the picture for ages, losing myself through the window of that little house, the details were tiny but so well observed. 'I can even see the paper fairy we made together, it's here on our tree now and it was there then in the window of 22 Hyacinth Road,' I smiled.

'Yes, it wasn't all bad... if you look hard enough there are always good times.'

'Like when we played snow angels?' I asked.

'Yes,' she giggled.

'Come on then,' I said, grabbing her hand and dragging her out into the night and the snow. She tried to resist but when she saw me laying there, my arms and legs outstretched, she lay down next to me. The two Angel sisters, both women, both mothers, who Tamsin said 'should really know better', lying side by side in the snow and screaming with laughter.

❄ ❄ ❄

That Christmas Tamsin and I and all our family spent the day together. With Richard, Jesus and Heddon and Hall there were nine of us and as I didn't have a dining room, we pushed the bakery tables together and threw a cloth over them. For Tamsin's sake I tried to stay with the white winter theme, but my glasses were blue and my napkins were red – and horror of horrors – made of paper.

'This won't be easy,' she said, holding a red napkin between thumb and forefinger, her lip curling in horror. For my sake, let's pretend it's a theme and call it a Christmas mash-up.' And as she dabbed her mouth with a paper napkin in the wrong colour, and ate frozen supermarket turkey instead of French organic goose – I knew she'd changed. A year ago she would have passed out at the prospect of mismatched (paper!) table linen and a non-organic turkey. The crackers were cheap and gaudy and chosen by my 'Christmas stylist', Jacob – and when we pulled them they cracked so loudly, Tamsin, Heddon and Hall all screamed. Jacob and Hugo read out the cracker jokes, Tamsin and the boys did an impromptu medley from 'White Christmas' and Hermione put it all on You Tube. And in a symbolic gesture, I asked Richard to carve the turkey. He seemed so delighted at my show of love and commitment, I thought I'd better take him aside and reveal just how committed I was. We were just about to sit down to dinner and I couldn't wait, so discreetly gestured to him to meet me upstairs in the flat.

'I couldn't wait to give you your present,' I said. I asked him to sit down and told him the news and we both laughed and cried with happiness and back at the table we exchanged secret glances. But as always, my sister had guessed something was going on and later, in the kitchen as we made Nan's rum sauce, she gave me a sidelong look.

'Sisters should never have secrets,' she raised her eyebrows comically. 'Do you have a secret you might want to share with your sister?'

I nodded, my face breaking into a smile. 'You know how I've been tired a lot lately... no energy, feeling sick - like I was in the first trimester with Jacob?'

I didn't need to say any more.

'I'm so happy... for you...' she said, hugging me and nodding through tears. 'It's happy tears.'

'Me too.' I wiped my face with a tea towel and handed it to her.

'Ooh tea towel? For tears? You've turned me into a right chav, our Sam,' she said, mopping her face.

This baby was our hope, our little crocus growing in that snowy winter of our lives. We'd lived through a time of sadness and loss, but now happiness was on the horizon for all of us. The secret was to allow happiness to enter our lives in its' own time - we couldn't chase it or change it. Meanwhile I had learned to let people in and my sister had learned to let them go.

For me it was like a first Christmas, I had begun to accept Steve's death, and was being a strong parent for Jacob. I was also beginning a new adventure with the bakery and Richard, who was already talking about marriage and a new place to live as a family – not too far from the bakery of course. For Tamsin it was also like a first Christmas. Her life had shifted on its axis, and through opening up about her past she had now begin to let it go and forgive. On this new journey, she couldn't allow the past to cast a shadow over her future... and she was working on that. And I would be there every step of the way.

Chapter 36

An Unexpected Guest at The Christmas Table

Tamsin

So there I was enjoying supermarket turkey and cheap new world wine on Christmas Day in a bakery window. We had cheap crackers that snapped loudly and had stupid jokes in them, the cutlery didn't match, the sprouts were cold – and I won't even start on the napkins. But you know what? Sitting there, with everyone around me laughing and eating, it was the best Christmas I'd ever had. When my phone rang I thought it was Jesus – he was late for lunch and Hugo was saying Jesus would be late for his own birthday, which just cracked us all up. But when I looked at my phone it wasn't Jesus.

'Alright Tamsin?'

My heart almost stopped and my mouth went very dry. 'Gabe?' I stood up from the table.

'Yeah... Happy Christmas.'

I was touched, also a little sad. I thought I'd got over Gabe, but just hearing his voice made me go all woozy.

'Where did you get to in the end?' I asked, imagining him on that beach, warm sand, his naked body.

'I'm where I always wanted to be...'

'Is there sand between your toes?'

'No.'

'Are you somewhere warm?'

'No... it's bloody freezing.'

'Really? Where are you?'

'I'm outside.'

'Yes but where outside?'

'The Bakery.'

I looked up and there he was through the window in a big overcoat, looking like a bedraggled film star, stubbly and rough and... I opened the door and ran to him. We fell into each other's arms.

'You're back? For how long?' I asked, burying my head in his chest

'A while.'

'But what happened to your beach?'

'I got to the airport and I hung around a bit and decided I didn't want to go anywhere. I don't need a beach, not now I've got you with your stupid shoes and your daft Christmas decorations.'

I had a sudden, uncontrollable urge to rub his bristly face all over my décolletage... thankfully I resisted.

'I missed you, Tammy,' he said in a moment of softness.

'I missed you too.'

We kissed and my heart soared above the snow, this was so wonderful, so unexpected. I heard jeering and clapping coming from inside and we pulled away from each other in embarrassment. Then I curtseyed and Gabe bowed. Through the window I could see my whole family gathered inside our little bakery. It was the perfect Christmas picture, love, laughter twinkling lights, mismatched crockery and hope for the future. And standing in the snow, Gabe's hand in mine, I knew this was it. The Christmas I'd been searching for all my life.

'Come on, Mum, bring Gabe inside, it's freezing out there,' Hugo called from behind the flaming pudding.

I smiled, took Gabe's hand, and led him into Christmas. I was finally home.

A Note from Sue

If, you're like me and that first line of 'Let it Snow,' has you lunging for the sherry and the fairy lights then you will appreciate what a joy it's been for me to write this book. I LOVE Christmas and have spent the whole summer wallowing in cinnamon-scented 'Christmasness.' I have written only to the sound of 'Michael Bublé's Christmas' album while inhaling gingerbread candles and sporting a reindeer jumper. I also sacrificed my diet and ate my own weight in mince pies, just so I could conjure the mood and spirit of Christmas and share it with my readers – you're welcome.

I really hope you enjoyed reading this book as much as I enjoyed writing it, and if you have a moment (in between buying cards and presents, writing cards, sending cards, wrapping presents, arguing with partners, refereeing children and cooking Christmas Dinner) do get in touch and say hello. My biggest thrill is when readers say my writing cheered them up, inspired them, or made them laugh, so please join me on Twitter and Facebook, because I love chatting to you. I'm @suewatsonwriter on Twitter and my page on Facebook is Sue Watson Books. Oh and if you enjoyed the book and want to tell the world, feel free to write a quick review – it's always very much appreciated.

I've started writing my next book now and I reckon after all that snow us girls need to feel sand between our toes and sunshine on our faces. So if you fancy some fun in the sun and want to know when my next book will be released you can sign up for email updates at:

www.bookouture.com/sue-watson

I promise I won't share your email address with anyone, and I'll only send you a message when I have a new book out.

Thanks again for reading – may all your Christmases be Merry and Bright – and overflowing with baked goods.

Sue x

 www.suewatsonbooks.com

 suewatsonbooks

@suewatsonwriter

Also by Sue Watson

Love, Lies and Lemon Cake

Fat Girls and Fairy Cakes

Younger, Thinner, Blonder